DRAGON LOST

DRAGON THIEF BOOK ONE

LISA MANIFOLD

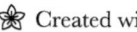 Created with Vellum

ENTER THE WORLD OF THE DRAGON THIEF...

DRAGON LOST

One last heist and I'm out of here. Except today I woke up as a dragon, and now someone is trying to kill me. Yeah, a dragon. You know, teeth, claws, blue scales, furniture exploding under my massive form... I don't have time for this.

LAGNIAPPE

(That means a little something extra!)
Want to meet Aodan before he exploded into a dragon? Click
the image below!
If you cannot click the link, please visit:
https://dl.bookfunnel.com/lw4j12jbcv

DEDICATION

Always to my family.
Jimmy, Cooper, Dale & Eve, Mom, Mom, Daddy, Dad, Dick, Liz,
Shannon, and Mike.
And my bonus family of Corinne & Rachel.

To Grandma Mazie,
Who took me in and squeezed my hand with love from the very beginning.

To my readers - especially Ms. Jan N. and Kristy.
All the folks I get to meet at events
and my Advance Readers –
I love you all.

And to Imagine Dragons, Lady Gaga, and BORNS. They carried me
through.

PROLOGUE

*T*he woman held the sleeping boy.

"Oh, my sweet boy. I am sorry," she said.

The sun moved across the room, and still the woman held the boy, rocking back and forth, singing softly and stroking his face and hair. Tears would fall down her face occasionally. Even more so, one of the tears would fall on the sleeping boy.

A knock on the door made her jump. She glanced up from the child at the door fearfully, tightening her hold on him.

He stirred a little. But he didn't wake up.

Inhaling deeply, the woman pulled herself up and wiped at the tears on her face. She looked at the child once more.

Blowing on her hand, she ran her hand over the boy's head. A faint blue glow sparked and then faded.

"You are still there," she said.

Then, still cuddling him, she went to the door.

A young woman with a brown bob, wearing a skirt and jacket with a white blouse and low-heeled shoes.

"Hi," the woman said softly.

"Hi Marion," the woman with the little boy said.

Neither spoke.

Marion said, "Can I come in?"

The woman stood back, and opened the door wider.

Marion walked in.

"Do you have the bag?"

The woman nodded. "It's over there," she pointed with her chin.

"You don't have to do this," Marion said, her words coming out in a rush.

The woman bowed her head, and brushed the boy's cheek. "I do. I know you don't understand and you have been wonderful, trying to help. But there's no other way. I must."

Marion pursed her lips. Then she opened her mouth as if to say something, but closed it before any words came out.

"All right," she said. "I'm ready to go whenever you want me to."

The woman looked up, and the tear tracks were visible on her face. "I'll never be ready, but since no time is good, let's do this now."

Marion took a few steps and picked up the duffle bag the woman had indicated a few moments before. Hesitatingly, she walked back to the woman, and held out her arms.

The woman pulled the boy close, holding him to her chest. Then with a muffled sob, she put the boy into Marion's arms.

"If you—" Marion began.

The woman walked to the window. "Just go. Please, go," she said.

Marion waited for a moment, then slowly went to the door, and let herself out.

The click of the door echoed in the room.

On either side of the door, a woman cried.

1

A noisy thief is a dead thief... so of course this was the moment that I was clinging to a dusty beam and trying not to scream for my life. This was supposed to be my last job—the one that would set me up and get me the hell out of here.

I clamped my hand over my mouth as I flattened myself onto the ceiling beam, trying to become invisible. Down below me, a circle of light popped into existence. It kept getting larger, until it grew to the size of a doorway, and then a man stepped out of it.

My practice of getting in—my skills, really—and stealing whatever I was hired to steal, then getting out without a sound or any sort of disturbance at all was being tested right now. I prayed that I'd make it through. The light was so bright it was making me dizzy. I squeezed my eyes shut, the refrain of "noise equals death" kept playing in my head even as my eyes tried to take in what I was seeing.

Focus, Aodan! The bag. Get the damned bag. Ignore the guy in the light.

Yeah, yeah, I know stealing is wrong. I closed my eyes again, and forced myself to breathe, in and out, in and out, quiet and steady. The breathing in and out was a challenge, too. I had the oddest sensation of smoke in the back of my throat that made me want to cough.

I didn't have a choice, however. I had a job. You got hired to do it, you took the deposit, and you did the job. That's how it was... that's what I was doing. I didn't get involved any further than that.

And the guy I was stealing from? A lot more wrong than me. I stifled the snicker creeping up my throat. The whole *I'm bad but you're worse* thing. Sounds like a crutch, right? Not really. The fact that I couldn't stand him was like the client sliding me a bonus.

Not to lean on the 'but he's worse' thing, but he really is worse than me. He's also a giant asshat.

I sent up a sorry to the heavens, or whatever. Wherever it was my foster mother Tina was. She hated cussing. When I would do it in front of her, her hand would whip out and flick the edge of my ear to remind me that a lady was present. How she managed to flick the same place every time, regardless of which ear it was, no matter the situation bordered on gifted.

Mea culpas to Tina managed, I thought about the job. I didn't think about the guy stepping through the wall of light, who was still down there. Was there a trap door in the floor I'd missed in my scan of the plans? Where the hell had that light come from? And why was this happening tonight?

I had planned this out. Nothing should have gone wrong. But it had. It had gone wrong in a way where I wasn't sure of my next move. So here I am, trapped on a beam in a warehouse. If I'm caught, I'm dead. There's no other outcome— either I get out alive, and life gets better, or I die.

That's it.

Damn it.

The disorienting light. The choking smoke... if I wasn't careful, I was going to fall. I swallowed back a sneeze and sent up another prayer to Saint Dismas, the patron saint of thieves. What? Just about every other sad case in the world had a saint.

Why not me? Not that I was normally a sad case, but at the moment, I most certainly was.

I don't understand why my body isn't working like it should. There's some weird stuff going on. I don't feel right, don't feel like myself. If I can't get it together, the very least of my worries is going to be falling off this beam. A fall and the subsequent noise would attract the attention of not only light boy, but the killer muscle that I knew lurked somewhere nearby. Even if they were on the other side of the warehouse, they'd hear me fall on my ass.

And when I say killer muscle, I mean three huge guys who kill when told.

Shit.

My continued need to sneeze is distracted by light boy. He's moving around, and then I see he's struggling with someone else, a woman. Her hair is flying, and she opens her mouth, but before she can say anything, he throws her off of him. Her hands reach out, and he pushes her away. Without warning, his voice rings out in the empty quiet of the warehouse.

"You stupid woman!" He pulls back his foot and kicks into the light. I hear a small cry, like an animal that's been hurt. I know it's the woman, and I want to help—but I can't. The man looks around, says something in a language I don't understand. But I get tone, and boy, is there a tone.

He steps into the light after her and then the light winks out.

I blink and I can still see the edge of the circle each time I close my eyes.

What just happened?

Why did I take this job, anyway?

*wo Days Earlier*

*T*his was it. One last score. One last time I had to squeeze into a too-small place, or some dusty hole, or any other shitty little hiding spot to steal for someone else.

This score would allow me—and Margrite—to get the hell out of here and start over. In a place where no one knew us, and no one would care. We'd have enough cash that we could live a life where no one cared what we did.

I thought about it as I made my way home. Luke found me in the nameless dive I frequented and told me that someone was looking for something that required a certain set of skills to retrieve. That there was one hell of a reward on the other side if I could get that something for them.

Just as my mind began to calculate how easy it would be to live with that much green on an island somewhere, Luke dropped the catch.

Because there's always a catch.

Caleb was the person had the something. Caleb. My nemesis. The asshole. The guy I would run over, and then drive back and forth over a few times, should the chance present itself. Why the bloodthirsty thoughts? Well, he was not a good guy, and he'd hurt a lot of people like me, like Margrite. Just people trying to get by, kids usually. Since kids aren't as good at fighting back. Maybe I had some experience with that, but I wasn't going down memory lane.

Except to say I wasn't a kid anymore, and I was a better thief than Caleb. I had actual skills. He was just lucky, with muscle and some major boss man backing him up.

I took the job. So now, I needed to figure out how to get the something.

The something turned out to be a backpack. I didn't care what I stole, or from whom. I did sometimes care who wanted it stolen, but the higher the payoff, the lower my ability to care. Not the best morals, I know. Sue me. Life in the street is what it is. Morals can easily take a back seat in a hurry if you're hungry, and there's no roof over your head.

Thankfully, I had a roof. And a bag of cheeseburgers. All I had to do know was sell Margrite on the merits of this job. Margrite should be back by now, and I'd need a couple of cheeseburgers to convince her this was worth it. Things were serious when I brought food. We'd gotten to the point where we ignored Caleb, and he ignored us. It was better for everyone that way. But this was just too good an opportunity to pass.

Stealing from Caleb, particularly on such a juicy score, would upset the truce. Margrite was even fonder of safety than I was. The childish side of me thought it would be great to pull one over on him.

I approached the building where we lived. It was almost a shell, except for the small apartment she and I had found, and spent years fixing up. I liked that the building looked ready to fall down. It meant that no one bothered it.

It also meant I had to be careful when I went home. I snuck in via our entrance and made my way upstairs.

"You home?" I asked quietly.

"Yes."

Margrite was lying on the couch, reading. She picked up everything she could find to read. "You brought food," she said.

I should explain. Margrite is my best friend. We've been friends ever since we were trying to steal the same lunchbox in school. Back when I still went to school. My mother died when I was two. I was in foster care after that. They never were able to find my family. I walked away from my last foster home when I was almost eighteen. Margrite, a year younger even though we were in the same grade, left with me. By that time, we were living in the same foster home and it sucked. A lot.

We've been on our own ever since. And we're both good thieves. I'm the better of the two of us. It's why Luke came to me. Since I was better, Margrite tended to manage what happened after we, or I, did the job. She drove a really hard bargain. I wondered if I ought to have her go back to Luke for me. She'd squeeze him for everything but his ratty-assed underwear.

"Yeah, we gotta talk," I said, putting down the bag.

"That sounds promising." She grabbed a cheeseburger and sat back, eyeing me warily. "Spill."

"Luke came to me tonight."

Margrite rolled her eyes. She doesn't like Luke.

"He has a job."

"He always has a job."

"Yeah, but this one is the one we've been waiting for."

"In what respect?"

I told her the price.

"Holy shit." Her hand holding the cheeseburger dropped into her lap. "Was he drunk? Did you get it in writing?"

"Don't be stupid. He's good for it."

She didn't respond, and I grinned as I ducked my head to focus on my own food. Really, though, it was so I didn't laugh in her face. She hated to be wrong, and in this case, I was right. Luke always paid. He was the only guy I dealt with anymore. But I still wondered if it was worth having her talk with Luke.

"You sure? Why would we want to leave all this?" She gestured around our little set of rooms.

The walls had chipped plaster and peeling paint. We stole electricity from a warehouse across the way. Same with the plumbing. I love the internet. You can figure out how to do anything on the internet.

It wasn't pretty. But it was warm, and comfortable, and safe. I had four different places in the building that I could use to stash things if I needed to.

"What's the job?"

"Get a backpack. From Caleb, who already stole it from who knows where? Luke said his guy didn't tell him how Caleb got hold of it."

"This is going to upset everything," she said.

"Did you hear me when I told you the amount?"

"Yeah, I heard you. When something is too good to be true, I generally don't believe it."

"Then come and talk to Luke with me. I know you don't like him. He's not fond of you, either. But you can see for yourself. Plus, Caleb is a bigger shit than usual. He took a job that someone else already accepted."

"That fuck," she took a bite of her burger.

"I know. Makes it all the better, doesn't it?"

We grinned at one another.

"It does, indeed. And we leave after that?"

I nodded. "Yep. We have the passports, and all we need to do is get out of the city, and buy a flight."

"We need to check the cards." She rooted in the bag for another burger.

Do I know my best friend or what? Bring enough cheeseburgers, and you can talk her into anything. Another souvenir of being hungry growing up.

"I check them every month. They're still good."

"Good. We won't get shit for a plane ticket without them."

I nodded again. "I know."

"Where's the thing?"

"It's a backpack. It's safety orange, and from what I hear, it's in his warehouse spot."

"What's in the backpack?" She asked.

"Does it matter?"

"It might…"

Margrite glared over her burger. I glared back. "Oh, all right," I relented. "A box."

"What kind of box?"

"A small one? One that fits in a backpack? One that the client wants?"

"Very funny. Where is it?"

"It's in his hiding spot on that one warehouse."

"Geez," she said. "That place is a pain in the butt to get into."

"I know. I need to think about it a little, and then I'll go in the next couple of nights."

Her eyebrows went up. "You have that much time?"

"Apparently the buyer isn't expecting it until next week. That's when Luke said he has to report in on any progress, good or bad. He made it clear he wanted to be able to call early with ugly backpack in hand."

"You don't know it's ugly."

"Come on. Safety orange? Is there any chance it's anything else?"

She laughed. "I want to meet with him. Get all the details."

"He'll love that. But this is such a big one, he won't mind."

And we got down to business. This was it. The last job. I wouldn't have to be a thief ever again. We'd get the hell out of here and live like normal people. Get a house. A laptop. An address.

I just needed to do this, and not screw it up.

Not that I ever did. I was the best. Everyone knew it, even that shitbag Caleb.

And I was going to prove it to him again. Steal it right out from under his fat, sloppy ass.

The thought made me grin. I think that was just as good as the payday.

She and I worked things out for the rest of the night, and after Margrite walked me through it three times, we went to bed.

Tomorrow we'd meet with Luke to get the final details. Then we would put the plan into action after we decided what night would be best.

Tomorrow our new life started. Just one more hurdle, and we were on our way.

resent Day
  On a beam
Wanting to sneeze

he wall of light and the strange abusive man had disappeared, leaving behind a tiny pinpoint like a flame that winked out in a puff of dust and cobwebs.

Shit.

No one was supposed to be here. What the hell was that light show? Was this a trap? Shit, shit, shit.

I crouched low on the beam again. I was spending more time on the beam than anywhere else. This late at night, there shouldn't be this much noise. Sure, it was quiet now, but with the light show and the poster boy for domestic violence beating up a woman, there had been a lot of noise. To me, it sounded like a herd of elephants. I could be a little sensitive about the whole thing. But noise made people come and take a look. I didn't want to bring any attention in here right now.

That might be a moot point. It was always other people who screwed things up. But I had time. I could wait.

I still needed to sneeze. Maybe I could sneeze quietly? I covered my mouth and nose with my hands, and let out a sneeze, immediately looking around. Thank god. I wouldn't have been able to hold it in much longer.

Holy... I couldn't even swear as I looked down on the warehouse floor. The pinpoint of light was back. It hung in the middle of the aisle a couple of rows over from me. It was small —but as I watched, it got larger. And kept growing. It was getting really bright—I was getting worried that I was going to be spotted. I still couldn't see anyone with the light. Was light boy coming back?

What the hell was going on? I did my best to push myself into the wood of the beam. Whatever this was, it made me really, really nervous.

Wide-eyed, holding my breath, I watched as a shadow appeared in the light.

It was the same guy as before. This time, there's no woman, and he's not flailing all over the place. He puts himself half in and half out of the light. It's clear he's looking for something.

But what?

I send a prayer to my new BFF Dismas that he's not looking for me. I don't know why he would be—I've never seen the guy before—but tonight has gone so far sideways, anything is possible.

He throws up his hands, and shouts in some weird language I can't understand.

Great. It's guaranteed Caleb's muscle guys heard that. They weren't nearby when I snuck in, but too much is happening here. It's going to draw their attention.

Streaks of red light fly out of his hands—there's no other way to put it. I shrank back—I couldn't get any flatter on the beam. Please don't let him see me. No sooner had I thought that, it felt like he turned and looked right at me. Creepy. He waved his hands and said something else I couldn't understand. I pressed myself so hard against the beam that I could feel the splinters digging into my skin. I couldn't let him see me. Even though I felt guilty as hell for leaving that poor woman on the ground at his mercy, the fact that he came back and she wasn't around made me feel even worse.

As I ignored the pain of the wood digging into me, and the feeling of my muscles beginning to cramp, I felt a spark run through me from head to foot. It surprised me so much I nearly let go and clutched the beam at the last minute before falling on my ass to the boxes below.

That would have blown my operation for sure.

I blinked once, and then again—and the man and the light disappeared. I blinked rapidly, still seeing the blotches from the light circle again. My night vision was going to be ruined if this continued.

Where did he—they—go?

I also didn't know how the noise hadn't gotten the attention of anyone else outside the warehouse. The guy hadn't been trying to sneak around.

I waited, breathing shallowly, and listening so hard that my ears ought to hurt. I could feel all the hair on my body stand up from the electric jolt that had run through me.

Tonight was getting weirder by the minute.

As I exhaled, my nose burned and a puff of smoke drifted across my hands.

What the...?

I inhaled deeply, and exhaled again, ignoring the slight burn in my throat and down into my chest. Smoke rolled out from my nose.

From. My. Nose.

I repeated this exercise a few more times, and the smoke got denser. It felt like there was a small fire in my throat, and I wanted a drink of water in the worst way.

At least I didn't need to sneeze anymore.

Now I could officially say that I was freaked out. Completely and utterly freaked out.

I didn't smoke. Not cigarettes, not weed, nothing. I saw too many people wasting money and life on that crap.

So why was I smoking like a barbeque?

I shook my head, causing dust to flare up around me. I rubbed at my nose, not wanting to sneeze. Although the smoke wasn't making my nose itchy. That was another tick mark on the weird side of things.

Knock it off, I told myself. Concentrate! *Get the bag and get the hell out of here! Then you can focus on your own shit.*

I inhaled again, trying to focus. I did have a job to do. I ignored the fact that when I exhaled, dark smoke blew out in front of me. Can't help that at the moment.

The bag. Get the damned bag.

"That's if you get your ass out of here without screwing it up," I muttered. When I'd planned this job, it had seemed a lot easier. No weird guys, no smoke... I stopped myself. Later. I could rehash this later. Bag, then payday.

How had the bag gotten here? I still didn't know what the connection was. This was Luke's gig. He didn't work with Caleb. Thought as little of the guy as I did.

But somehow, Caleb had discovered the job. I'd gone into the local bar, and Caleb had been trash talking, like he does. Normally, I don't listen. But after learning from Luke that he'd gotten to something I needed to acquire, I listened hard.

And I have exceptionally good hearing. Freakishly good. Even in the dive bar I was standing in, nursing a beer.

"So I heard, from a source," Caleb said to one of the flunkies that hung around him like flies on a zapper, "That there was something special coming in. Something that held a lot of interest for..." he looked around, deliberately over my head than at my eyes, and continued. "For a lot of people. Which means an easy sell," Caleb shrugged. "Boss is paying *really* well for this."

That shrug made me want to rip his head off his shoulders. Even as I noted he referenced his boss. The scary badass or badasses that no one messed with.

I didn't know how he'd heard. Worse, I didn't know how he'd gotten to it first. Along with the juicy payday.

I knew him well enough to know that his trash talk was letting me know he'd beaten me.

Yeah.

He was a jerk. And outside the payday, I didn't care what it was that I was stealing. Luke did right by me, no matter what Margrite thought of him. He'd said I needed to get a box that was in a grubby backpack. I had pictures of both of them. The backpack was raggedy. The box was pretty, but nothing special. What I cared about was that I'd been given the job, and someone snaked it from me.

I grinned, picturing Caleb as a snake in the road.

That I ran over with my bike.

"Speaking of which, your bike is missing you, jerk," I whispered to myself.. Another concern on my already long list. I found that a plain old bike was the easiest way to get around. No records, as I'd need with a car, or a motorcycle, and no one paid attention to a kid on a bike.

I talk to myself. It's a habit. Maybe a bad one.

I eased along the beam in the warehouse. Now that strange angry guys who made the get-off-my-lawn guy look like a picnic had stopped showing up with a light show, I might be able to sneak over to where I knew Caleb stashed his goods. Everyone knew it was here although they didn't know the exact location.

Although I did now.

But he also kept a pack of goons that would beat you down first, and never ask questions, so it didn't really matter that everyone knew.

No one would try to steal from him, that bastard.

Except me. Not only for the payday, but because I liked to

steal from him. And because after this was over, I'd never have to see his stupid face again.

It was a satisfying thought. However, none of all the glory or the riches would rain down upon me until I got the box.

As I inched along the beam, heading for the other side of the warehouse, I tried hard not to picture the small metal box that held my cash. I hid it in a floorboard of the house that I squatted in. It was the picture of urban decay. Not even the junkies would go there to hide out.

Perfect for me.

The box was getting pretty light, even with my frugal living. I kept only what I needed, what we needed, to get by. Everything else went to our escape plan.

That last bit made me laugh. Frugal living was all I knew. And it—

Wait.

I flattened myself on the beam, willing myself as invisible as possible. There was something making noise—had the light thing returned? I'd be picking the splinters out of me for days with all the quality time I was getting up here.

A thin, golden glow came to life on my left as a door opened. A shadow, and then another, and another entered through the light, casting large monsters on the wall to my right.

Great.

Now someone else was here. What the hell? No one was supposed to be here this time of day. This was the third time in what seemed like less than five minutes. I'd cased the place for the last two days. The goons hung around outside, burning up Caleb's money with smokes, and weed, and forties—sure.

Not in the warehouse.

I held my breath as I heard footsteps coming closer.

"Boss said there might be someone trying to get in," a low voice rumbled.

Great. It was one of the goons. I'd rarely heard them speak, but when they did, they all seemed to have this deep bass voice that was barely domesticated.

A laugh, and then another.

"Who'd be that stupid?"

"Someone looking to make a score," the first goon sounded bored. "Doesn't matter. Just look around, let's get this done. I don't need him breathing down my neck!"

The guy sounded annoyed. It was nice to know that someone else found Caleb annoying.

"There's no one here," a third voice said. "Come on."

Good. Be lazy. Perfect. And yes, get out.

I could feel an itch developing in my leg, and felt the need to cough, all at once.

The twin desires made me tense up, and I heard the drag of my coat on the beam.

Not a lot of noise, but enough to make the trio of guards stop twenty feet away from where I was clinging on for dear life above them.

"What was that?" One said.

They all stayed silent. Listening.

I held my breath. I could feel my ears getting hot, and then my forehead. I wanted to cough. My cheeks puffed out, and I pursed my lips together.

Don't, don't, I told myself.

The spot on my calf felt like spiders were dancing on it.

Jeesh. Couldn't I get a break here? Sneezing, smoke that I couldn't even think about, and now an itch?

"It's nothing," one of the guys said. I couldn't tell them apart at this point. "Probably just a rat."

"Hate the friggen rats," said another.

"There's no one here. Let's go."

"Yeah, we'll be back here in an hour," I heard as they walked by my hiding spot and towards the right side of the warehouse.

Laughter, and then words, but I couldn't understand them. They'd gotten too far away.

I let out the breath I was holding. It was safe to breathe, at least. I reached down and scratched the back of my leg.

They stopped again.

Damn it. *Come on,* I thought. *Get out!*

Finally they opened a door on the right, and the light shone in and then it went dark once more. The door closed firmly behind them and the warehouse was quiet again.

It could be a trap. They weren't entirely stupid, appearances notwithstanding.

I stayed where I was, counting to five hundred. That might be pushing it, but since they were suspicious, no need to add to that.

When I felt I was safe, I continued slinking along the beam. I got to the other side, and swung down, landing softly on a crate.

Convenient. Thankfully, I was able to be quiet as I dropped. I crouched down, looking around.

According to all I'd heard, there was a safe, or storage box of some kind on this side. Caleb had trust issues like I did and hid his stash accordingly.

But ever since he'd stolen the backpack with info he'd weaseled from somewhere that was meant for me, I'd made it my business to find out how he did business. I hoped that no one had lied to me along the way.

This was going to hurt otherwise.

I jumped down from the crate to another box and nearly fell on my ass. It made more noise than I liked, and I crouched in a seriously uncomfortable position while I waited to see if someone would come rushing in.

No one did.

I carefully eased down onto a third box, and then onto the floor.

Excellent. I was near the wall with the small storage door in it. I'd talked to a former girlfriend of Caleb's who said she'd dumped him after he locked her in one time. She had said that it was more comfortable than she'd thought because there were big laundry bags of stuff. She hadn't bothered to look, being too mad and screaming her head off.

Made sense to me that was where he hid his stuff.

I got to the door, and there was a big Master lock on it.

What an ass. Like any thief on the street couldn't handle this. Size wasn't everything.

Something a short guy like Caleb wouldn't get.

I pulled out my tools and picked the lock. Took a little longer in the dark, but I'd been doing this since before I was ten. The skills you learned in foster care.

The lock clicked open, a sound that echoed in the warehouse. I paused and then tucked it in my pocket. I'd be sure to lock the door when I left.

I ducked into the room and pulled out my flashlight. Just like Melinda the ex had said—there were a bunch of dirty white canvas bags that looked like big laundry bags.

So where would he hide the backpack?

I kept the light low, holding it in my mouth. Methodically, I went through the bags. He had some good stuff in here.

When I opened up a box that held jewelry, I found a black pouch. That could only be loose stones.

I opened the bag and shook some stones into my hand. They sparkled in the light, and I pulled a plastic baggie from my pocket and put the stones into it. Then I shoved them into the pocket of my jeans. I closed the black pouch and put it back. Hopefully, he wouldn't notice a thing until I was long gone.

"Payment for my troubles, jerk," I mumbled around the flashlight.

There were only four bags left. What if my hunch was wrong? What if the damn backpack wasn't here?

I opened the next bag. "Bingo, sucker," I said.

Carefully, I went through the backpack. There was nothing

in any of the outside pockets. I opened it up, and I could see a wooden box. Pretty fancy one, too, with metal edges and some crystals or some kind of thing on top. It looked like the one in the picture.

I reached in to grab it. I'd leave the backpack here and—

"Ouch!" I snatched my hand away. I looked down at my hand and I could see a scorch mark. I must be in some kind of shock because this should hurt.

But it's not hurting.

As I'm assessing how bad this latest issue is, I'm thinking, *Why is this not hurting?*

I shine the light on my hand, and it doesn't look burned, but something burned it when I touched the box. Nothing's burning now, and nothing is hurting, and I don't see any burns on me, but—I shook my head. What is going on? Things are not what they should be. I'm getting a bad feeling in the pit of my stomach and that's never a good sign.

As though someone snapped their fingers in front of me, I shook my head. *Snap out of it, jackass,* I thought. *Kind of on the clock here.*

Ignoring the pain that flares up as soon as I'm ready to get going, I shoved the box into my backpack, and zipped it shut. Hopefully the shirts in my pack would muffle any rattling from the box. I'd already been here too long. Much longer, and I would be caught. Interesting that the strong box I'd heard about was not here at all. I made another note that ex-girlfriends probably had the best intel even if they might be a little nutty.

I crouched down, looking to make sure that I could get out the way I'd planned. You know, when this job was risky, but simple.

A burned hand made it risky, and potentially complex. And I didn't do complex. Complex just made everything tangled. As one of my many foster fathers—I use that term loosely—used to say, *Keep it simple, stupid.* That was usually accompanied by a slap to the head or shoulder region, so there's no way to forget it.

I listened. I didn't think, even if I had yelled when I mysteriously burned myself, that anyone heard me. If they had, if they were waiting, I would be done for.

So what did I have to lose? I put my hand on the door and lifted the latch. The door eased open, and I held still, listening. Nothing. I opened it a bit further and slid out of the door, closing it behind me in a smooth motion.

Now I had to get away without attracting the attention of any of the goons. I crept along the side of the warehouse, taking one slow step at a time.

You'd think it was best to run like hell and get away from the scene.

I'd thought so too and nearly gotten my head beat in when I tried it. I'd found that after… liberating whatever I was after, I went slow and silent. That way, anyone listening was able to shake off their concerns and chalk weird noises up to nothing major. Running alerts people that something's up.

Running is not something you can do quietly.

After what seemed like fourteen hours, I finally reached the fence that ran around the warehouse. I ducked down and wiggled out through the hole I'd found when I'd scoped things out yesterday. I didn't jump fences if I could avoid it. Too easy to get caught up in the air, a perfect target. Slinking along the ground was a lot safer.

I hoisted my own black backpack onto my shoulders—no way I would have taken that safety cone orange thing—and walked away, making sure to stay in the shadows.

I snickered, thinking about the orange backpack. Caleb would be in deep shit when he went to hand it off. I'd stuffed it with some women's clothing I'd found in the big bags—serious hooker stuff. Yeah, that would go over well.

It was totally deserved, too.

Now I just needed to figure out whether I would contact the person after this before or after Caleb was scheduled to hand it off. Did I shame him now, or later?

As much as I wanted to, I didn't leave any indication that it was me who got one over on him. He was not the brightest guy, and a complete ass, but he would kill you without a second thought, and I found that I was attached to living. For the most part.

Lost in thought, I let down my guard.

"Out a little late, aren't you?" A voice hissed in my ear as a hand came down on my shoulder.

3

"What the—" I whirled around, ready to take out—- "Oh, it's you." I rolled my eyes and shoved the hand off of my shoulder.

"You're lucky as hell it's me," Margrite, my one and only friend rolled her eyes right back at me.

Amazing how you could see these things in the dark. But I could. I could see as well in the dark as I did during the day. Freakish, like my ability to hear. I would have heard her, had I not been so lost in thought on getting away without being caught. Or dying. I didn't even think about how easily I navigated in the dark anymore. Everything that happened in the past hour had thrown me off my game.

"What do you want?" I asked. I wasn't trying to be an ass, but I really didn't want her around. I kept walking, head down, not waiting for an answer.

"What have you been doing? Something's gone wrong! I can see it all over you!" She hissed, hurrying to catch up with me.

"Well, since I have a need to eat regularly, and not be naked in the streets, I've been working," I answered, not slowing up.

"Whatever," she said. "This wasn't the plan, Aodan! You know this is not what we talked about—"

At that I did stop and hold up a hand. "I don't want to talk about it. No, it's not what was in the plan. But I took a look at what the situation was, and I made some changes. I'm good with where I am." I started walking again. "And keep it down, will you? I'm trying to make a quiet getaway. What are you doing out here, anyway? Did you follow me?"

"Of course, I followed you. I wanted to be available if the cops showed up. Or Caleb," she added snottily.

I made a 'whatever' kind of noise, which meant I didn't want to answer her in any way.

"Yeah, that's what I thought." She made her own noise. "The least you could do is go get something to eat with me."

For people like us, people who lived on the street, lived by our wits, food, shelter, and keeping the other people like us away from us were the paramount concerns. Everybody talked about what they'd do if they hit some big score—because while not everyone I knew was a thief, everyone I knew wasn't exactly on the right side of the law—I wondered if any of us really could get away.

I was only twenty-three, and I didn't see me getting away. I just didn't see how it could happen. Not that I didn't keep trying, but the kind of cash it would take to get out of here for good looked really far away.

Until this job came along.

That had been six days ago.

I'd gotten the text, and after I talked Margrite into it, with her eating most of the cheeseburger bribe I'd brought, we made our way over to his place. Luke had nearly been quivering with excitement when I showed up at his house. If he'd been a dog, he would have already peed on my shoe.

"Hey, man, I got something for you." He waved me in and handed me a can of beer. He offered one to Margrite, who shook her head.

"Yeah?"

"Yeah, and big payday, too."

I raised my eyebrows. Luke always seemed to talk a big payday game, but funnily enough, there was always a reason that it wasn't as big as the pre-theft hype. Listening to Margrite, I'd started to find all the skepticism in the world.

Still… "How big?" I asked. We'd talked about it briefly before, but I wanted to see if he said anything differently now.

"Enough that you could get out of here and get into some kind of real life where it's warm," he said, all excitement gone.

"What?" How in the hell did he know about that?

My expression must have shown on my face because he waved a hand at me. "You think no one else knows but you and the skinny chick?" Normally the fact that he was open about their mutual dislike made me laugh. Not now.

"I know why you steal anything I ask you to. I know why you live in that shithole. I know what you're saving for. You've told me. You know, like friends do?"

"We're friends?" I asked, sitting down in his office. When had I ever told him?

Luke put a hand over his heart, drawing back slightly. "That hurts, Aodan. We're always friends."

"You must give me the friend percentage then," I looked down at my can of beer.

"I give you all I can, and still keep enough for me," he shot back with heat behind his words.

That made me look up. He actually sounded as though he cared.

"We're here. So tell me more about the job."

He settled onto the ratty pleather seat across from me in front of his disreputable desk. That desk was a monument to defying reality. Any sudden moves and all the crap on his desk might fall over and kill him. Or me and Margrite. Or all of us.

Luke wasn't bothered by the leaning tower of potential death on his desk. "It's a backpack, and it's bright orange, and the client told me it's probably dirty-looking, too. Like I told you before. She just wants it back. I asked her what was in it, she said it was an old family heirloom, a keepsake box. No biggie, but I guess someone stole it when the original owner died." Luke nodded at Margrite and I with a slight movement of the head. "Who knows? You know how people get when someone dies. It's like a blood bath." He shrugged. "As long as it's not illegal shit, I figured it was fine." He knew my limits.

At that, he looked right at me, a question in his expression.

I waited, not meeting his eyes. This part of things, the hesitation—it was important. Even if Luke and I both knew the deal.

I sighed. "Okay, I'm in. But tell me how big?" This was important. I needed a number now. It's why I brought Margrite. She would never let him get away with anything once he'd offered a number. He'd teased me before, but now it was time to get hard numbers.

He gave me a number, and I clutched at my can of beer, feeling the sticky residue hit my fingers.

"Say it again," I whispered. "There's got to be—"

He shook his head, earlier excitement resurfacing. "Nope. I did the same thing. Nearly shit myself when she tossed out the number. It's enough, even with my cut. You can get the hell out of here. Take Skinny with you," he referred to Margrite. Why did no one call her by her name, I wondered? Because they were afraid of her? She was petite, but she could kick all sorts of ass.

I also thought it was interesting that everyone we came across talked about us as though we were an item rather than best friends.

I ignored the irritation that brought. "You think this chick is good for it?" People talked a lot of crap.

Luke leaned in. "I got a down payment, man," he whispered. It was weird how he was whispering in his own house.

Which decided things right there for all of us. Not even Margrite could argue with a down payment.

And that's how I found myself here, outside of Caleb's warehouse, trying to get away without getting my ass kicked and ignoring whatever it was Margrite was hissing at me. Again, with the hissing. What was she, a snake?

I still didn't know where the three guys had gotten to. That made me nervous as well.

"You want to ease up with the pissy snake impression? I'd like to get out of here in one piece," I whispered.

A punch between my shoulder blades was my answer.

I smiled. Pain-in-the-ass she might be, but Margrite took no shit from anyone, not even me. I liked that about her. I understood it. Just like that, my annoyance passed.

We walked in silence, clinging to the warehouses and abandoned buildings we passed, living in the corners of the shadows. For all her bitching, Margrite got it. It's why I didn't tell her to hit the bricks. Well, that and she's my best friend.

When we'd gotten about ten blocks from Caleb's hidey-hole, I turned to her. "I'll go get something to eat, but I need to see Luke first. I don't want this," I shrugged my shoulder against my pack, "Hanging around any longer than it has to."

"What is it?" she asked quietly.

"Wooden box, nice decoration. Exactly what the client said it was. No surprises."

"Anything good inside?"

I shook my head. "I don't know. I didn't look. I don't care. Still seems too good to be true, so I want to hand it off and get paid. Even if something goes wrong," I added, thinking about what else I'd taken, "Everything is going to be fine."

"What does that mean?"

Caleb was going to be pissed.

Which made me laugh.

"What?" Margrite asked.

"Tell you after. Let's go get rid of this."

Like she did every time I did a job, she reached down and squeezed my hand. Just once, just enough to allow me to feel the warmth of her skin and the strength of her muscles. Just enough to let me know that we were a team and in this together no matter what.

Like always, her touch was gone in an instant.

"You're buying," she said.

I smiled. Right now, I felt like I could buy the whole world a drink.

We hurried, not speaking. After what seemed an eternity, we reached the small ramshackle house Luke called home. That made twice in one week. We might be risking it with the desk of doom.

The lights were on in the front, so I went around the back. I didn't need to be seen walking in his door even though he fenced everything. People here knew. They knew you, knew what you did. But there's a difference between everyone knowing something and giving them proof.

Three knocks, and he yanked open the wooden screen door. "Yeah?" He peered out and then recognized me. "Oh, come in." He stood back to let me enter, and Margrite followed on my heels.

"What is this, date night?" He asked with a leer.

"Bite it," Margrite said.

"Gladly, sweetheart. When you get an ass."

She raised a hand, but let it drop as he moved away from her.

"You get it?" Luke asked me.

I nodded. I'd told him he'd see me again once I got it. I'd never failed him before, and I had no intention of starting now. Not even with Caleb the douche getting in my business.

"Where is it?"

"I have the item," I said. "I left the backpack. No sense in advertising that Elvis left the building," I shrugged.

"Weird. He was expecting you tonight," Luke said, turning away.

I followed, knowing where he was heading. "You knew this?" I asked his back.

"You couldn't warn a person?" Margrite asked from behind me.

"You heard that? Why didn't you tell me?" I demanded.

His shoulders went up once. "Would it have made a difference?" Luke didn't even turn around.

"It might have," I answered. "I saw something weird tonight. I think he had more than just the normal goon squad there tonight."

Now Luke did turn around. "Who was it?"

I shrugged, loving the look of irritation that crossed his face. "I don't know. I saw a light in the warehouse, like someone was having a smoke, and walking down the aisles."

"You get spotted?"

I gave him a look.

"Okay, yeah, yeah, not you, whatever, asshole. Where's the box?"

I set down my backpack and carefully pulled out the wooden box. In the light, it was gorgeous. Stones winked on the top, and there was a raised piece in the middle that I was pretty sure was gold. A shudder of something ran through me as I touched it. I'd forgotten that it had burned or shocked me or something when I first picked it up. I felt a small shock, like when you rub your feet on the carpet and then touch a light switch. But it didn't compare to the shock I got in the warehouse.

Luke took it and examined it. "You open it?"

"Nope. You know I don't look."

"I hear differently, we're done." He turned from me and went about opening his safe.

Code of thieves. I stole the whatever, but I had to get the entire whatever it was to the client. Luke fenced the whatever, but he got the client exactly whatever they'd requested. We didn't steal from clients. Luke and I knew each other well enough we didn't steal from each other either—well, not much

—so his questions were merely a formality. But he knew I never looked. His question was always the same, just like my answer. He liked to be able to tell the clients he'd done due diligence.

Once I knew I had the thing I was hired to get, I didn't care.

I smiled as I always did. It gave me a laugh that there were rules among thieves. But there were. At least, the thieves I dealt with. It was even funnier that Luke stuck to this charade when he knew all the answers.

Probably why I hated Caleb. On principle, in addition to the fact that he was a douchebag.

"All right. I'll let the client know now." Luke set the box down and opened the safe. Once he'd put the box away, and hidden the safe again, he pulled out his phone, and I could hear the ringing.

"Yes?" A strong voice, the voice of a woman, rang out even though he wasn't on speaker with her.

"Got it," he said shortly.

"Intact?" the woman asked.

"Looks like it," Luke answered.

Silence, and then, "I'm transferring the funds to you now. I'll be there in ten minutes. Is the thief still there?"

Luke's surprised face met mine. I could read the question in his expression. Did I want him to lie? Or was I all right with meeting the client?

I shrug-nodded.

"He is."

"Keep him there. I'd like to talk with him."

Luke raised his eyebrows at me. I nodded again.

"Okay."

The woman hung up.

"What the hell?" Margrite asked.

"I don't know. She didn't mention that," Luke said, and stopped as his phone chimed at him.

"That's ridiculous," Margrite snorted, crossing her arms. His notification was the SpongeBob SquarePants theme.

"My kid likes it," Luke said. "You sure you're okay with this? You don't have to," That was directed at me.

"Yeah, I'm fine." He had kids? Where did they live? In the desk?

"Holy shit," he breathed. "I'm transferring yours right now," Luke's eyes didn't leave his phone as his fingers tapped it rapidly.

"Get enough cash to eat for a couple," Margrite said to me as she walked out into the small living room.

"No prob," Luke said absently. Then he looked up. "What are you gonna do now, A?"

"Meet your crazy client, then go eat," I said.

I felt a buzz from the phone in my pocket. That meant that I'd gotten an email letting me know a deposit had been made. I felt a warmth spread over me I had never felt before. I glanced at the email, loving the fact that there were more zeroes than I'd ever seen after the first number. I'd never seen that much money in conjunction with my bank account ever. But it was there now.

I was set. A few more moments, and then it was *Asta la vista, baby.*

4

———

$\mathcal{W}$e were all sitting in the living room when the rap landed on the front door. I couldn't be sure, but I thought all three of us jumped.

"I got it," Luke muttered, getting up.

"Your house," Margrite said, rolling her eyes.

I gave her a WTF look. Tonight was strange enough without her being all shitty.

A woman came in, and I sat up straight. A similar jolt like I'd felt in the warehouse when the abusive guy showed up raced through me.

Why?

I didn't have time to consider it because I was too busy looking at her.

She wasn't old, and she wasn't young. She had long, curly hair and that look that really rich chicks have—like, they knew who they were, and where they were going, both short-term and long-term. It was a look I envied. She was also gorgeous, the kind of woman who drew looks and attention simply by walking out of her door in the morning.

"Where is the casket?" She demanded.

We all looked at her. Her next move could involve snapping her fingers, or stomping her foot. She was that kind of woman.

She tried again. "The box?" Without taking a breath, she looked around the room. "Which of you retrieved it?" As she came in, I got a glimpse of a man who stood outside, obviously with this woman.

"I got it," Luke all but ran from the room to respond to her request.

I could see why, if he met her in person, he was practically peeing himself. She had that effect. Next to me, I could feel Margrite's temper rise, like the hackles of a junk-yard dog.

"I did," I said. I didn't get up.

"Was there anything difficult about getting it?" she asked.

I got the impression she wanted to ask more, but was restraining herself. I also got the impression that this wasn't a normal thing for her.

I shrugged. "Is stealing something ever easy?" I met her gaze.

Her cheeks flushed although I think it might be anger more than shame. "It's important that no one saw you, human."

What? "This human—" I emphasized the word, "Got in and out with no problem." I wasn't telling anyone about the light show.

She looked at me, and I could tell that she was dying to say something. Her eyes narrowed as she took me in. Her mouth pursed. Whatever she wanted to say—I couldn't tell. But I was familiar with the look of someone biting their tongue.

The man behind her must have been able to tell as well. He came up and put his hand on her shoulder. She turned her head so fast I was surprised she didn't hit him.

She said something in a language that I didn't know. He looked at her, and then at me.

He responded in the same language, and I felt the weight of both of their stares.

Her brows furrowed, and she turned and asked him something, looking back at me carefully.

He inhaled, and I could tell that he was considering. Then he shook his head.

"We need this," he said quietly in English.

I didn't know if Margrite heard him. He barely moved his lips. But his words calmed the woman, and she gave a single tiny nod. That did not, however, stop her from watching me from under her lashes. She didn't take her eyes off me.

I knew enough to know that she wasn't checking me out. This was something more. I didn't like it. It was weird, and I avoided weird like the plague.

Luke was coming in with the box in his hands, and Margrite studied her nails or something. Whatever it was women did to show they were bored to tears.

I had to smother a smile. I knew her faces, and this was one that she put on when she wanted to piss off someone. Which meant she didn't like Miss High-and-Mighty any more than I did. She looked up at me then, and I grinned fast and then let the smile fall from my face.

"It's right here."

"Where is the bag it came in?" High-and-Mighty snapped.

"It's still in the warehouse where I found it," I answered before Luke could say something. "I thought it would be better to let him think he still had it."

She was about to rip my head off, but the man with her spoke first. "Thank you for your consideration. It is better that no one know where this is." He was smooth, practiced.

"You're good. As far as anyone who knows it was in the warehouse, they think it's still there."

"And you weren't seen?" The woman asked again.

Margrite huffed.

"No." I kept it simple.

"Thank you," the man said, giving me a sketchy bow. "We

appreciate your discretion. Come, my dear. We're done. Let's go home," he added.

For whatever reason, those words affected her, and she gripped his hand. "Yes," she breathed.

Without another word, without a backwards glance, the pair walked from the room.

Margrite, Luke and I just stared. What else could you do?

"Well, that was weird as fuck," Margrite got up. "Let's go eat," she said to me.

"You sticking around?" Luke asked.

"I'm not sure," I said. I knew we were leaving, but I wasn't advertising my plans to anyone. Not even to Luke.

"You want me to call—"

I shook my head. "No. I'll let you know if that changes."

His shoulders dropped a little. I knew he didn't want to hear that, but I'd made the call that once the job was over, if the pay was what he said, I was getting the hell out of here. Or rather, I'd told him I was done with any jobs for a while. I hadn't mentioned we were actually leaving the city. And changing our names.

Now I just needed to do it on the quiet so that no one knew. So how Luke knew, I wasn't sure. It made me nervous.

Margrite didn't say anything to Luke as she walked out the door. I followed her, raising my hand to him in farewell.

Finally, it was time to go eat.

---

*A*t the diner, we ate in silence. When Margrite had finished her burger, she sucked noisily on her milkshake. We were splurging.

"So, you think that's it? You think he's going to just let you go?"

I nodded. "He won't know anything other than we're

moving away from this. He doesn't know all the rest," I waved a hand to encompass all of our plans.

"I hope you're right."

"I am." I hoped that Luke had made merely a lucky guess.

"Okay, when do you want to put this into action?"

"Let's get a bike, and get all the things we need, and say, maybe two days? I want to be gone before Caleb finds out," I dropped my voice. "You know it's not just him."

Caleb, in spite of being the biggest douche ever, worked for someone. No one knew who, but they were big. I'd seen people come to see him from his boss, and it's the only time I'd ever seen the little pissant look frightened. In public, too, so the boss had to be some big, scary bad ass.

I wanted no part of that.

Margrite nodded. "I'll start packing."

Neither of us kept all our valuables in one place. We'd learned the hard way that you put all your shit in one place, someone only had to find your one spot. Another awesome foster kid legacy.

So packing, for us, encompassed visiting the hiding spots. I knew where Margrite stashed stuff. Unlike me, she went outside of our ratty building. I disagreed with her philosophy. Scattered hiding places made it tougher to get out in a hurry, but it wasn't my shit, so I let her be. Besides, as she was happy to remind me, we'd never had to run.

"I'll get a bike," I said.

"You think you can?"

There was the small problem of no ID, no driver's license, and it went without saying that plates would need to come with the bike. But I nodded. "I have a guy. I've been talking to him."

We had the fake IDs—but I wasn't going to share my new name to anyone here. No way. That was a sure-fire way to have someone track you down and do less-than-positive things to you. Once I shook the dust from this place off me, I never wanted to come back.

As we left, I asked her, "You heading out for a bit?"

She nodded. "I'll be back later."

We split up and after stopping at one of my hidey holes to grab some cash, I went down to the garage of the guy I'd been talking to.

"You still got that bike?" I asked him as I got to his office at the back of the building.

The guy, whose name was Keene, looked up from the paperwork he was surrounded with. "Hey, Aodan, I didn't know if you still wanted it."

"Yeah, if you have it. If not, another bike, something similar," I didn't want to let on that this was a big deal in any way.

"You still need some plates?" He shuffled some of the papers.

As much as I wanted to do something other than stealing for a living, I was really glad that I didn't have a job that had a lot of paperwork. "Yeah," I said again. "I'm getting tired of hoofing it."

For years, I'd used a bike. As in, pedal my ass around bike. Much easier than trying to keep something motorized, and if someone lifted it, I just got another one. It wasn't a huge hassle.

Okay, in the rain it pretty much sucked. My latest ride was stolen two days ago.

"'Bout time," he grumbled. "Come on back here. I put it aside for you. I have a nice, clean plate for you, too."

"Already?" I was surprised.

"'Course. I told you I would." His tone was gruff.

I remembered that I'd stolen his daughter's diaries back a couple of years ago. She had a really shitty boyfriend, wrote all kinds of stuff like teenagers in love do in her diary, and then he stole them and threatened to blackmail her. At least, that was what Keene told me. It was why he asked me to steal them back for her.

I had a lot of problems with people taking advantage of

kids. Blackmail happens, but to a teenager? I told him I'd take the job for nothing.

I hadn't looked in them when I got them—I never looked—but Keene had been pretty grateful. She'd gotten into Stanford, I remembered him telling me.

"I appreciate it," I said. "How long do I have with it?"

"It's registered to me," he said.

"What?"

"You buy it from me, and if you ever get questioned, I'll say I let you use it, with no idea that you had lawbreaking in mind," he grinned at me suddenly as he unlocked a gate on the other side of the garage. "And you use it for as long as you want," he added.

"That's—you don't have to do that," I said. I wasn't used to this. Kindness, generosity—they'd been long gone in my world.

"You helped my daughter out of a pickle," Keene said. "I been looking for a way to thank you for that. I can do this. Just don't screw things up too bad, okay?"

"You sure I'm going to be breaking the law?" I asked with a small laugh.

"Don't you?" He went in and brought out a bike. "This is a generic, no attention-grabbing kind of bike. Plain, simple, looks like every other motorcycle out there. Now how you dress... well, I can't do anything about that," he said. He looked my coat up and down.

I smiled. I loved my coat, but it wasn't exactly low-key. Red never is.

Back to the bike. It was lovely. It was shiny black, but Keene was right. It was an older Kawasaki Ninja. It wouldn't attract attention, and while it was worth something, it wasn't anywhere near top of the line.

"It's perfect," I said. "This is kick ass, Keene. What do I owe you?"

We'd agreed on a price before, but I wanted to give him the

chance to up it if he felt he needed to. He was seriously doing me a solid.

"Same as we agreed to two months ago. What do you think I am?" He actually sounded insulted.

I handed over the cash and took the keys. I started it and grinned as the sound echoed around the mostly empty garage. In another corner, I saw a guy quietly working on a nice BMW. I ignored him. Not my business.

"She's in good shape. Try not to kill yourself," Keene put the money in his front shirt pocket.

"Thanks, man," I said.

"Good luck." He studied me for a moment. "Get out of here," he waved and turned around, heading back for his office.

I watched him. Is that what fathers were like? Did the right thing for their kids? Tried to help others who'd helped them? I felt envy for his daughter. He might not be totally honest, but he was a good guy.

"Fuck this," I muttered. There was no reason for me to be moping around about what I didn't have. Because what I did have was exactly what I wanted, and I'd be able to make my life what I wanted. And I'd done it on my own, with the help of only one person.

I gunned the bike out of the garage bay door and headed for home. I had the perfect hiding place for this. No one would ever find it, and in two days, we were out of here.

The wind on my face made me smile even as it stung at my eyes. I'd have to get helmets. Not because I was overly safe—I enjoyed the wind across my hair—but because it would be easier to hide my identity.

When I got to our building, I wheeled the bike around the back, and into one of the ground floor apartments. There was a big hole in the wall, so I wasn't sure it counted as one anymore, but it would work. I headed for the far corner of the apartment, and put the bike in a closet, in a busted-out wall. Then I threw a tarp over it, and then a ratty blanket, and piled trash and other debris I found around the place.

Once it was concealed, I moved several steps away, looking it over, satisfied with my work. This wouldn't be a good long-term solution, but it only had to last for two days. Forty-eight hours.

"Let's just get through this," I whispered.

As I was leaving the apartment, I heard someone whisper.

Come to me.

What the fuck? "Who's there?" I whispered, trying to throttle the anger that raged up within me.

No one answered. But I'd clearly heard it.

I stood still, listening. There was no one. Nothing, not even the garbage and crap all over the place, stirred. If someone was in here, I'd hear them.

I thought about the voice. I didn't recognize it, but it was said with command. With an expectation of being obeyed. I knew that tone just fine.

"No," I said out loud.

Aodan, is that you? Have I found you at last?

I stopped in my tracks. The voice was back. And this time, it sounded hopeful, and slightly unsure. Like they—whoever this was—couldn't believe they were speaking to me.

What the hell? Was I really debating my imaginary voices?

But I'd heard it. As clearly as though someone was standing near me.

"Who are you?" I whispered. I peered into the darkness, looking for someone, anyone. Any sign that someone was fucking with me.

I have finally found you! I've been searching for a long time, the voice said. *Where are you?*

Oh, no, I thought. I'm not saying shit. Looks like forty-eight hours with peace and safety might be asking too much. I ignored the voice and sprinted upstairs.

We were leaving tomorrow.

5

"You get everything?" I asked as I walked in. Margrite was sitting on the floor with a couple of small bags.

She nodded. "This stuff will all be one fat backpack when I'm done."

I didn't inquire. Her stuff was her stuff. Besides, I was too rattled about the voice in my head.

"It's got to be comfortable on the bike," I said. "I got it, and it's hidden. But I heard someone whispering outside, so let's move things up to tomorrow, okay?" It couldn't have been in my head. It had to be someone prowling around.

Margrite looked up, instantly on alert. "You look around?"

"Not really. But I stood and listened—whoever they are, I think they left. We'll hear if someone tries to get in here, or look around too much."

Another benefit of our building. We laid booby traps, for lack of a better word. Just shit all over the place so that anyone who was wandering around would step on it, and wake us up. We had black curtains on all the windows so that you couldn't see our light. We each took turns looking at the place at night occasionally to make sure that everything stayed blacked out.

I know, I know, what about letting sunlight in? I could safely say that Margrite and I preferred a comfortable, dark safe place.

Her shoulders relaxed. "Okay. Everything go okay with Keene?"

"Yeah, he even gave me a clean plate."

"Really?" Her eyebrow indicated a lack of belief.

"He said he owed me for the job I did for him a while back."

She smiled briefly. "That was nice. Good. It'll make it easier when we go."

"You'll be ready tomorrow?"

"I have all my shit. You're the one who needs to go dig yours out," she shot back.

"Stop nagging. I'm heading to bed, and then I'll pack." I gave her a big smile. Another benefit of hiding all my stuff here, around the building. I didn't have to go far.

She rolled her eyes and went back to ignoring me. That was one of the great things about her as a best friend. You say whatever, and it's over. We'd never had a fight, ever. We worked well together, on the few occasions where I needed help.

I tossed my coat on a chair, and stripped down, leaving my clothes where I could grab them easily.

Then I turned off the light and crawled into bed. I was really tired all of a sudden, like I'd been doing a hell of a lot more than I had been.

The last thing I remember was the soft, questioning voice in my head.

Aodan?

I woke up to Margrite's scream. I nearly fell out of the bed, and it broke as I scrambled to get up.

"What's wrong?" I said.

My voice came out in a growling, snarling tone.

"What the fuck?" I said.

Margrite stopped screaming, her mouth hanging open in an '*O*'.

"Did you just say something?" Her hand crept up toward her mouth. She whispered, "Where's Aodan?"

"It's me!"

Her shock gave way to anger. "Did you *eat* him, you bastard?"

"Margrite! What the hell are you talking about?"

Her mouth fell open wider if that was possible.

"What did you say? Say it again," she hissed.

"I said," I made myself speak slowly, not sure why my voice sounded like I was growling, "What the hell are you talking about, Margrite?"

"You know my name," she whispered, edging toward the door.

"Of course, I do," I put my hands on my hips and looked down—

"What the fuck?" I fell backward as I shouted—roared, really—while crashing onto the already damaged bed. The floor creaked alarmingly.

My hand wasn't a hand. It was a claw. A blue-ish green claw. And I wasn't me. I had the body of a lizard, something with scales. I was big, bigger than I'd been.

What the fuck?

I looked up. Margrite was hovering by the door, obviously scared, but not able to run away screaming.

Train wrecks were kind of like that. And whatever this was, it was definitely a train wreck.

"Margrite, it's me, it's Aodan."

"Whatever the fuck you are, it's not Aodan," her voice was hard as nails.

"Trust me, it's me. Ask me something. Anything."

"What was in the lunch you tried to steal from me?"

"A ham and cheese sandwich, and you tried to steal it from me."

Her mouth opened again, but nothing came out. She

blinked, and closed it, inhaling deeply. "Aodan?" She said. "How—what?"

I held up a hand—a claw. "I have no idea. What the fuck am I? An iguana?"

Her eyes widened. "No. You're..." she stopped, coming into the room. "Stand up."

I did, and my bed gave up and collapsed even more. I didn't think there was any more that could break, but apparently, I was wrong.

"Jeesh, you think the floor is going to hold?" She asked.

"Thank for the confidence," I grumbled, and it was the growl when I spoke. Wow.

I finally stood. I didn't feel like me. I felt like anything but, and I didn't like it.

I didn't have any clothes, either. What the hell was that about? Although I supposed it made sense—nothing I had would fit me at this size. My head brushed the ceiling.

"You're not going to believe this, but you are definitely not an iguana," she said, a slight smile on her face.

I didn't care that she might be laughing at me. I was glad she wasn't looking at me with fear.

"What do I look like?"

"You look like a dragon," her smile widened.

"What the hell?" I looked around. I had a tail.

A. Fucking. Tail.

"What is going on with me?" I asked, feeling panic as I looked at her. The floor creaked alarmingly under me.

"I don't know. Let me get you a mirror. You're really..." she stopped and then hurried from the room.

With all the creaking, I was afraid to move. If I moved, this whole thing might blow up somehow, so I held still, barely breathing. Worse, I might fall through the floor.

Smoke came out of my nostrils.

Just like in the warehouse.

"What the fuck?" I whispered. "What am I?"

Aodan! The voice from last night shouted.

It was in my head.

That's what I'd heard downstairs last night. In my damn head. It wasn't someone outside. It was inside—inside my head.

Okay. So, I had a voice in my head. Normally I'd write this off as crazy, but I was a dragon who was breathing smoke, and I had a tail.

Voice in the head was nothing big.

What is going on with me? I asked.

What are you? The response was immediate.

I'm sure as shit not me anymore.

There was silence, and then I heard how it sounded when another grumbling growl laughed. It was a deep rumble, and it lasted longer than I liked.

This isn't funny, asshole.

No, the voice was serious instantly. *It's not. I'm not there with you, and you must do this on your own. Until you can get to me.*

Oh, you mean come to you? I asked.

Yes. You must. You will need my help to manage it. Since your parents are not there.

You knew my parents? I asked, heart beating faster. It was like listening to a drum in my chest and my ears. My senses were on overload. I struggled to keep everything from swirling away from me like paper in a wind storm. That's how it felt. I was in the middle of a tornado, and I had no way out.

Yes. The one word carried a wealth of feeling.

"Look!" Margrite had come back in, holding a mirror. "Look at yourself. You're really beautiful. Like one of those dragons from the fairy tale stories." A frown creased her forehead. "You're... ah, not hungry are you?"

"What the hell, Margrite?" Wow, my voice sounded intimidating.

She took a step back, her hands holding the mirror dropping down. There was fear on her face. I hadn't seen that expression from her in years, and it made me want to cry and break shit that she was looking at *me* in that way.

"Let me see," I rumbled.

She came forward, holding the mirror out in front of her. I could tell she didn't want to get close.

Damn it.

"Margrite, I'm not going to eat you. I can't even deal with being hungry. I'm scared, and I don't know what's going on. I need your help. Please." I locked eyes with her, hoping to convince her that it was still me in here, no matter how I looked.

Even though I got it. I scared the shit out of myself.

She took a small step toward me, and then another, still holding the mirror in front of her.

I reached for it and then let my hands—claws—drop. "I think you need to hold it," I said.

Aodan! The voice in my head was insistent.

I ignored it. Peering at myself, I thought that being an attractive dragon, despite the admiration in Margrite's tone, wasn't a plus.

Because I was still a damn dragon.

"What am I going to do?" I looked up at Margrite. "We can't leave with me like this."

"Well, you changed somehow. Lay down... well, maybe just lay on the floor, and let's see if we can reverse this." Her voice sounded calm again, more like the Margrite I knew.

Thank God. I couldn't bear this if my best friend walked away from me, and I wouldn't even blame her if she did.

"You have got to be kidding," I said.

"You got a better idea?" She was mad.

"No." Slowly, I lowered myself down, first to a sitting position, and then onto my side. I had a ridge of vertical scales that didn't allow me to lie flat.

How the hell do I change back? I thought. *I don't know how to be me again.*

Imagine yourself in your form as a man, the voice was there instantly. *See yourself as you know yourself in human form.*

It was the last thing I heard from him. I could hear Margrite shouting, but she seemed very far away.

Not only did I hear and smell and sense everything around me, I could sense a presence in a dark room—a cave? And I was tired, very tired. How did I manage to keep my eyes open?

We were at battle. There was smoke, and I could see fire and flames in the distance. The tang of blood—there were different types. I didn't know how I knew that, but I knew. I could smell it. Dragons were flying in the air, and there were men on the ground below, tossing spears, and some of them threw light. When the spears hit a dragon, the dragon burst into a green flame. Same when the light hit them. Some dragons fell, and the rest still in the air roared and sprayed flame across the men as far as I could see.

Then I saw bars in front of me. As though I were in jail.

The scene shifted, and a dark man was in front of the bars, then a woman. Then another woman, and another. Too many women to keep track of.

An overwhelming sadness and anger came over me. I was so angry I wanted to destroy everything in front of me. And so sad that I wanted to crawl into a corner and weep.

Then a small, dark-haired woman was in front of the bars—sometimes alone, sometimes with a dark-haired man. I felt a wash of emotion that was so strong but it passed by me so fast I couldn't identify it. The small woman stuck with me. I felt like I should know her.

What the hell was going on? What was I seeing?

Aodan! The voice said again. More like yelled in a growl.

"I don't want this shit!" I yelled as I opened my eyes to see the cracked ceiling above me.

The room went still as though someone had taken a picture. Everything was captured in that moment. "I want to be me," I said.

Aodan—

"Shut up! Get the hell out of my head!" I wanted this to go away, and I just wanted to be *me* again.

Margrite said something, but I couldn't hear exactly what she said.

Then I felt it, and I've never felt anything like it before. My bones moved. It felt like I was standing on top of where an earthquake was happening, except the epicenter was my body. Things were moving, and I could still hear the voice in my head, but it was quieter, like someone was talking from behind their hand.

And then, the pain came.

I opened my mouth, to scream, maybe? But it hurt so bad, I didn't have breath.

Without warning, the earthquake and the pain stopped all at once. I opened my eyes slowly and Margrite was staring down at me in horror.

I was naked.

"Clothes," I croaked. My voice wasn't the deep rumble I'd heard when I was in dragon form. Thank god. It meant that I'd come back to me. That I was myself again.

Margrite remained frozen for another moment and then she sprang to the box where I kept clothes and threw some at me.

"Turn around, would you?" I asked. I felt that I'd lost enough dignity. I might fall over if I tried to stand and put my pants on, so I wanted a little privacy and time to manage it.

Finally, I got my pants on, and although I struggled with the button, I managed. I put on a tee shirt. It made me feel a little more normal. "You can turn around now," I said.

She did, and her hands were still over her mouth. "What the heck was that?" She spoke in a whisper.

I got scared then. Margrite never spoke in a whisper. I hadn't heard her muffle herself since we were kids. She figured she had the right to be as loud as she wanted to be.

"I don't know. Did you hear anyone else other than me in here?" I had to know if the voice was just me.

She shook her head slowly. "I think you made enough noise for the entire place. We'll be lucky if the cops don't come."

We stared at each other. "Did I really—"

"Yes," she answered before I could even get the words out. "You did. You were beautiful, but it scared the living hell out of me, Aodan. Why did you ask about someone else?"

I told her about the voices, both before and then after I woke up. I tried to tell her some of what I'd seen, but it made me feel an overwhelming sadness, so I skipped a lot of that, telling her that I thought I was seeing things that happened to someone else, or a pretty big hallucination.

She didn't speak after I finished.

"Say something," I said.

"I don't know what to say. Normally, I'd tell you everything was fine and then haul your crazy ass to a looney bin, but I saw you. I *saw* you," she repeated. "I know I'm not crazy."

"Thanks for the vote of confidence," I said.

"I don't understand," she said. "I think you need to close your eyes and see if the voice talks to you. I can't believe I just said that," she shook her head and slid down the wall to sit on the floor.

"I can't either. You think the voices are a good thing?"

"I don't know. But it seemed to know what this—" she indicated my now wrecked room, "Was all about. I think you need to at least ask."

I glared, and she glared back.

"Fine," I said. "Fine." I squeezed my eyes shut, and thought.

What was that all about? Start talking now. I sent my thoughts out, willing someone to answer.

Aodan?

Were you expecting someone else?

Are you human once more?

Yes. Why wasn't I human?

There was silence and then I could swear I heard a sigh.

There is so much I need to tell you. I may be able to come to you, to bring you here.

Bring me where? What the hell is this? Did I hit my head?

"What's he saying?" Margrite asked.

"Nothing important, yet. Shut up," I said, without opening my eyes. I felt a kick on the bottom of my foot. "Abuse isn't going to help," I added.

She made a noise of deep disgust. I forced my face not to smile.

Where the hell is here? I'm here in a shitty building.

What happened to you?

What do you mean? I felt a wariness at his question.

I know that your mother brought you back. What happened?

Why don't you know?

Another silence, and then the voice spoke again. I could actually hear sadness in it. *When your father died, I lost the ability to know what happened to you, or your mother. I tried to pinpoint you, but you were in the Human Realm, and I couldn't sense you.*

Why now?

Something has changed. The tone of the voice changed. *What has happened to you recently? What has been out of the normal for you?*

Other than waking up as something other than myself? Gee, I don't know.

Don't be sarcastic. This is important.

I felt a reluctance to give this voice—I thought it was a him, but with the growling voice, who knew? It could be a girl dragon, for all I was able to tell.

For someone who wants all sorts of information, you're not giving much up. I tried to keep the resentment out of my thoughts.

I could say the same thing.

We were both silent.

Then the voice said, *I suppose we are at an impasse. Let me take some time to decide the best way to come to you. I can bring you here. Then I can tell you everything.*

Maybe.

Don't you want to know? The voice was impatient.

Maybe.

Don't be foolish, boy. You either come with me to find out or don't.

That sounded rather threatening.

I forced myself to shove the voice out. I pictured a door closing with the mysterious man? Dragon? Behind it.

I could hear the voice again, but it was faint, like hearing a radio in the distance. I ignored it and got up.

"Are you all right? What happened? What did he say?" Margrite scrambled up, following me.

I needed water in the worst way. I went to our kitchen and got a bottle of water out of the ancient refrigerator. We lived in a condemned building, but like I said, you can learn how to do anything on the internet. Electricity was one of those things.

After I sucked down almost an entire bottle, I felt a little better. I grabbed another one and then wiped my mouth with the bottom of my shirt.

"Ew," Margrite said. "Is that dragon slobber?"

"Really? This is where we're going to go?" I glared.

"I'm sorry. I can't help it. Are you going to tell or what?"

"Let's sit down. I'm tired." I headed for the sofa. We had a couple of them, which was nice.

"Okay, spill." She flopped down opposite me.

"It's weird, and it doesn't make any sense. Before I... changed back to me," I still couldn't believe I was saying that, "the voice was telling me to imagine myself as me again. Then, after I changed, the voice came back but... it was different. Almost like I wasn't talking to the same person. And he, because I do think it's a guy, was all about getting me to come there, wherever the hell there is. He said something," I remembered, "About me being in the Human Realm. He said it like it was a known place, or something."

"The Human Realm? What other realm is there?" Margrite shook her head.

"Right? Margrite, you really don't think I'm crazy?"

"Do you?"

"Thanks," I said. "I don't know, or I sure wouldn't be asking you, Ms. Nice Bedside Manner."

"I don't lie to you, Aodan. You know that. I don't think you're crazy, but if you tell me differently, I'll go with that. The only thing that stops all of that, for me, anyway, is that I saw you become a dragon, like right out of a story. There's no unseeing that," she added with feeling.

"Try being the dragon," I muttered, leaning back and opening the other bottle of water.

After taking another drink, I looked at her. "We need to get out of here. If I am crazy, I don't want to be around when Caleb finds out—"

"Don't even say it," Margrite held up a hand. She was superstitious.

I thought it was nuts. Things happened, and that was it. You influenced what you could and dealt with it when you couldn't. Pretty simple, no star charts and hocus pocus shit involved.

But since I'd just turned into a dragon, I thought that maybe I wasn't able to just brush all that shit off anymore. That might have sucked even more—I'd have to admit Margrite was right about this mumbo jumbo. I sighed. As if things didn't suck enough.

"I wonder," she was tapping her teeth.

Which was never a good sign?

"What if we went to see Nala?" Margrite sat forward. "She might have an idea!"

"I am not going to see some chick named after a kids' movie," I grumbled, and I could hear the growl of my dragon voice in it. That was new. I wasn't sure I liked it. "And I don't want to tell anyone. No one, Margrite! No one! We have to get out of here, and today. Or tomorrow. What time is it?"

"It's four-thirty in the morning," she said. "You're sure you don't want to talk to someone?"

"What would the cartoon girl fake psychic know that my weirdo voice doesn't?"

"Maybe she could tell you something, which is more than weirdo voice seems to want to do!" She glared.

AODAN.

Holy shit. I nearly fell off the couch.

What? Why are you yelling?

I've been yelling since I tried to tell you how to change. Did you change?

Now Weirdo Voice sounded normal, not on the verge of angry and out of patience, like he had before. Great. Weirdo Voice also experienced multiple personalities. Normally I wouldn't care, but I needed info, and such a thing seemed like it would get in my way.

And I didn't have time for this. No time at all.

I managed, I said in my head.

Good. Where are you? Are you safe?

Except for the part where my roommate and I were both screaming, and probably will have the cops on us in a while, yeah, we're fine.

What are cops?

It doesn't matter. What am I?

The voice laughed, and there was nothing but genuine humor in it. *You have to ask? Didn't you look at yourself?*

Well, he got me there. *Yeah.*

What color are you?

Blue-green?

Your father was a bright blue, with green eyes. He was not as dark as I am, but we are from the same line.

What are you, some kind of family?

I am your grandfather.

I leaned back, my eyes closed. I couldn't take it all in. *What? You're my what?*

Your grandfather.

That would have been great to know when I was running away from the latest crappy foster family.

What are foster families?

It's where they put you when there's nowhere else. Where the fuck have you been all my life?

In a cage.

I stopped. I'd seen the bars. *Was that you? With the bars in front of you?*

You saw that?

I saw a lot of shit.

I'm sorry. Waking to your dragon mind is difficult under the best of circumstances. You haven't grown up with it.

"Wait, wait," I said getting up.

"What?" Margrite asked.

I shook my head at her, mouthing the words, "Hang on," and continued the conversation in my head. *What are you talking about?*

I'm guessing you saw parts of the rest of us.

The rest of you? How many are there?

There are eleven full dragons, and one half-dragon. Well, a bit less than half, but I think that can be—

Wait. There's more like me? Why only eleven?

That is a long story, Aodan. I would like you to come to the Dragon Realm, and we will talk.

No.

Why?

I have my life planned out, thank you. You weren't there for me growing up, when I was getting my face rubbed in the dirt, or cigarettes put out next to my arm. No, I don't want you, I don't need you.

I was angry, and there was no stopping it. I could feel the anger well up inside me like a huge wave, the kind you saw in movies right before the wave destroyed a city. That's where I was right now. Ready to destroy a city.

I am sorry, came the voice.

Yeah, well, sorry isn't cutting it right now. Just go away. I have shit to do. I pictured myself shutting a door, and while I could hear talking behind the door, it wasn't up front in my head.

"Let's go see her," Margrite said.

"What?" I hadn't been paying attention. It was a sign of how out of whack things were that she hadn't punched me for ignoring her.

"Nala. Let's go see her."

"You're still on about that?"

Margrite crossed her arms and said, "You turned into a dragon. I think being all judgey about mumbo jumbo shit is pretty much out the window right now."

I opened my mouth to shut her down, shut her up when I realized that she was right. I'd lost the battle to be all superior. Because some pretty mumbo jumbo shit was going on with me.

"Fine," I sighed. "Let me get cleaned up and we'll go. But we're leaving tonight."

"Absolutely."

"No matter what she says, right?" I knew I needed to make this point. Margrite really believed a lot of what Nala said.

At the moment, I couldn't recall the chick's success rate with anything, and I sure as hell wasn't getting into that discussion with Margrite.

She was like a shark. She'd sense my weakness, and I'd have to live with blessings on the room along with other oddball rituals forever and ever. No way.

"All right. You can probably go back to sleep for a while. I'll get you up in time to get there when she opens." She left the room.

I sat back down on my ruined bed.

What the hell was going on? Why did the voice in my head say it—he—was my grandfather? The thought gave me a pang. I'd never had any family other than Margrite. Anything more felt… weird.

And fake.

I shook my head, forcing myself to look forward, see what had to be done today. We needed to hit up the psychic chick, do a check around the building and make sure that nothing that could lead to us was left, and get out.

There wasn't much I could do to save my bed, but I lay down on the mattress and closed my eyes.

As my heart calmed, and my brain stopped racing, Margrite came back in.

"A," she whispered. "There's someone out in front."

I sat up, instantly alert.

"You see anything?"

"I heard them. I turned off my light and came in here."

I moved out of bed, taking care not to step on the remains. I felt in the dark for her hand and pulled her close to me.

"We'll go out and see if we can see or hear anything from the hallway. If they come in, we're going across the hall."

The apartment across the way was beat to hell, but we'd made a hiding place in one of the closets in a room.

Carefully, we moved through our apartment and out the front door. There was a window that was broken at the end of the hall. It was a good lookout point.

I crouched down and closed my eyes. I focused on listening.

There they were. They were walking.

"Did you hear a car?" I whispered against Margrite's head.

She moved her head back and forth.

Okay. That meant they were parked on the next street over. If they'd driven right up to the building, we would have heard them. The road was always covered in trash.

I could tell they were talking. They weren't really bothering to lower their voices, or be discreet, or anything that would suggest they were supposed to be doing this on the quiet.

"… you think he's here?" One said.

"He's been seen here," Two answered.

"That doesn't mean anything. He's a crafty little shit."

"Whatever."

I could nearly see Two shrugging.

"Well, let's leave a message," One sighed. "And then let's finally get back, so I can get some sleep. He's got to lay off, or I'm going to die."

One was kind of whiny.

But if this guy worked for Caleb, I felt a stab of satisfaction that Caleb was freaking out. I hoped his big bad boss kicked his arrogant mouthy ass.

The wall next to me shuddered, then shuddered again.

"What the hell?" Margrite whispered.

"I don't know."

A few more shudders, and then I heard them talking again.

"It'll be a miracle if that holds," One said.

I could hear his admiring tone.

"Well, boss said to make it hurt. One wrong move, and this is going to hurt." Two chuckled. "Come on. Let's go."

Their footsteps moved away.

"What did they do?"

"I think they knocked down something. Maybe a wall, or structural support? I don't know," I said.

"We need to check," she said.

"Not tonight. We need to stay here, and move carefully, and make no noise."

We took our time making our way back, not only because we didn't know if someone had stayed to watch over the place, but because we had no idea what kind of damage had been done.

Anger burned in me hot and fiery.

Whoever did this would pay.

6

I lay down for about an hour before the sun came up, making further sleep impossible.

I kept seeing things that I knew weren't my life every time I closed my eyes.

A woman holding a baby, and then a dragon leaning over her.

A different man taking the baby away. The woman crying.

The dragon that leaned over the woman lying on the ground. It wasn't moving, and the sadness that overtook me as I saw that was so strong I felt tears slide down my cheeks.

Finally, I'd had enough. Reluctantly, I rolled out of bed. Once I'd gotten dressed, and spent a little time getting myself back together, I felt more normal. I wasn't sure that normal would ever be a thing again, but for the time being, I'd take it.

"Let's go," I said, coming out of my room.

Margrite jumped up, and we silently walked out of our place, and then down the stairs. Years of caution and practice made us quiet. You could be standing outside the building and you wouldn't hear us coming down the stairs.

I peered outside out of habit and didn't see anyone.

Although it was clear that some sort of shit had gone down. The front of the building where I'd banged around with the bike looked like hell. But the guys who'd come along before sunrise made it worse.

They were right, too. Damn it. We would be lucky if this side of the building didn't collapse.

"We'd have to leave if we were staying," Margrite remarked, casting a glance over at the wreckage.

"Good thing we're leaving," I said.

She nodded, and we continued on in silence. Heads down, but aware of one another. We'd always been this way. It was why I liked being around her. There wasn't a lot of need for words, for all that extra talk that people liked to indulge in.

Margrite led the way. I didn't go to her magic shoppe, or as I called it, the woo woo joint. After fifteen minutes, she turned into a doorway of an older building.

"I called her. She has time to see us right now," Margrite said.

"What?"

"Nothing. Come on," she made a sighing noise.

As we entered, I remembered why I didn't care for these places. Too much scent, heavy incense burners. It made my nose tickle.

And it bothers your dragon.

Wait. What? I stopped, waiting to see if the thought would come to me again. It wasn't the voice I'd heard earlier, but it was... something.

"Are you coming? You promised," Margrite said from about ten feet in front of me.

"Yeah, I'm coming," I said.

She turned and walked through a curtain, and I followed her. It was a darkened room, a bunch of candles around. The incense wasn't as strong in here, thank god. If I sneezed too hard in here, I'd set the place on fire.

"Hey, Nala, thanks for seeing us," Margrite said.

I'd been so busy looking around I hadn't seen the small woman who sat at a round table in front of us.

Stereotypical, I thought. She's just missing the crystal ball.

"I am glad to. I need to make sure that you're all right," Nala said, eyeing first Margrite and then me. "You sounded out of sorts when we spoke."

She was young. She had curly dark hair that wound out from her head in every direction. I heard a light tinkling sound, and I could see that Nala wore stacks of bracelets on each wrist that made a noise as she moved. She was holding a deck of cards, idly shuffling them. Her eyes were on us, so I thought it might be habit more than anything else.

Nala was pretty and didn't give off the woo woo vibe. I met her gaze, and I could feel power in hers.

Wow.

Not what I expected at all. As I thought that, her mouth lifted into a smile.

"Sit, and we'll see if there are any answers for you."

"You mean you can't guarantee the answers?" I asked.

Margrite elbowed me. I thought I'd kept the sarcasm down but I guess not.

"Never any guarantees," Nala said with a shrug. "But you get nothing if you don't even bother to look."

"Yeah," Margrite said, elbowing me again.

"Hey," I said in warning.

She ignored me. "We're… well, we're okay. But some things have come up that I really want some clarity for."

"For yourself, or the both of you?"

"Both," Margrite said. "I need it for me, and Aodan sure as hell needs it, even if he'll die before admitting it."

I glared at Margrite and then turned back to Nala. "I would like some answers, if there are any."

"Which you doubt?" Nala's smile widened.

"Yep," I said.

She laughed. "I prefer honest skepticism. I can't guarantee anything, Aodan. But we'll try."

That was good. Making this a 'we' thing, rather than just her. I nodded.

"What I want to know is what does—what do the new developments mean?" Margrite asked.

That surprised me. I didn't think she'd be all out in the open.

"And you? What questions do you have?"

"Uh," I said. I didn't realize we'd have to do anything other than sit here. "I guess along the same lines as Margrite. What does it mean, all this new... info we've gotten? And what does it mean for our plans?" I added.

Nala held up a hand, stopping me from adding on. "Don't ask anything else. I like to have a general question in mind and then see what the cards say. Who will choose?"

"Aodan," Margrite said. "He needs to be the one doing all of this. I think, and I'm not trying to presume," she smiled at Nala, "That a Majors only would be the best thing for him."

Nala stilled and looked from Margrite to me. "You do? Why?"

Margrite looked like her cheeks were red, but it was hard to tell in this light. She ducked her head down a little. "He's not really into this, and I think a smaller group of cards to work with, cards where the meaning can be seen more clearly, makes it a little easier."

I was astounded. I hadn't seen Margrite this uncomfortable in... ages. Like, I couldn't remember the last time.

"What are you talking about?" I asked.

Margrite didn't look at me. What the hell?

Nala nodded, a slight smile on her face as she looked at Margrite. But she didn't answer one way or the other. She pulled several decks of cards from under the table and set them between us. "Choose your deck, Aodan."

"Why?"

"The deck is part of this. Choose the one that speaks to you."

I looked them. They had different patterns on the backs of the cards. Nothing really stood out—then I saw the last deck, the one that was closest to where I sat on the right side of the table.

"That one," I said. It had a gold medallion, or something on the back. There was a red dot in the center. I couldn't see exactly what it was, but I found the pattern pleasing. As though it called to—no. Those kinds of thoughts had no place with me. They opened you up for suggestion. Which is what this place specialized in, right?

Nala smiled as though I'd given her the right answer.

"Let me separate them, and then," she moved her hands quickly, so that I couldn't see the images on the front of the cards. "Don't look. Just shuffle." Then she handed me the smaller pile she'd pulled out of the larger one. "In whatever manner you would like, for as long as you want. When you are satisfied, hand them back to me."

I took them, and the room felt heavy and quiet as I shuffled. I could hear the snick of the cards against one another, and hiss of the candles, along with a light floral scent. Every one of my senses seemed heightened, more aware.

When I handed the cards back, she took them in both hands, and closed her eyes. Then she opened them, and began turning cards over on the table. There was some sort of pattern, but it made no sense to me.

I heard Margrite make a small gasping noise. I choked.

The deck was full of dragons. Every card had a dragon on it. Large, beautiful in the intensity of color on each card, and powerful. The images themselves radiated power. That was something I understood. You didn't survive without projecting power.

Was that what I looked like? I'd been so knocked back, I hadn't really had time to look at myself.

Nala glanced at us quickly and then went back to studying the cards.

After what seemed like an age, she leaned back, and regarded both of us.

"This is interesting. Are you ready?"

"Sure," I said. "But before we get started, why do they all have dragons on them?"

"It's the Dragon deck," Nala answered. She held up a card from the part of the deck she hadn't given me to shuffle. "See? The dragon on the back?"

I hadn't realized the gold medallion was actually a dragon.

Nala continued, "That means all the cards will be shown via the artist's interpretation of how dragons look."

Here comes the drama, I thought. We gave something away with our response to the images on the cards.

"This is the spread called the Celtic Cross. It tells me a little about what has happened in the past, and what's coming for you in the future. This is more about you, isn't it?" She peered at me.

"Yes," Margrite said before I could answer.

I was still stuck on Margrite's reaction when the cards were shown.

"Do you want the overview, the high level, or do you want me to get into it?" Nala asked.

"How about somewhere in the middle?"

She smiled. "Okay. These first two cards," Nala indicated the ones in a cross in the middle of the pattern, "Are you," she tapped the one on the bottom, "And your current situation." Another tap, this time on the card on top.

"So. You. You're this one, the Emperor. It's interesting. The Emperor is the boss, the man in charge, the dad in the house. But you didn't grow up with your dad, did you?"

I glared at Margrite.

She held up her hands. "I didn't say anything. Nala is just good!"

"Uh, huh," I grumbled.

"Your life doesn't follow the typical idea of this card—you aren't conventional, or a believer in doing what's expected. That's the no dad figure," she said, almost to herself. "But because of that, because of the chaos you have lived, now, when you make your own choices, you do follow your routines. You have rules. Schedules. Patterns. These are very important to you. And you are the boss in your world. Also very important."

"No kidding," Margrite muttered.

"Now your situation," Nala continued. "This is the Death card. Before you start looking over your shoulder, stop your ideas of what death means. This says, to me, with what I see in the rest of this," she waved her hand over the other cards, "That your life is about to change. Think of this more as a closing of life as you know it. You're not going to die," she looked up at me, "Although you might, because no one ever knows when Death will appear, but in general, you will experience an entirely new life, a new path, something that is so foreign from what you know now, it can seem a death. That's not a bad thing, and I think that this is saying you should give the new a chance. Which is not something you normally do, is it?"

"Taking chances is dangerous. I've built a good life," I said. Maybe this was a sign that all that we'd been planning for would actually happen? I hoped so.

"All I'm saying is you should be open to what's coming." She smiled at Margrite. "No matter how foreign."

"This third card," she pointed at the card below the first two, "The High Priestess, indicates that in your past, there is a... well, for lack of a better word. A mentor. But since he—or she—has been your mentor, it brings you to where you are now. I think maybe it's a mentor that was supposed to be? But wasn't? I don't know, but that seems what this is saying." She tapped her lips, thinking.

"A mentor? What the hell is that?" I asked.

"Someone who helps and guides you," Nala said.

"Kind of like the dad you mentioned in the first card? The dad who wasn't there?" I couldn't keep the sarcasm from my words. "This is an imaginary person, too. Unless you're saying that the person fell down on the job. Because they did."

"That could be," Nala said.

She didn't seem bothered by my attitude.

"You should have a mentor, according to this. But I'm not sure you did—"

"I didn't," I interjected.

"And he—or she—has contributed to where you are now. Either by involvement, or lack thereof. But it shaped you, helped to make you who you are."

"Definitely lacking," I muttered.

"Moving on," Margrite said.

I didn't know when she'd done it, but Margrite had pulled out a notebook out of her bag and was taking notes, even drawing the pattern the cards were laid out in.

"You're taking notes?"

She nodded. "Yes. I like to be able to remember what was said."

"This one, the fourth card, this is Strength. Think of this as your more recent past, the past that has shaped you. You're very strong. I think you've had to be, haven't you?" She looked up.

"If you're not, you're dead," I said. I didn't know why I felt compelled to keep bringing this up, but I couldn't stop myself.

Margrite nodded next to me. You learned that early on.

"It shows. It makes you who you are. But it also tells us that we have to be unafraid to be who we are. Trust yourself, Aodan. In spite of your past, you can trust yourself, and trust yourself to be open to who you are. Part of Strength is being able to accept the new, or things that are outside our norms."

"The fifth card, this one," Nala touched the card above the crossed pair, "this is what's happening in the short-term. Think a couple of months. Like, don't make major, year-long plans based on this. It's more immediate."

"This would be the more pressing issues?" I asked.

"Something like that," Nala smiled. "You're pretty calm. This is the Devil. People who don't know tarot may find this alarming, but it's not. In the next couple of months, you're going to find that you have things that have structured your life, and while you have felt them necessary, they have become chains. Chains that may be holding you back. The Devil is telling you that you need to look within, to see if those things you've been committed to are in fact dragging you down. Most of all, don't be afraid to step way, way out of your comfort zone. Remember, you're the Emperor, and you like routine, habits, and structure. The Devil asks that you look outside of that, and see the positive, even though you may not have seen the positive in doing so before. It can also mean freedom of your sexual self, and I feel like I need to mention that." She smiled. "I don't see anything specific, but the Devil is also there to free us to be who we are intimately."

I flushed. I didn't have time for girls. Life was all consuming as it was. Margrite stirred next to me as she made notes.

"The sixth card," Nala didn't press the sex issue, thankfully. "The sixth card," she repeated. "You can say this is the present state of things. Based on this," she pointed at the second card, "Is saying your current status is. Now this is interesting. This is Justice, and what it means for you, basically, is that things are right. They are where they are supposed to be. Things are happening as they should. Even as your situation is indicated by the Death card, what is coming from that is supposed to be. I also feel that when you see Justice, it's because any wrongs are going to be righted. They may not happen as planned, or expected, but it happens. Justice likes the balance of right. If there is a wrong in all of this, Justice says that it will be righted, and balance will be restored. Achieving that, however," she looked up at me, "Isn't always easy. Right and balance often require work and sacrifice so that is something to be mindful of."

Nala sat back, sighing. "This feels like a really big thing, Aodan. I don't know why, but sometimes when I read, I get a hint that this isn't just an ordinary reading."

"What makes an ordinary or not-so-ordinary reading?" This was mystifying to me. The whole thing lived in mumbo-jumbo land, to me.

"There's not really a good way to describe this, but I have that feeling. The feeling that this is important in your life, to you. For you. I'm glad that Margrite is making notes. I'd love to hear if any of this plays out."

"Doesn't that kind of set the stage for me looking for validation?"

"No. Most people forget their reading. You may, or may not," she shrugged. "But I wanted to mention this to you. We're almost done, so let's move on. The seventh card," her fingers brushed the card at the bottom of the row on my far left, "is the Moon. This indicates the outside influences. It's the things that are happening to you, for you, against you, and around you. You can't control them, so don't try. The trick with the seventh card is to see when it's influencing the situation, and work around it, or with it, whatever it takes to move you forward in your concerns. The Moon represents things in the shadow, things that are hidden. I don't know if they will be revealed, but there are secrets. Here's the thing with the Moon—there can be an illusion in what is hidden, and it can be hard to see the truth. So, in this, pay attention to your instincts, and don't let your fears win —and you will find what is real and true." She leaned forward. "This is important, Aodan. Fear is powerful with regard to secrets. Don't let fear be the driver of the bus with this."

"What the hell does that mean?" I spent a lot of time afraid. There was always fear. Fear made you strong because it made you prepare for what could happen. And how to survive it. I generally felt good about my ability to survive but I wasn't stupid enough to let my guard down.

"It means don't let fear be what leads you. Take fear into

account, but don't allow it to overrule everything else. Now the eighth card, this is also interesting. Your whole spread is interesting. I realize it comes with challenges for you, but I can say this as the reader," Nala smiled, and her dimples flashed at me.

"This card, the eighth card, is the Hanged Man. This card represents your internal influences. Given who you are, as represented by the Emperor, this is a challenge within you. If you are not careful, you will be working against yourself. The Hanged Man means that you must surrender yourself. You are successful in the life you have chosen, and I believe you will be so in the next chapters of your life—but the Hanged Man is telling you that you must let go, allow yourself to let things go as they will. There may be sacrifice involved—"

"What, like a goat?" I asked.

"No, stupid, not a goat," Margrite sounded exasperated. "Like in your thought process, or one of your precious habits, or things like that. When have you ever even seen a goat?"

Nala laughed. "If you don't have regular habits of being around goats, I doubt that a goat sacrifice will be called for. No, this is very much in line with the other things in your reading. You must see the new aspects that are entering your life and be open to them. Be willing."

I shook my head. This didn't make sense. But I could see that I wouldn't get things that did make sense, so I let her move on. Her words making no sense was part of the woo woo.

"The ninth card represents your hopes. What do you want? What do you dream of?"

"I can tell you that," I said.

Margrite hit my leg. "Stop it."

"It's all right, Margrite. I don't take any offence to his skepticism. I just want to hear, later, if these things came true. Or not. Margrite will keep you honest," Nala said with a laugh. "So. The ninth card. It's the Magician. You want to be in charge of your own life. In spite of all this, all these things that stem from your being the Emperor, you still fear the influence of others on your life. It's interesting—I think you have come to who you are because of this—but when you begin to see all the changes to your path, this will be your hope. That you, and you alone—not your past, or the outside influences, or even your own fears—will choose what is next for you. It will be new," she added. "Don't let the fact that it's a new thing for you allow you to ignore it. And it also represents creativity and resourcefulness. I think it means that you must embrace your own creativity to help you get what it is you hope for."

Her words shook me. More than anything she'd said. Because in this, she was right. I felt very much at the mercy of various aspects of life. My only choice was to react. I didn't have the luxury of anything else.

"Any ideas on when this will happen, with all these new things coming at me?" I asked.

"Well, let's look at the tenth card. This card is a statement of all the things that we've seen so far. It represents them all, in a way. I'd say a time period of up to the next year?" She looked up. "Over the next year, this is what will happen—if you take heed of the things we've talked about here, and work towards what it is you want. It's the Judgement card. And what this means, Aodan, is that with all these new things, you will have to make a choice. You will have to choose whether or not you're going to live in this new way, this new path, that has opened up for you, or not. There will come a time when you must make that choice. You can get what you want, this whole new life, a new perspective—but you must accept the challenges that come with the new, and rise to the call. If you do, you will find success."

The only sound I heard was Margrite scribbling into her notebook.

7

*N*either of us spoke as we walked away from the shop. I couldn't take it anymore. Too many things were running around in my brain like hamsters on crack.

"You believe any of that shit?"

"Do you?" Margrite was quick to shoot back at me.

"I… I don't know. Seems like a lot of vague stuff that can be applied to most people."

"No. I think a lot of it was totally you. Your schedule, your rules, your habits? So you, Aodan. And secrets? I mean, really? Can we say dragon? There's totally a secret there!" She hit me in the arm for emphasis. "How about how you chose the Dragon deck? And that weird voice?"

"Keep your voice down," I hissed. "No one else knows that!"

"Well, what if that's the mentor? The High Priestess? And that sure as shit goes along with secrets!"

"Okay, you're making some sense. But I'm reserving the right to question it."

"She said if you go along with your instinct, and you embrace the new things coming, you will get what you want, and you will have a positive outcome. That's all well and good," she added, "But it makes me think there's a heck of a bumpy road ahead."

"Why do you think that?"

"I don't know—the way Nala told you about it, the way she said this was important, that her gut told her this was big—and most things that are worth it aren't easy? Since when has anything we've ever done been easy? I mean, the shit that was worth it?"

"See what I mean? This shit can apply to anything!" I threw up my hands. "I can't believe you made me pay forty bucks for that! That's like a lot of burgers," I poked my finger at her to make my point.

"She gave us a discount."

"That's a discount?" I couldn't believe it.

"Yep. She loves me, so I get the friends and family discount."

"You've never told me about this."

She shrugged. "I don't have to tell you everything."

"We don't tell each other everything?" I was astounded.

"Do you tell me everything?" Margrite didn't look at me.

"Yes! What the hell would I keep a secret from you?"

"Whatever you wanted."

"What else aren't you telling me?"

"My innermost thoughts and what I'd put in a diary entry, if I had one," she said.

I stared as she marched forward. She was offended. I could tell. Margrite wasn't one of those people who hid her emotions —well, not from me. But I had no idea why. I did tell her everything. It didn't occur to me to not tell her things.

"Are we good?" I asked. I wasn't sure what else to say, honestly. I didn't want to go further down this path.

"Yeah, we're fine."

She sounded like herself again.

"Okay, let's go home and go through the place, and make sure we're not forgetting anything."

*T*hree hours later, I could hear my stomach grumble as I thought about food. A late lunch, of an early dinner. We'd stripped the place bare. While I was thinking about where we could go, I heard people outside our building. I stilled from instinct.

I whistled softly. Margrite's head popped out around a door frame from the room where she was.

"People," I whispered. Twice in twenty-four hours? This wasn't good. It didn't matter what or who it was—this wasn't good.

She nodded and her head disappeared. As the voices came closer, I carefully crept to an apartment that was next to ours. We'd made holes where we could see out. We never opened the windows up for sunlight or anything else in our rooms—and I wasn't about to start now, even though we were almost out of here.

I could see a small group of people—it was one, two, three, four, five—from what I could see, men. Great. They had the look of thugs, but it wasn't Caleb's thugs, so that was something.

As they studied the building, their conversation got quieter. That wasn't good.

I don't know how long they stood there. It felt like forever. But they all took one last look at the building, and I could see that the expressions on the faces of two of them hardened.

"Fire," I heard one of them say. "That'll solve it."

Shit.

They left, and as I watched, they got into an older model Cadillac and spun tires as they sped away.

"Douchebags," I muttered, getting up. Why was it this kind of guy always had to spin tires? And *fire*? Really? Like the beating of our poor building earlier today wasn't enough. It was either going to collapse or be burned down.

I headed back for our apartment. "They're gone," I said as I came in the door.

"Who were they?" Margrite joined me in the main room.

I shrugged. "I don't know. But I heard them mention fire, so it's a good thing we're out of here. You all done?"

She nodded. "I am. Like I said, my backpack is fat as hell, but I have all the things I want."

"Me, too. Let's get out of here. I don't like whatever it was that just happened."

Margrite didn't answer, just went and gathered her bag. Whatever had happened between us after we left the tarot reading seemed like it was gone. Or maybe she just hid it from me. I didn't like that feeling, either.

Everything that I thought was solid wasn't. My home, my best friend—what else was going to happen?

I ignored my feelings of unease as I got my bag, and we turned out the lights, and headed down to the first floor where I'd hidden the bike. I wheeled it out of the building, looking around as I did so. Everything seemed quiet.

"Did those guys really do all that?" Margrite gestured to the damaged wall

It looked bad. Really bad. It pissed me off all over again. I forced myself to try and calm down. I needed to stay calm and get through this. We were almost gone. I loved our old place, but it wouldn't be home ever again.

"I don't know. I guess so," I said. "One more reason to leave."

"We've been here a long time. It stands to reason that it might not be safe anymore. Nothing lasts forever, Aodan."

She was right, but that didn't mean I liked it. Nor did I want to admit it right this minute. We'd worked so hard to carve out a little piece of safety, of a home.

I got on and started it. Margrite sat behind me. I took one last look at the building that had been the only home I'd ever known, and then I started the bike, and drove away.

$\mathcal{W}$e stopped at a restaurant outside of the area we normally stayed in. Neither of us said anything, but I knew that Margrite wasn't any happier with the thugs showing up than I was. It was better to get the hell out of the neighborhood. It bothered me that I didn't have any idea of who had come prowling around, or planned to set fire to our building. It really bothered me that there were two different sets of people.

"You ready?" I asked her. We'd talked about this for so long that it almost didn't feel real.

She nodded, her mouth full of—what else—a burger. "Yes," she said finally. "We should have left before now. But we stayed. And now, I'm tired of always looking over my shoulder."

"Yeah. Who do you think they were?"

"Who have you pissed off lately?"

"How can you be sure it was me?" Her question annoyed me.

Margrite gave me one of her rare smiles. She looked like a different person when she smiled like that. "Because in spite of my legendary anti-social personality, I don't discriminate. I'm unfriendly with everyone, and they know it's not them. It's totally me. With you, you take shit personally. And you don't hide it. So, it makes more sense that you've pissed someone off."

She leaned forward, lowering her voice. "You think they are with Caleb?"

"The ones this morning? Yes. The guys I saw later? No. None of them were his regular guys, and I think that Luke would have warned me if he'd gotten a visit from Caleb. But it was obvious they were looking for me."

"Even a dead watch is right twice a day," she countered.

"Yeah, well, there's a lot more time that it's not. You know he has no control. He'd have already beaten the hell out of Luke."

"Okay, then who were the guys wanting to burn it?"

"I don't know. It makes me edgy." I was worried that it was somehow connected to the guy that Caleb answered to. Margrite was rubbing off on me. I didn't want to say it out loud for fear it might be true.

"I'm glad we're out of here."

"Me, too. I didn't like that they mentioned fire as they were leaving. Once you finish, we can leave," I said, indicating all the food in front of her. "Did you get one of everything?"

"Stress makes me hungry. For once, I can indulge."

I rolled my eyes, but I didn't respond. She was right. We sat in silence until Margrite finished.

She pushed her plate away. "Okay, I'm done."

"I might be able to cover it," I teased.

"Well, you know how to do dishes."

Laughing, we paid, and headed out to the bike. This was it. We were out of here. Night had just fallen.

Despite the weirdness of the last few days, I hadn't heard the voice in my head. That wasn't entirely true, I realized. I knew it was there, but it wasn't upfront. I'd been able to keep a door closed between me and the voice.

I'd slept, and I hadn't turned into a dragon again. Thank God. That was a problem I didn't need.

The tarot reading was something that kind of bothered me, but just as with the voice in my head, I'd put that over to the side, and focused on the immediate things. No need to make my life harder than it was. While it was clear that Margrite believed every drop of what Nala had told me, I was not willing to give it a lot of credibility. Like Margrite was fond of reminding me, even a dead watch was right twice a day. Nala may have hit on things that were coincidentally correct—and that was all it was. I wouldn't allow myself to get all caught up in something I thought was a bunch of woo woo nonsense.

The night air felt great in my hair. The further we got from the downtown area, the clearer the air smelled. There was a miasma that hung around cities even if they were fairly clean. It went without question that Margrite and I lived in the less than clean areas.

I spotted a sign and pulled the bike over.

"Why are you stopping?" Margrite leaned around me.

"This is it," I gestured at the sign. "This is the limit. I've never lived anywhere else that I know of. My whole life has been here, a lot of it in a crappy situation, or with a bad family. Not everything was bad. There was some, okay, a lot of good." I smiled at her. "But that's part of the past now. I don't know," I looked at her, feeling stupid now. "I just felt like I needed to stop."

"Well, it's fine to look back. But not for long. We have to get down to DC, and catch our flight," she said.

We'd booked flights for the islands out of DC. We were heading for a couple of places, in order to keep anyone from picking up our trail. We each had a number of passports, and each of those people planned a trip island hopping. This planning had taken us a while to put together, but after all this time, all that we wanted would happen.

When we finally stopped, I hoped that we'd done enough to keep under the radar. If not, I had a plan for that, too.

I was never coming back here.

"You ready?" I asked her.

"Yes. Let's get the hell out of here."

I smiled and got that rare smile back. Starting the bike, I faced forward, ready for the future. While this city was my home, and the place where I'd lost my mother, and presumably my father, that wasn't my life. I couldn't hang onto that.

The time had come for me to take full control of my life. In spite of the tarot reader's words, I was only in control of so much. Much of my life depended on the decisions of others. I didn't want that anymore. I wanted full control. If things went sideways, I wanted it to be my fault, not because I had to react to someone else's bullshit.

I hit the gas, intending to race past the sign, a kind of fuck off gesture to all the shit in my old life. I felt Margrite hold my waist tighter as we accelerated. As we passed the sign I smiled. I'm free, I thought.

Then the blackness hit like a baseball bat to the face, and I didn't know anything else.

8

I had no idea where I was. Everything around me—there was nothing around me.

What in the hell?

Aodan! Are you all right?

Great. The god damned voice apparently burst through the door.

Who are you? I asked.

I told you, I'm your grandfather.

What's your name?

I don't want to say it aloud, even as we talk like this.

But you say my name.

That cannot be helped.

Why won't you tell me your name?

Because I am unsure who is listening.

I thought that over. *You mean that this is some sort of open channel?*

The voice chuckled. *I think I know what you mean, and yes, I believe it could be. Stop talking and listen for a moment. Tell me what you hear.*

What the fuck, was my first thought. Then I stopped and allowed myself to listen. To open the door, the one I'd kept shut in my mind since I'd first heard the voice and see if I could hear anything else.

I could. While he was the only one talking, I could feel others. Listening in the background. Waiting.

What is that? I asked.

You are feeling us, the voice said.

Who is this us? Who are you? Why won't you tell me what is going on?

We are like you. Well, I am like you. You and I, and your father... the voice stopped.

What about my dad?

The three of us can shift. We are both dragon, and fae.

Oh, fantastic. I have no idea where I am, what has happened—I'm supposed to be on a plane—and now you're telling me I'm a dragon. And a... whatever else you said.

I felt like I did when I got a headache. I just wanted to close my eyes and close out the world.

But the noise in my head was too loud.

What is all that noise? I yelled into the blackness in front of me.

Aodan, close your mind!

What?

Close it! The voice boomed, and then it was gone.

I tried to get a grip on my location, hell, on any location. I could see nothing. In front of me, all around me—nothing.

I know they—whoever they are—are still there but now it's like there are a bunch of doors between me and them.

This keeps getting weirder and weirder, and I have no idea what I'm dealing with. For me, that's damn well crisis level.

The voice returns, and now, rather than fear, or panic, or concern, I hear calm confidence.

Aodan, is that you?

Who else would it be? What's going on? Where are you?

I am close by. I can help you if you will let me.

There's a different tone to the voice now. He doesn't seem to have the same concerns he did just a couple of seconds ago, but he also seems to have lost his ability to be warm, or anything other than all business.

That, I understood. That, I could deal with.

I have no idea where I am, or what happened. Margrite and I were leaving, and then everything went black.

The voice made a noise of impatience. *The human is of no concern. What is important is that you are cared for and returned to your rightful home.*

What do you mean, she's of no concern? Have you lost your mind?

Do you want to learn your truth, Aodan?

You know I do.

Then you must put aside the human concerns, and the humans.

I'm human!

There is so much more, the voice said.

There was a hint of secrets to be shared. Of promises to come. Of a better life. It was all right there, like just behind a curtain. How did he do that with a voice?

You are so much more. The voice sounded sure of himself.

What, humans don't mean anything?

Not in the scale of things. There is a reason that the Human Realm is the Realm we all hide from.

This didn't make any sense. None at all.

Let us meet, Aodan, and I will explain all. You will see who you are, who you are meant to be, and where you truly belong.

I didn't say anything.

The voice came in my head again, louder this time. *You will come back with me, Aodan. Share with me where you are.*

I could feel a command in the words. Why wouldn't I do as he asked? The voice had only been good to me even if he wouldn't tell me shit. Well, he was kind of telling me things now… what had changed?

Aodan! Show me where you are!

The force of the words startled me.

I don't know.

What do you mean, you don't know?

I told you. The last thing I remember was riding my motorcycle across the city line. Then, nothing.

Open your eyes, Aodan. Let me see what you see.

I couldn't find my eyes. I had to think about where they should be. Then I saw a pinpoint of light.

You know when you see the movies, and a character gets knocked out, whatever, and the film wants to show you what it's like to come to? That's how this felt.

The pinpoint grew, just a little. Then an explosion of color, light, sound and smell hit me like... well, once again, like a baseball bat. It all went from this small circle in front of me to so much around me I didn't know where to look, or what to do.

Let me see, the voice commanded. He sounded angry.

I blinked, trying to orient myself to wherever I was.

"Aodan?" Margrite was near me. "Are you awake?"

I tried to talk, but when I opened my mouth, my voice wasn't working. I closed my eyes again.

Let me see!

Shut up, I thought. *I'm tired. I think I almost died. Go away.*

I envisioned kicking some douchebag out of a door and slamming it behind him. The voice faded instantly although I could tell that he was talking.

I didn't have the energy for this. Now that the voice wasn't demanding shit from me, I could relax. And then I couldn't open my eyes again. I'd just lie here and rest for a bit.

The next time I tried to open my eyes, it wasn't so bad.

Margrite was leaning over me. "Are you alive?"

She didn't sound so good.

"I think so. What the hell happened?"

Margrite got up and walked around the room. We were in a room I didn't recognize— "Where are we?" I asked.

"I got us to a hotel. It's sketchy, but I didn't want to attract any more attention." She grinned, but it wasn't a happy grin. She was stressed. "The clerk wanted to know if I was booking for the entire night, or a certain number of hours."

"That was good," I said. I had no idea whether it was good or not, but I wanted to hear the rest of this, and Margrite was visibly upset. That didn't happen often. "Wait, what? By the hour?"

"Never mind that. It's not important, although we'll think it's funny later. When we were leaving, we were just about to go past the city limits sign. When your body moved passed it, it was like you were hit by lightning, or something." She crossed her arms in front of her, rubbing her arms as she looked at me. "Then you fell off the bike, and I half-jumped, half-rolled off it as it fell. I grabbed you, but the bike fell on you."

"Oh, hell. Where?" I tried to sit up and look over my body.

"It fell on your leg," she pointed at my left leg, "But you won't be able to tell now."

"Why not?"

"Because it has already healed."

"What? It must not have been as bad as you thought."

"Oh no?" Her nostrils flared. "Let me show you, smart ass." She stomped over to the bathroom, banging the door open. When she came out, she held my black pants, my favorite pants —and the left leg was in tatters. I could see the dark stains— whoa! Holy shit, that smelled! I covered my nose. "You smell that?" I asked.

"No. I mean, they're a little funky, but it's not horrible."

"So you say. Those stink." How could she not smell it? It was almost making me gag. It smelled like copper, and dead plants, and something else I couldn't identify. I didn't want to identify it.

Margrite gave me an annoyed look and took the pants back into the bathroom.

"You don't have to save them," I yelled.

"I'm not going to. But I'm not going to leave them for the maid, either," she yelled back.

"There's a maid here?" I looked around. A place that rented by the hour had a maid?

"Yeah, she banged on the door yesterday, and I told her you were sleeping."

"Yesterday? How long have we been here? Shit, Margrite! Our flight!"

She held up a hand. "Who are you talking to? I had your nurse call and let the airlines know that you'd come down with a wretched flu, and there was no way you could travel. Then I asked for them to please cancel the flight, but keep the funds as a credit, since we still wished to use them. I did that for each of our legs of the flight, and I was able to get all of them to cancel and hold a credit."

"I should let you handle this stuff more often," I said. I couldn't believe she'd talked all the airlines into it.

"You should, but maybe you shouldn't fall off the damn bike and scare me to death!" She nearly shouted at me.

"I'm sorry. I don't even know what happened."

"Did the voice talk to you?"

"Yeah, how did you know? Did you hear it too?"

"No, I didn't hear it. You were mumbling and thrashing around—"

"Did I... did I change?" I asked. I was almost afraid to hear the answer.

"No, but I thought you might. You opened your eyes once, and even though I was right there, it was like you didn't see me. Your eyes were glowing, Aodan! And you were growling. We need to figure out what is going on with you, and it needs to happen now. We can't leave here and then have you freaking out on the plane, or something! We're lucky this happened at night, and I was close enough to this place to drag you in!"

"Lower your voice," I said. "The walls aren't that thick."

"I'm scared," she said bluntly, sitting on the bed across from where I was. "I didn't know what to do, and honestly, I have no idea how to handle this. We need to get a grip on this."

"You should go," I said.

Margrite looked at me, and then made a noise—I couldn't

tell what kind of noise, but it wasn't good. She wasn't happy with me. She got up again, and walked out of the room, closing the door behind her in something a little less than a slam. Enough of one to let me know she was pissed.

I got it. I understood. But it was stupid for her to stay here when we had no idea what was happening, and I was hearing voices in my head. Not to mention the possibility of sprouting a tail in moments of stress. That was on top of the whole black out thing. What if that had happened when I'd been at full speed? I would have killed us both.

I couldn't let anything happen to her just because my life had gone apeshit and sideways all at once.

She stormed back in, and this time, she slammed the door. I guess keeping a low profile wasn't a concern anymore.

"You are not dumping me off," she said, her breath coming heavily. "I didn't save your ass for you to go off on your own and be all noble, and stupid, and get yourself killed."

I couldn't remember the last time I'd seen her this angry. "M, I don't want you—"

"What you want doesn't matter anymore. I'm in this with you. We've always been a team. That's not going to change now just because—"

"I've got a tail?" I asked.

She took off her shoe and threw it at me. "You don't right now, and even with the tail, you're still you. Just shut the hell up with this whole noble go off on your own thing!"

I held up my hands. "Okay, okay, simmer down. I feel like I have to offer. I don't really want to split up, either. But I would feel like an even bigger shit if I didn't give you the chance to leave. I don't know what's going to happen, but I…" I stopped, looking over her head. "I don't know that this will end well. And I'll beat myself up forever if you get hurt."

"Well," Margrite came over, and snagged her shoe off the bed, sitting on the opposite bed to put it back on. "We've been dealing with each other's shit for a long time. I'm not going to let you do this alone. Don't be stupid, Aodan."

Part of me was not happy that she wouldn't take herself out of the way of danger. The other part was relieved that I wouldn't be alone in this, whatever this was.

"What do we do?" Margrite asked.

I sighed. "I need to talk to the voice again." I didn't tell her that the voice had dismissed her and my worries over her without a second thought. There'd be time to deal with that if it came up again.

It probably would, but this fell under the heading of I was too tired to deal with more.

"What did it say?"

"It, or he, because I think it's a guy, wanted to see where I was. He said he needed to come to me that he had to see me."

"How do you feel about that?"

I shrugged. "Not great. I feel like something has changed. He's not as nice."

"Was he really nice before?" Her eyebrows went up.

"Yes. He said…" I hesitated.

"What?"

"He said he's my grandfather," I said. "That was before. Now, though, he's kind of bordering on being a dick," I admitted.

Her eyes were wide. "Your grandfather?" She asked slowly. "Really? Do you believe that? Can you trust him?"

"Can we trust anyone?"

"True," Margrite said. "Outside of each other."

"What do I do? He wants to show up here. I don't have a good feeling about him anymore. I can't get a handle on who— or what—this is! Why the hell is someone in my head?" I was so frustrated.

She tapped her lip. "That's weird. You didn't feel bad about him before."

While I couldn't have stopped my outburst, I'm glad she ignored my bitching.

"Yeah, something has changed. But let's not talk about that for a minute. We have bigger problems."

"Like the fact you got knocked on your ass?"

"Yes. What happened there? You said it was like seeing me get hit by lightning? What does that even mean?"

She sighed. "So, we're moving forward, and I think you'd just hit the gas, and then as soon as we went past the sign, there was a blue flash and you fell off the bike and we went over."

"More of shit that's weird," I said. "I don't remember any of that."

"Did you hear the voice? Anything?"

I shook my head. "Nope. I was thinking about how finally we were the hell out of here," I shot her a rueful grin, "And that's the last thing I remember."

Margrite had an odd expression on her face. "I think we should try again."

"What do you mean? I've been out for nearly two days! I don't want to do that again!"

"No, I think we should go to where the sign is, and try it again."

"You think the sign is what did it? Did you hit your head?" This made no sense to me.

"You have a better idea?" Margrite shot back. "Because as the only person who was conscious, that's the only thing I see that might have done it. Maybe I'm wrong. I might be. That's fine. I can admit it. I don't have to be right all the time, like some of us," she rolled her eyes toward the ceiling. "But if I'm wrong, you'll be able to walk past the sign, and no biggie. It was a freak accident. We redo our flights and get going."

"I don't know. What if it happens again? Like when we're on the plane, or whatever?"

"Then we deal with it. First thing is to rule out that it was the place we were in. Then we try something different."

Listening to her discuss this crazy stuff with logic calmed me. This was how we'd approached nearly everything since being on our own. Look at all the angles and decide what made the most sense. That's how you survived. Too much emotion, or anything, and you were just waiting for a screw-up. I took a deep breath and forced my mind into the consideration phase.

Margrite was right. We had to start eliminating what might have caused my accident. Once we'd whittled down what hadn't, that would tell us what had.

"Can you get back here again?"

"It'll be better now that I'm prepared," she said. "You walk past it. If you fall down, then I drag you back. I won't have to deal with a bike trying to kill me."

"Let's do it tonight," I said. "Can I nap some more?"

"Why not now?"

"I don't want to be all out in the open. It makes me less nervous if we go at night. I don't feel like myself," I added. Which was pretty much the understatement of the year. If not the century.

She looked at me and then sighed. "All right, control freak. Go back to sleep. I'll get you up later."

I didn't feel good about this. About any of it. It was logical, it made sense. But it felt like shit.

But as much as I didn't want to admit it, this was the best plan we had. We needed to figure out whether this whatever would happen again. I mean, we could just ignore it, but that wasn't my way. It never made anything better.

I was so used to shit going off the rails that I preferred to just roll on through the shit and clean up on the other side.

In other words, same shit different day.

I closed my eyes. I might as well take advantage of the time to sleep. I thought about the door I'd shut in my head earlier. I focused on making sure it was closed and then allowed myself to relax.

I floated in a darkness. I'd never felt so calm, so easy. My life was a matter of trading one set of adrenaline for another. I'd do a job, and then keep my head down, stash money for getting the hell out of here, and then do another job. That was it.

Here, in the darkness, it was nothing. Nothing was peaceful.

The darkness exploded in my head like fireworks, and the voice was back.

Aodan! Do not shut me out.

Oh. It was the angry voice. It made me sigh. This side of the guy took a lot of energy.

What?

Where are you? I need to come to you.

Not now.

It must be now.

Then it must not need to happen, I thought.

Silence, as though he was considering what to say next.

That's right, asshole. Think carefully. I'm not a stupid kid to be impressed with a firm tone. That ship sailed.

It does need to happen. I need to see you, and we must speak. I can tell you your history, of your parents—and what you are born to.

You can't tell me now?

No.

Then we have nothing to say. Go away. I'm busy.

I envisioned shoving a rich guy (because this guy reminded me of bossy rich guys who occasionally showed up in our part of town) through a door and locking it behind him. I didn't have time for this crap right now.

I forced myself to ignore what I knew was somewhere in my head. After a while, I felt myself begin to slip into sleep.

Then Margrite was shaking me. "It's time to get up."

I looked at her, my eyes bleary. I rubbed them, feeling the burn of being tired. "Already?"

"Sorry, Sleeping Beauty," she said. "Come on. I have our stuff all ready to go."

"You think we'll make it out of here?"

"If we do, we're done."

I nodded, and got up, taking time to brush my teeth, and ignore the noise in my head. It was like white noise, except it was annoying white noise. He was there, on the other side of my mental door, and he was pissed.

Tough shit. I had things to do, and I didn't care for the fact that he didn't respect that. I wondered what had changed. He'd been nicer at first. Still formal, like he had a stick up his ass, but not as impatient as now.

I could feel the mean streak in him.

Which made my level of unease intensify. Why had all this happened with me right as voices started camping in my head? Logically, they were not connected, but somehow, I knew they were. If I'd been a dragon all my life, why did the dragon come out just as I discovered people—one person, really, with dueling personalities—in my thoughts.

It made me all kinds of nervous that I couldn't figure out why.

I finished packing my stuff. Margrite was waiting by the door.

"You ready?" She asked.

I nodded. She headed out to the bike and as we got on, stowing our stuff like we had before, I had a sense of déjà vu. But I had my fingers crossed this would go the way it was supposed to, and we'd finally be out of here.

I drove up to where we were before, next to the city limits sign. Parking the bike on the side of the road where it wasn't easily visible, I got off and turned to Margrite.

"Can you get this thing out of here if you need to?"

She nodded. "I'll move it and then get you on. Unfortunately, I have practice dragging your ass around."

I smiled, but there was no humor in it. What was it that Nala had said? That she felt the reading was important somehow, but she didn't know how? That's how I felt now. This was an important moment, but I wasn't sure how. I just knew it was. Was the reading trying to tell me that?

Oh, no. I stopped myself and focused on the task in front of me.

"All right. I'm just going to walk over and try to get past the sign."

She nodded again. I could tell that she was nervous. So was I.

I carefully stopped well before I hit the place where the sign was next to the road. Took a couple of deep breaths and then started walking. This time, now that I wasn't on the bike, I guess, I could tell that something was going on. A tingle, or a feeling like your skin itching from the inside, started in my arms. Then it spread to my body, and my face.

This was different.

I might not have noticed this before because I was on the bike.

As I made to pass the limits sign, I saw a flash, and then everything went black.

Like before, but with less pain.

But I couldn't stop my fall into the darkness, or the fact that I couldn't keep myself aware.

I only hoped that Margrite was up for it.

9

When I woke, I didn't open my eyes immediately. I tried to take stock of where I was, what I was.

I listened in my head, and like before, I could hear the muttering of voices behind the closed door. I was thankful that whatever had happened, I'd managed to keep the door closed.

There was something or someone moving around near me —I could hear the shuffling. It didn't smell good, either. But then, nothing had smelled really all that good to me since the first time I changed into a dragon. So that didn't mean much.

It didn't feel like anything was broken, or anything else, so I opened my eyes. The intensity of the sun in the room, the dust motes floating in the sunlight, the sharpness of the corners of the dresser at the end of where I was—presumably in a bed —struck me.

"Margrite?" I whispered. My voice had the dragon rumble.

She appeared from the bathroom—we were back in the same ratty motel.

"Aodan?"

I could hear the worry and the fear in her voice.

That sucked. Big, huge, hairy suckness.

"Yes," I said.

She came closer, a hand out. I don't think she realized she'd put it out there.

"How are you feeling?"

"Should I say I feel a little dragon-y?" I asked, the rumble more apparent.

"Yes, I think that would be an accurate description," Margrite answered.

"What happened?"

"You put one foot beyond the sign, and there was some kind of spark, and you fell down. I was able to get you back here, but things were different this time. It was like your body was humming, and I broke every speeding law to get you home. Good thing, too. You changed about five minutes after we got here."

Because it was safe, the nicer voice said in my head.

Jesus. No rest from this guy.

Really? Me passing out again and changing? That's safe?

It would have been better in the open?

It would have been better if I didn't pass out and lose all control! My irritation and anger spilled out.

We don't change out in the open if there is a danger, the voice said. While the words were stern, the tone was not.

What was going on with the Jekyll-Hyde impression this guy did? First, he was all right, then he was a douche, and now he was all right again.

We need to meet, the voice said. *Then I can help you.*

Help me how? Why can't you help me now? I found this insistence off putting. To say the least. Things were too unsettled, too out of my normal for me to feel good about adding one more thing to the weird shit happening folder.

Because this is not the easiest thing to do this way. It will be easier and there will be less chance of misunderstanding if we can meet.

I didn't respond, doing my damnedest to keep my mind blank. *All right,* I thought, feeling myself sigh. *Then let's meet.*

I'd work it out with Margrite. She had even more suspicion than I did, so I'd work out... well, I didn't know what, but I'd work out some kind of plan with her so that I didn't end up screwed.

That's good, the voice said. *I will be able to help you with the transition, and then we can speak of how—*

How I got this fucked up? I thought before I could help myself.

What do you mean?

The question came after a moment of silence.

I mean this is not normal! I'm a dragon! When does that happen, except in books where magic is real?

How do you know it's not?

What the hell are you talking about? I was getting irritated.

Magic. How do you know it's not real?

Well, why wouldn't it be? I rolled my eyes even though I knew he couldn't see me. Because what the hell? I'm a dragon, after all.

Is this the first time you've been aware of this?

What?

When did you first shift? This is the first time since your birth I've been able to contact you, but that doesn't mean your dragon hasn't woken before.

No, this is it, I thought.

"Hey," Margrite said.

She had a look of concern on her face. That wasn't good. She usually kept that shit to herself.

"What?"

"What are you doing?"

I frowned. "What do you mean?" I swear, I couldn't turn around without interrogation headed my way.

"Is he talking to you?" The look of concern increased.

Oh. "Well, yeah. He is. He really wants to meet."

Now she frowned. "How do you feel about that?"

I shook my head. "I don't know. I don't feel good about any of this. What the fuck, M? As soon as we get all of it together, and we're ready to leave, this happens? Doesn't that seem a little too coincidental for you?"

"I don't think it's coincidental at all."

"How so?"

"I think this is supposed to be happening. When did you notice that you were feeling different?"

I remembered I hadn't told her about when the weirdness began. "When I was stealing the box thing."

She nodded. "What did you feel?"

"My nose was itching like crazy, and I wanted to sneeze, and my throat was scratchy. I…" I stopped. This part was too weird.

"What?"

"Smoke came out when I let out a breath."

Her eyebrows rose. "Has that happened before?"

"No!"

"Calm down, touchy. I'm trying to pinpoint things. This goes along with Nala's reading."

I threw up my hands. "Great! I have Jekyll-Hyde in my head, insisting on getting together like a stalker date, and you're trying to pin me into woo-woo land! Not sure things could get worse!"

Margrite stared at me for a moment and then burst into laughter. After a moment, she reached out and patted my hand. "I realize that this is tough on you. You're wound so tight, I'm surprised you haven't imploded. I get it, you know I do. You grow up in a shit show, then things went all right, and then they went to hell. So you want to control everything you can. And now you have this big, dragon-sized thing you can't control." She stopped because she laughed again.

"So glad I'm here to provide the comedy." I crossed my arms and stared over her head.

"I'm sorry! I'm not trying to piss you off, and I'm not lying when I say a lot of these things scare the shit out of me, but that this happened to you, the most anal retentively controlled person I have ever met, is funny. Come on, Aodan," she said, smiling. "Don't be mad. We have to maintain some kind of sense of humor or we'll kill ourselves with the weight of it all. Does the voice seem more... normal?"

"You mean he's not being a douchebag? Yeah, he's nicer. If you promise not to laugh for two minutes, I'll admit that he gives me the creeps when he's in his do it now or shit will rain down on you in doom mode," I said.

"I can't figure it out," she said. "I've been going over and over it, everything you've told me, and there's no reason for him to be a dick. So something is setting him off—but what is it?"

"Do we care?" I asked.

"I do. He doesn't spare you from his dick self."

"True," I agreed.

"So are you really going to meet him?"

"I think I need to," I said slowly. "I wanted to talk to you, try to set things up so you can get me out of there if things go bad," I added. I hated admitting that because she was right. I liked my control. That was one thing the tarot reading got right. I was the Emperor. My domain was small, but it was mine.

"If you're a dragon," Margrite said, "I'm not sure I can get you anywhere."

I didn't reply right away. It was so surreal to hear her say that like it was no big deal, part of daily business.

I supposed it was. I was a dragon at times although I didn't seem to have any control over it. At the moment, I couldn't even remember what happened when the shifting occurred. But there was no changing the fact that this was happening. Maybe it was a good thing that Margrite was accepting this as part of our normal.

But it wasn't. And I didn't understand it. And no one would give me any info without a big effort and risk on my side of things. Which made me nervous, and extremely suspicious of my weirdo voice buddy.

"I wish that I could remember something—anything—that happened when I change," I said. I hated that I felt whiny.

Margrite shrugged. "Shit happens, Aodan. I know, I know," she waved a hand at me. "It doesn't happen to you. You plan for all things, blah, blah, blah. But you can't plan for everything. I think you need to talk to the voice."

"What do you mean? You give me shit when I do," I jumped in.

"No, stupid. Ask him how you are supposed to get a handle on this. Explain, without getting all up in it, how this doesn't fly in your world."

It wasn't a bad idea. He wasn't willing to tell me anything about me, or my parents—the thought of my mom brought a pang as it usually did. It's why I didn't think of her much. It was easy to put her aside because according to my foster parents, and all the guardians that supposedly oversaw my early crappy foster parents my mom had been a drug addict, and no mention of who my father was. Tina hadn't said that, but Tina wasn't the same as the rest of my foster parents.

I moved thoughts of Tina aside. I didn't want to think about her, or what could have been.

But a grandfather—maybe he'd help me with dragon management.

The idea made me smile, just a little.

"Maybe," I said. "If I phrase it as dragon management, or something like that. He's pretty closed off in terms of sharing."

Margrite burst out laughing again. Twice in one day was some kind of record.

"Are you drunk?" I asked.

"No, but I think a drink would be nice. No, I'm just stressed all over the place about your… situation."

I laughed with her at that. "Try living with it."

"I am!"

I laughed harder.

She hit my arm. "You think it's so bad being you? Try dragging your ass around!"

"I'm sorry," I said when I'd gotten out my humor. "I think your manner of handling the stress is getting to me."

"What, totally lost control?" She teased.

"Yeah. It's making me crazy like you. I'll be suggesting a tarot reading shortly."

"Hey, don't make fun. I've never heard her talk to anyone like that. I mean," she added, "Not that I listen to other people's readings. But she was worried for you, I think."

"Worried I wouldn't pay, maybe."

"You're all kinds of stressed, and still an asshole," Margrite got up. "OK. What's the plan, oh guru?"

I didn't answer right away.

"Uh-huh," she muttered, heading toward the bathroom. "Got lots to say, and not a plan in sight."

More muttering as she walked in and closed the door.

It was a good question, and it made me crazy I didn't have a good answer. It was apparent that something had to change, or I wouldn't be able to get beyond the city limits. But what?

Hey! I concentrated on the image of bars, and a dark cavern. Something about that made me think that was where the guy with the voice resided.

I forced myself to wait.

Aodan?

Yes. I want to talk. I need your help.

Of course, you do.

Well, I do.

Very well. What do you want?

Great. He was all shitty now.

I want to manage how and when I shift.

Silence, and then laughter. It wasn't the fun laughter between Margrite and I, either.

Those who shift can and do work for years to master their ability to shift. And you wish to learn it right this moment?

How would I know that it's a long process? How do people not kill themselves? The thought of not being able to manage this scared me more than anything I'd heard or seen lately. And honestly, nothing had really scared me, not even the shifting—well, OK, when I actually shifted, and saw myself as a dragon, that did scare me—but I'd assumed this could be managed and my inability was merely a matter of lack of knowledge and basic skill.

All of which could be learned.

But what he was saying—that it would take years? I wouldn't last years. Somewhere, sometime, someone would see me, would report me to—I didn't know who you'd report this kind of thing to—and I would be finished. I'd be hauled away to some secret government lab, and that's where I'd die.

OK, maybe I read one too many end of the world books. But wasn't that what the government whoever did to people who didn't fit the mold?

I laughed to myself a little. This was definitely in the category of didn't fit the mold.

Those who have the ability to shift are identified early. I would guess that being around humans for so long delayed your shifting.

He sounded thoughtful, and somewhat less douchey.

Aren't you human too? When you're not a dragon?

Silence.

I am not human.

What the hell are you? Because I am definitely human.

No, Aodan, you are not human. Not entirely.

What am I?

Maybe I'd get him to tell me a little something. Was he saying that mom wasn't human? That would be great. I'd love to hear something other than the fact that she was a druggie who met the inevitable druggie end.

There is some human in you, but you are fae and dragon.

I'm what?

Fae. Your father was half fae, half dragon. Your mother was human.

So I'm only half human?

Yes. And part fae and dragon.

The dragon I get. What is a fae?

Fae are the people of the Fae Realm, the people who rule the Fae Realm over all, and the Goblin Realm. A fae man is also on the throne in the Dragon Realm.

I could hear some anger creep into his words at the end there.

So how do I manage the shift? All this talk of Realms, and people ruling... not helping me any. Right now, that was my priority.

How do you manage the shift? He mocked me. *Sorry for boring you with the history lesson.*

There's no need to be shitty. I'm happy to learn history, but my pressing concern is not going dragon in the middle of a crowd of people. I don't know how it is there, in the realm or whatever, but here, you do not pop in between a human and a dragon without causing problems for yourself.

What problems are you having? His manner changed abruptly.

Thankfully, none, but luck doesn't hold that long. I need a plan.

I can appreciate that, he responded, and I could hear the pleasure in his voice. I'd passed some sort of test, apparently.

So how do I manage this? I can't have people knowing I'm... I'm what I am.

He was silent and I could feel that he was considering my words even if he didn't want to hear them.

No one liked to hear the bad. But he was a dick, and he needed to hear it.

You might think I was extraordinarily forceful, given that I needed something from him. But I did need something from him. And I was going to get it. One thing that I'd learned was that people really didn't enjoy saying no to someone else. People wanted to be seen as the good guy. Even where I lived now. People said no because they had to, they felt they couldn't say anything else.

It was why Margrite and I trusted only each other. Because everyone else would sell you out in a heartbeat for what seemed like pennies.

I can help you, I finally heard in my head.

That's why I'm asking for your help, I thought.

More silence. My instinct was to push, but this guy was touchy. Maybe it wasn't a surprise that this was my family, that is, if he was telling the truth.

Very well, he said. *What do you need?*

I need to know how to manage this, and then we need to meet. You have things to tell me. Things I need to know.

I made myself sound firm. I didn't want him to know that I was really nervous, in a way I hadn't been in a long time. I was also annoyed. Wasn't he the one pushing to meet, telling me he'd help me? And now he was acting all reluctant?

We will need to pick a safe place to meet. Somewhere that I can come through and not attract undue attention.

What do you mean, come through?

I'm not in the same place as you, boy. You're in the Human Realm.

I hated this side of him. He sounded contemptuous. It made him sound like a complete dick.

Let me see where we can find some privacy.

Do you not have a dwelling? He asked.

Who the hell spoke like that? I mean, really.

Not at the moment. You'll have to deal.

I was tired of his attitude.

Very well, he said again. *Let me know when you have secured a location.*

I could feel him exit my thoughts. This must be what it felt like when I practiced shutting the door.

"Yeah, I'll do that," I said out loud. I wasn't sure I wanted to meet someone who was so shitty even if he was my grandfather.

First things first. I needed to find a private place.

10

It took me two days of prowling around the warehouse district, searching to see which ones weren't in use, or being squatted in. It's harder than you might think. Two days of camping out in the hourly no-tell motel when I wasn't out searching. Margrite was going spare being stuck there.

But finally I found one. I spent most of the second day sitting in various places around entrances to the warehouse, waiting to see if anyone came in, or around, or near it in any way.

No one did. I figured this might work.

At the end of the second day, I crept in, and spent time exploring. I didn't want to be surprised when my mysterious grandfather came on through from wherever it was he was.

There was no one here. It was a dump, which explained why. It was also perfect. No one would notice anything because there was no one around. I planned to invite him in evening hours since one of the neighbors was open for business during the day.

Once I'd finished going through the place, I thought about what he'd said about controlling the dragon. I couldn't have a part of me that took over that I wasn't aware of. I couldn't black out every time I shifted.

We shift when it's safe, he'd said. We control our shift.

That must mean there was a way to control this, make it part of me? Since there didn't seem to be any chance of getting rid of it.

What had made me change? Trying to leave the city. So… stress? I was stressed now, and there was no sign of a tail.

Okay. I took a deep breath and concentrated. I'd seen myself with consciousness as a dragon. Not for long, but enough that I knew what I looked like.

You're part of me, I thought. Let's bring all the parts together. Because the separate parts sure as shit aren't getting on an airplane, and that is the ultimate goal.

I closed my eyes and imagined myself as I'd briefly seen me. Tall, a bright, glorious blue. Margrite said I had green eyes, and I already knew how low and rumbly my voice became. I had claws, too. Impressive ones.

I pictured me, and I could feel the scratch of smoke in my throat that had been with me since I'd pulled the job at Caleb's warehouse. Every inch of my skin tingled, and I felt… something. My eyes flew open as I held out my hands and looked down to see… my hands.

No claws in sight.

Damn it.

How was it that I changed at the worst possible moment, and I couldn't manage it now?

I closed my eyes and envisioned myself again.

It was as though the dragon stood right in front of me… he —I—was there! But when I opened my eyes again, it was just me in a dirty warehouse.

"All right, damn it," I muttered. I closed my eyes, and I thought about my body making a shift. I didn't remember actually changing. I had no idea what it would be like. As I thought about it, I wondered if it would be painful.

Then, in a flash, I saw her.

A woman, dark-haired like me. She was beautiful, and I could tell that she wasn't happy. I don't know how, but I could tell. She looked up, and I saw——-

Nothing. My eyes opened.

"What the hell was that?" I asked the empty room.

All I wanted was simple, easy, and direct. Every move I was making made things more complicated and made no sense.

The woman, beautiful though she was, had no bearing on my here and now. I needed to start to get a handle on the dragon—on myself. I was the dragon. The dragon was me. That was the first step. Me and the dragon were the same.

I was a dragon. I, me—not he, or it. I.

My mind was having a problem with it. I scrubbed at my eyes with one hand.

Then I closed them again and concentrated on seeing the dragon side of *myself.*

There was no getting around it. Part of me was a dragon.

Without warning, I felt a—stirring? Shifting? In my bones. Oh, wow. This didn't hurt, but it felt really, really weird.

"WAIT!" I shouted.

My eyes flew open and my concentration fell to the floor. But it needed to. If I changed right this moment, then my clothes would be torn to bits. I didn't care about my jeans and shirt. I tended to wear all black and stuff I got from the thrift store. But my coat? The coat I'd carried around since I was a kid? The coat that belonged, so I was told, to my father? The coat that came with a note and carefully wrapped? I still had the note and the wrapping.

No, that couldn't be ruined.

Well, shit. Did I need to get naked?

I didn't want to risk it, but this was something I'd have to manage, too. One more thing to ask the grandfather guy about. I really hoped he'd tell me his name at some point and stop keeping secrets.

I took off my coat and piled my clothes on top of it. If I could get my dragon shit together, I'd need to start carrying a bag with extra clothes in it. What a fucking pain in the ass.

Okay. Please don't let anyone come in here, I thought. This place was a dump, and abandoned, but it would be my luck these days that I would be in here all naked and exposed and someone would come strolling in.

Normally I had better luck than that, but I wasn't counting on it at this point.

I closed my eyes, ignoring how cold my ass felt with no clothes on. While I was thinking about the fact, I'd need more shoes, too, just in case—the tingly, weird feeling returned, and I could tell that something was happening.

The urge to open my eyes was almost overwhelming, but I fought it, and kept the vision of me as a dragon in my head.

There was a pop, like a grape had just exploded. It knocked me out of concentration, and I opened my eyes.

When I looked down at my hand, it was blue and ended in a claw.

"Yes!" I shouted.

Okay, growled. Roared. I could feel the reverberation of my voice in the open space.

Aodan!

Jeez, not even two seconds to enjoy my own newfound dragon-ness.

What?

You've done it? You've shifted of your own accord?

This was the nice guy voice. Guess all I had to do was a change on my own? That kind of pissed me off.

I have. I kept my excitement muted. I didn't want to share it.

That is wonderful! Do I see right? You saw another?

How the hell did he know about the woman?

I see a lot of things I don't get, I thought.

There is much to tell you. I am sorry I have not been as forthcoming

There are forces that are working against us, and I must be careful how I share like this.

He sounded apologetic.

Yeah, well that's not a lot of help to me right now. I have to keep my shit together and try not to get killed—

Who is trying to kill you? Have you been contacted by others?

I'm contacted by people all the time. I don't know what you mean by others.

There was silence.

I waited, but it stretched on and on.

Do not worry about the others, he said.

I could sense the shift in tone immediately.

Why not?

It was amazing. I could pay attention to the crazy in my head, and I could hear *everything*. There were mice, or rats, running around the warehouse, and I could hear *every* one of them. I could smell them, too. And other things. Holy shit, did this warehouse *stink*.

Because the others do not matter. Humans, fae, dragons—they don't matter.

Wait. Others like us, other dragons, don't matter?

No. I know this makes no sense, but it will become clear once I explain.

He was right. It didn't make sense. It also made me really uneasy. There was something in his words, something that wasn't right.

I'd known that all along, but I didn't want to admit it. And now while in dragon form, I couldn't ignore it. It was like someone was screaming in front of me.

You're not being honest with me, I thought.

What do you mean?

I could hear surprise from him.

I can tell. You're lying to me somehow.

If you mean that I am not telling you everything right now, you're right. I'm not. We must meet, and I need to see if you can be trusted.

If I can be trusted? I felt my anger rage up within me. *If I can be trusted? I didn't invade your head, asshole!*

I must be careful.

No sign of any apology now. I could picture someone flip me the bird.

Yeah, well, that makes two of us. Go away.

No, Aodan. You cannot indulge as though you're a child. We must meet, and then I will explain everything.

Yeah, if you can trust me, I thought bitterly.

I couldn't explain why, but the thought of having to prove myself to someone claims to be family pissed me off to no end.

You will understand once I explain.

If you do.

If I do. If you persist in behaving like a child, then I shall treat you as such.

Fucker. I pictured the door shutting, just so I could bitch to myself about what an ass this guy was. Just when I thought he might be decent—every time I did, in fact—he showed me that he was kind of a douche bag.

Great. Did I even want to see him?

I didn't want to if only to spite him. But he had info, and I needed info. Even if I never saw him again, I needed to understand how this happened, how or why I was like this.

Then I could decide.

I allowed the door to open.

I am a child, I thought. *According to you. And you're dropping a lot of shit on me all at once. You haven't been kind or gentle about it. But I'll meet you. Then you can decide if I'm whatever it is you think I need to be.*

Good. That is the mature decision. When shall we meet?

Tomorrow night. I think I've found a place.

Go there and shift. I know you haven't shifted on your own—

What? He kept talking, but my head was whirling....

I shall focus on your location, and will join you.

It took me a minute. Had I imagined our earlier conversation?

Um, yeah, okay. I'll be at the place, and I'll call.

I hoped that was what he said.

Good.

Then he was gone. I could feel the lack of his presence in dragon form in a way I didn't as a human.

What in the ever-loving hell?

Did we not just have a mind meld kind of thing about the fact that I shifted? How had he forgotten that fairly important fact in such a short period?

I was missing something here, and I didn't like that.

But at the moment, I wanted to focus on me, and my dragon. I shut the door in my head and looked at myself again.

I *was* gorgeous. A deep, intense blue. My claws were a smooth, milky ivory, and as I flexed them, I could feel the muscles up into my arms? Front legs? I didn't have just two legs anymore, which was weird.

Maybe trying to walk would be a good thing. I dropped down onto four legs and tried to walk.

I promptly fell on my deep, intense blue face.

So much for having too much pride. I had gifts, but instant grace wasn't one of them at the moment.

I got up. This whole four-legged thing was not instinctive. I practiced, very slowly at first, walking around the warehouse floor.

Then I forced myself to run. Or gallop. I had a lot of weight on the backside—was this what it meant by junk in the trunk?

I fell again while thinking about it.

"Damn it," I said. It came out in a husky growl.

Stopping, I stood up, and inspected myself to see if I'd done any damage. My scales were shiny and showed no sign that I'd fallen twice in the last five minutes.

Okay. So I could sort of run. I liked sitting back on my haunches but that wouldn't help me if I had to hustle.

Hustling would need to wait. I took a breath, feeling the scratch of wanting to do something in the back of my throat.

Dragons breathed fire, right? I could feel my heart beat faster. This would be so cool if—

I exhaled, and a decent cloud of smoke blew out. I coughed, and the strength of my coughing made my eyes burn.

Not so great at the fire then. But it had to be possible—why else would I feel like a cigarette all the time?

Maybe more concentration was needed? I closed my eyes, but opened them again because I wanted to make sure if I did breathe fire, I didn't set my clothes on fire.

That would suck.

My clothes were safely piled up far away from me. So I closed my eyes again and thought about breathing fire. I had no idea why or how this would work, or even whether it should but I had to try.

This time, I felt a burn come out when I blew out my breath, and a warmth in my chest. It didn't burn *me*, but I could feel the warmth.

A bit of trash about ten feet from me was on fire when I opened my eyes.

"Holy hell."

I concentrated again, this time keeping my eyes open, and aiming for a pile of trash to my left.

Fire shot from my mouth, almost just as you'd expect it to, and hit the trash, catching it on fire.

While I felt the tickle or the itch from the smoke, the fire didn't burn me. I had to see if it would. I took a breath and carefully breathed onto my own hand. Claw. Whatever. I needed to know if any part of me could catch fire.

Fire shot out although not as strongly as before. It passed over my claw like water. I didn't even feel it.

So I tried to set my back claw on fire.

Didn't notice anything with that, either. Then I leaned down and slowly stood back up, breathing fire all along my body.

Nothing.

Well, this was pretty fucking fantastic. I could burn things, but I wouldn't burn.

What I did notice was that I could control the intensity of the flame by how hard I exhaled. Good to know.

A movement behind me caused me to whip around, crouching down on all fours. My mouth opened and I was ready to flame broil anything or one who came near me. I scanned around, seeking out movement, smells—and I didn't sense anyone but the rats. Or mice.

Wow. Dragon-me had faster reflexes than I realized. I hadn't even thought about it, but I moved without thinking.

I took a deep breath through my nose and nearly choked.

This place stank. Badly. There were a lot of dead things around, and it made my stomach swim for a moment.

Okay. So I could do this, but how to get back to me?

I sat back on my haunches and closed my eyes. There had to be a better way to do this, but until I spoke to Grandpa Asshat, and got some tips and tricks of the trade, this would have to do.

As long as I didn't have to do it in a hurry.

"Okay, let's go back to the human," I said quietly.

I felt, rather than heard, my dragon laughing.

That broke all concentration. Not that it was stellar but what the hell?

"Are there two of us in here?" I asked out loud.

There wasn't a reply, not even in the crazy-person-voice-in-the-head way I'd become accustomed to.

But something in me heard my question, and I felt my dragon shift.

I fell backward and something hard hit me right in the butt.

"Ow!" I yelled.

My voice was mine. My non-dragon voice.

"What was that?" I asked.

Then I got myself up because one, I was naked and needed to remedy that immediately. Two, I needed to make sure I wasn't bleeding. Looking around, I saw that I'd fallen on a rock.

But I wasn't bleeding. I'd probably bruise, though.

Great.

I moved to where I'd left my clothes. Taking a deep breath, I realized that I couldn't smell all the rank nastiness I'd been able to smell as a dragon. That was a good thing. The heightened sense of smell would take some getting used to.

But as I dressed, looking around to make sure no one had snuck up on me in the middle of my dragon problems, I couldn't help but feel pleased.

I'd done it. I'd shifted into a dragon and then back to myself. There were problems. No speed, even though my dragon was wicked fast. There was also what to do with clothes. If I needed to shift quickly—and part of me wondered what sort of occasion would call for that, even as my mind worked on the logistics—I couldn't really stop and say, Hang on, let me get naked.

Yeah. No. That wouldn't work. Maybe Margrite would have some ideas. She was the planner after all.

I'd always said I have gifts. Now I could add 'dragon' to that list, and boy, was it awesome.

Scary, but awesome.

It was time to go home and plan some more.

For that, I'd definitely need Margrite. I didn't trust Grandpa, not at this point. He was too all over the place.

And we still needed to figure out what was up with the people wanting to burn down our building.

It had to be us because no one else lived there.

That was on top of how to get out of here.

I sighed as I left the building. For a moment, I'd been able to forget my problems, and just enjoy being me, checking out the new me.

Back to real life.

11

With all my concerns over the group of people who seemed to want to kill me, or us—I took a long way home, and kept to the shadows. I hoped no one had been able to follow us, but we'd been found twice in a day by people with definitely bad intentions.

I went past our building, and I spotted two different people hanging around, watching.

That wasn't good.

It also meant that I wasn't just being paranoid. Thankfully, these guys seemed bored, and weren't paying attention, because they should have spotted me.

They didn't—at least, I hoped not—and I kept going, heading back to the motel.

Margrite was waiting when I shut the door behind me.

"Where have you been?"

"I was looking for a place to meet up with Grandpa Asshat."

"You find something?"

I nodded. "I did. I want you to be there, too. We're meeting tomorrow night. I also went by the apartment. People are watching it."

Her brows furrowed. "Which people?"

"Looks like the guys who were there the day we left, but I don't really know. Who else would be watching it?"

"Are these Caleb's guys?"

I shook my head. "I don't know. It's not a good sign that I haven't heard anything about him and haven't seen him around. He's always around."

Margrite rolled her eyes at me. "We haven't been around, Aodan. We're hiding out, remember?"

"Oh. Yeah," I said, not wanting to admit that I'd completely forgotten that. The hiding out piece was kind of further down my list of important shit at the moment.

"So what's the plan?" She asked.

"What do you mean?"

"What do you need help with tomorrow night?"

"I don't trust him. I'm not going to tell him you're there, but I want you there in case something goes sideways."

Margrite didn't answer.

"*W*hat?" I asked.

"Normally, I'd say no problem, and not worry about it. But I don't know what this guy is, what he might do. I don't even know what you might do, Aodan!"

"You're just going to let me go it alone?"

"No. But I'm worried. There are a lot of unknowns here."

Margrite hated the unknown. She liked to have a reasonable probability of how things would go. I felt like she overdid it with planning for the worst, but I hadn't gotten shot or killed in the five years we'd been on our own, working together.

"You're good at improvising," I said, smiling at her. "That's why I want you there."

"You could just tell him you don't want to meet," she said with a frown.

"What? Are you kidding? I don't think this dragon thing is

going away," I said. "Even if he is an ass, I'd like to at least know what I'm dealing with. I can shut him out when I want to, for the most part," I added, more to myself than her.

"What do you mean?"

"What are you talking about?" I looked up.

"You can shut him out?" Her hands were on her hips.

"I hear him in my head, you know?"

She nodded.

"So when I don't want to talk, I think about closing a door, and putting him on the other side. I know he's there, but I don't have to listen."

"That sounds… annoying," Margrite said.

I shrugged. "It is, but it's nice to be able to turn him off. He likes to go on," I thought about how when he got into jerk mode. Yeah, it was really nice to be able to shut the door on his rambling. Or snotty commentary. I wasn't going to mention to Margrite that he didn't seem to think much of her, or any humans. It would piss her off.

"Good thing you have skills, huh?" Margrite asked with a small grin.

I smiled. "You know it." It was an ongoing joke with us, but I did have mad skills at the things I wanted to.

Margrite accused me of picking and choosing what I wanted to be good at. She wasn't wrong.

"Okay, so what do you want me to do at this meeting?"

I didn't answer right away. "This is going to sound crazy, and I don't want to hear any woo-woo stuff, but I don't have a great feeling—"

"Then why are you meeting him?" She threw up her arms in frustration.

"Didn't we just go over this? He has info. I need it. Not meeting him is not an option. When he's being nice, he's good, but he gets a lot less nice at times, and I don't like it. I don't trust it. He's going to have to show me that he's not going to screw me over and…" I stopped. Took a breath.

"I don't have enough control of the dragon. He has a lot of control, and I'm worried he'll be able to control me."

Ever since Tina died, I'd been vigilant about not allowing anyone to take control of my life, of my choices. No one but her had ever shown me where it would be a good idea, and even Tina didn't try to tell me what to do. She knew it would be like hitting her head against a brick wall. Instead, she focused on helping me to make a good choice, with all the information possible. She always said that information was what gave someone control.

That was certainly the case here.

With my grandfather, I didn't always get warm and fuzzies that he'd help me do the same thing. Well, sometimes I did—but not recently. He'd been in full-on ass mode.

Margrite nodded. I didn't have to explain to her.

"What do you want me to do?"

"As far as I can tell, he's going to show up. Like, in the flesh, not just the crazy voice in my head. So watch him. I'm not going to tell him you're there. It's better he think that it's just the two of us. And if he tries anything, tackle him."

"What? Have you lost your mind?"

"What?"

"This guy is a full-grown man, and a dragon? And I'm supposed to just tackle him? And do what? Use bad language?"

"I don't expect you to do anything other than distract him, so that we can get away."

"Oh, nice to know that I'm part of the getaway plan."

"Don't be stupid. We'll go over tomorrow before we meet him, and you can get an idea of where to run to if you need to."

She made me draw a picture of the warehouse from what I could remember, and then we finally went to bed.

I dreamed of a battle. There were dragons—bigger than me, and fierce looking—flying through the skies. Men were on the ground, with spears, and bows and arrows, but bows and arrows that were out of some kind of sci-fi movie. They were glowing, and when they hit a dragon, there was an explosion of light. Sometimes the dragon fell, sometimes it didn't.

I could feel my heart beating and I wanted to be up in the sky with them, shooting fire and killing the men who were killing the dragons—killing the creatures like me.

In spite of the magic, or whatever it was, the dragons were doing well. They seemed to have some kind of magic of their own, you know, outside of the breathing fire. I thought the dragons were going to win until a man showed up and stood on a hill a ways back from the battle area.

He had a shining pendant on a thick gold chain around his neck. It hung down to his chest. It was a bright, reddish-yellow, and reminded me of looking into the sun. It was hard to see the man with the brilliance from his necklace.

He held up his hands, and while I couldn't hear what he said, I could tell he was shouting. His hands began to glow the same shade as the pendant, and the light got brighter and brighter.

There was a moment when everything seemed to stop, like someone took a picture. The dragons were swooping and diving, breathing fire with every breath. There were men that got hit with the fire on the ground, and they flew backward and forward with great force when the fire hit them. I could tell that they screamed, but I couldn't hear that either.

Then the man back on the hill disappeared in a ball of light.

And the dragons fell from the sky.

"NO!" I shouted as I sat up in bed. I was covered in sweat and my heart raced.

As I looked around the darkened room, the sounds that hadn't been clear in my dream echoed in my head. The cries of wounded and dying men, and the roars of dragons.

So much death, so many hurt and in pain.

I wiped my face and felt the tears mingled with the sweat.

What the hell had I seen? It was like I'd been there.

What was that? I thought.

You saw our end, came the immediate response. *We dream of it still. You see what we see.*

They're all gone?

Not all. There are ele-twelve of us left. Perhaps thirteen, now.

I stopped, realizing that he was referring to me.

That's it? Thirteen? There were so many—

No more, his voice cut me off, and I could hear the anger and pain in it. *We are but thirteen. There are no more.*

I'm sorry.

This is not the present, Aodan. It was long ago. You have nothing to be sorry for. You must keep yourself safe until I can get to you.

I wanted to talk to you about that, I thought. I had the nice Grandpa at the moment. I wanted to keep him.

Yes?

I found a place. Let's meet tomorrow around six.

What? I do not understand your time.

Around dark, I thought. It was nearly spring, but it was still dark by six-thirty.

Sunset, then?

Yes.

You have only to call me, and I will be able to—he stopped.

I waited, but he didn't continue.

You'll be able to what? I asked.

No answer.

Hey!

I am sorry, his tone was more formal. *You were saying?*

Great. Asshat was back. What happened to this guy?

I'll call you when I get there. It'll be just getting dark here.

I will wait for your call.

He was gone. I don't know how I knew, but I could tell that he'd stopped the connection.

That was so strange.

I listened, letting my breathing relax, and my heart return to normal.

He had a door, too. I could hear a lot of things behind the door, multiple voices.

Why was he shutting me off from them? From the other eleven dragons?

There had to be a reason. I was going to find out, since he'd been pretty careful not to talk about them, or mention meeting them.

Was I a secret?

I was glad that Margrite would be with me tomorrow.

Something told me that I'd need the help.

I rolled over, closing my eyes, and thought about how amazing it had been to see the dragons in the sky, rolling and swooping. They were both frightening and beautiful to watch.

I wanted to be one of them.

12

When I woke, my eyes flew open, and my heart beat faster. I lay still, listening. Margrite was sleeping still, her breath light and steady in the other bed.

There was a smell I hadn't noticed before, one of damp and decay. This was an old motel, and I didn't even want to think what was making the room smell like that.

I didn't notice any smell when we checked in so that must be part of my dragon.

Now it was invading me? The non-dragon me?

I sat up, stretching. I could feel my muscles protest as I kept stretching, and my bones felt like they were popping as I moved.

The people next door were fighting. I could hear every other word. She was accusing him of trying to flirt with the waitress from dinner last night.

I shook my head and rubbed at my ears. How was I hearing this? If they were really this loud, wouldn't it wake up Margrite? She was a light sleeper. I looked over, and she didn't stir.

Sliding from bed, I pulled on my pants and a tee shirt. I walked to the door, and unbolted it, sticking my head out a little.

Nothing. No noise, even though now the fighting of the couple next door was joined by all sorts of underlying noises.

It wasn't that the world had all decided to yell. I closed the door, leaning against it after I locked it.

It was me.

I could hear better than I'd ever been able to. I glanced at Margrite again.

Nothing.

I'd never get back to sleep now. I headed for the shower and took my time getting ready. It was nice to have a shower that didn't run out of hot water.

When I came out of the bathroom, Margrite was sitting up in her bed.

"What happened? You're never up early."

I toweled off my hair. "I woke up, and I was wide awake. So I decided to do the thing right. You know, get up, and take a shower. You hungry?"

"I could use coffee," she rubbed her eyes.

"You want to get up and we'll go have breakfast?"

"What, you get up once and now you're the early morning person?" She grumped at me. "Are you done in there, princess?"

"Maybe I'm turning over a new leaf," I teased, snapping my wet towel in her direction.

"Keep your new leaves away from me," she got up and went past me, shutting the door hard.

I smiled. She was right—I wasn't a morning person. But I felt like it this morning, and if this is how people who liked getting up felt, I could see why.

I prowled around the room while Margrite got ready. I could hear everything. The couple next door were—well, it was better not to go into what they were doing. Apparently the waitress had become a non-issue.

There was someone smoking outside below us.

I could hear the humming of the housekeeping staff a

couple of rooms down (I had to peek out the door to see where she was.)

My hearing, my sense of smell—both were heightened. It felt like my skin was crackling with energy. I felt alive and ready for anything.

Was this because I'd shifted on my own last night? I had to wonder.

Maybe Grandpa would be in the nice-guy mode, and I'd be able to get some answers from him.

Finally, Margrite came out of the bathroom looking a little more cheerful. Not much, but a little.

"I need to eat and get some coffee before I murder something," she muttered.

"Okay," I said, trying to keep the cheerful tone out of my voice.

We headed out, not speaking, and walked down the street to the little diner on the corner.

"I'd kill for an IHOP," Margrite said. "I want some ridiculous pancakes with all the fruit and whip cream and stuff."

"I bet they can add something to your pancakes," I said.

"Shut up," she walked in ahead of me, and went to a booth.

A waitress, pretty and almost as cheerful as I felt, came and put menus in front of us. She had a big smile for me.

Maybe this was the waitress who caused the argument between our neighbors at the motel? I could see why if so.

Margrite was scowling at her.

The girl's smile faltered when she saw Margrite's expression.

"Were you working last night?" I asked before I could stop myself.

She turned to me, and the wide smile came back. "I was! I closed, and I'm filling in for someone who's sick," she added.

"Probably sugar overdose," Margrite muttered.

"I'm sorry?" The waitress whipped her head back toward Margrite.

A dangerous proposition, to be sure.

"Coffee, please," Margrite said.

"Make it two," I added.

I could tell Margrite made the girl nervous. She nodded and hurried away.

"How the hell are people so chipper this early?" Margrite met my eyes and rolled hers.

"I feel pretty good," I said.

"Shut up. You've got... reptile issues."

"What, that doesn't count?"

"Nope."

"Be nice. You could be a waitress."

"No, I couldn't," she said immediately.

"Then be glad it's her and not you and she can smile at your grumpy ass."

Margrite looked at me for a moment. "You want to ask her out?"

I burst out laughing. "Why do you have to go there? No, I'm in a good mood, and I'm glad neither of us has to wait on grumpy asses like you."

She glared and then smiled. "You and me both. I would be in jail."

"Maybe not. You could have unlimited coffee," I added.

"That would be the only good thing."

We were both laughing when the waitress returned. "Here you go," she set down cups with steam rising off them. "What are you having for breakfast?"

"You guys put fruit and whip cream on pancakes?" I asked.

She thought for a moment and then nodded. "I know the cook has some fruit in the back. What do you want?"

"Whatever you have. And top it with whip cream."

"And for you?" She turned to Margrite.

"That was for me," Margrite smiled, but it wasn't her nice smile. I could tell the waitress grated on her nerves. That was another point for her being the topic of discussion with the neighbors. Even though most people got on Margrite's nerves.

"I'll have the American," I said before Margrite could skewer her. I knew the signs.

The girl made a note on her pad and hurried away.

"Stop. You probably don't mind scaring kids, either."

"What, because you like them?" Margrite was stirring her coffee and not looking at me. "What's up with you this morning?"

"I feel... different," I leaned forward. "Ever since I got up this morning."

"I thought dragons were supposed to be moody, and sarcastic, and all-around grumpy bastards."

"Is that what you'd prefer?" I asked.

"Right now, yes," she said.

I smiled.

"But what do you mean, you're different?"

In a whisper, I told her the things I'd noticed this morning. I also shared my suspicions about our waitress.

That brought a genuine smile from Margrite. "She can't help it, annoying as I find it."

"That was my thought, too."

"So you can hear everything?" She changed the topic back to the important one.

"I can."

"What are they saying in the kitchen?"

I pretended to listen although I hadn't really been focused on it before. It was like background noise.

"The cook is asking our waitress if she wants him to spit in your pancake mix."

"What?" She slapped her hands on the table and shot out of her seat.

I grabbed her arm. "I'm kidding! Kidding! Sit down, crazy!"

She glared at me. "Jerk. Don't do that."

"I'm sorry."

She didn't change her expression.

"No, seriously, I mean it! Sit down, and I'll listen for real."

Slowly, Margrite sank back down. I took a breath, and let my focus move outward,

The waitress was talking to the cook, but she was talking about what fruit he could use.

The surrounding people were talking quietly, just as we were. Nothing major, just conversations about whatever.

Nothing that would create a danger for us, which was my chief concern.

I shook my head as I met Margrite's eyes.

"I don't hear anything of importance. Just people talking about whatever. The waitress is talking to the cook, but she seems more worried that you won't like the fruit."

Margrite raised a brow.

"I mean it," I said.

She sighed. "You haven't noticed this before?"

"Nope. I thought something was wrong when I woke up this morning. Particularly after…" my voice trailed off.

The waitress had returned with breakfast.

She set a stack of pancakes that had peaches and strawberries and whip cream in front of Margrite, and then my eggs and bacon American plate in front of me.

Margrite smiled. I could tell she was making an effort, but it scared the waitress.

"Um… do you need anything else?"

"More coffee, please," Margrite said sweetly.

The waitress ran.

"You're just making it so I have to leave her a big-ass tip," I hissed over the food. "Stop it."

"You're in a great mood with the world," Margrite said as she cut into her pancakes. "Don't be cheap."

I rolled my eyes. The waitress came back and filled our cups and hurried away again. I hid a grin behind my food. If I didn't know her, Margrite being friendly could be intimidating.

We ate in silence. I was still ridiculously cheerful, in spite of all the crap I had to sort through. And the fact that I was the best eavesdropper on the planet at the moment. Eavesdropping had its uses.

I stopped with the fork halfway to my mouth.

"What?" Margrite noticed.

"What if we—I—could get close to Caleb, or some of the punks who work for him? I could eavesdrop, see if it's them who are after us and plan on burning the building."

"They can't be that stupid to talk about it all out in the open like that," she said. "Besides, why do we care at this point? Aren't we leaving?

I didn't say anything, only raised an eyebrow.

"No."

"Yes," I said. "They really are that stupid. How do you think Luke found out about where the box went? It wasn't through keen detective work. One of the punks blabbed. And I'd like to think we're leaving, but things keep stopping us. We might need the building."

"How has that guy not gotten killed?" She ignored my comments about our former home.

"I think his boss protects him," I said.

Maybe I could get a read on his boss, too. See who it was. The thought of all the things I could discover hit me with the force of a sledgehammer. I sat back in the booth.

"Don't tell anyone about my hearing," I said slowly.

"Whatever. Who would I tell?"

"Nala," I said. I didn't think Margrite had friends closer than me, but she was closer to Nala than I realized, and she'd told me she kept secrets from me—so I felt like I needed to say it.

"I talk with her, but I don't tell her a lot."

I gave her the stink eye. I'd seen the two of them together. They were close.

"Okay, I tell her more than I tell most people, but she'd never hurt me."

"That does nothing for me, Margrite. If people knew... I could get killed."

"You could get killed now," she pointed out. "But I'll keep my mouth shut."

"Thank you." Why did this have to be so hard? "Until I—we—know more about this, don't say anything!"

She held up her hands. "Relax. I won't say anything. I never do. Why are you so worried about this now?"

"I didn't know you talked at length to Nala."

She looked at me while chewing on her pancakes and then swallowed. Laughter bubbled out of her. "At length? What is going on with you? I talk to her, a little."

"And you keep secrets," I added.

"Now we're getting to it. You're upset that you think I don't tell you everything. Do you tell me everything, Aodan?"

I opened my mouth and then closed it. "Pretty much."

Margrite leaned forward, pointing her fork at me. "Pretty much? That's not everything. So there are some things you keep to yourself?"

Reluctantly I nodded.

"So do I. It doesn't mean anything. It means that you and I are the same as we ever were, but now we both know that we don't say every single thing that comes into our heads. That's it. You need to get over this, A."

She went back to her food, studiously ignoring me.

Damn it. She was right. I didn't want to admit it. Maybe because my life had exploded into something I had no control over was why this was getting to me.

I decided that I didn't want to keep on with this topic and finished my breakfast. I wouldn't get anywhere anyway.

The waitress dropped the check at the speed of light, and I left her a big tip. She'd earned it. We went back to the motel, and I went through with Margrite what I wanted her to do.

I wasn't going to let her expose herself to Grandpa, or

anyone else. While we were a team, this was something I needed to keep focused on me.

"Can you shift again?" Margrite asked.

"In here?" I looked around. "I don't think there's enough room."

She got up and moved the beds, pushing them away from each other so there was a fair amount of space between them.

"I still don't think that's enough," I said.

"Try."

"If something breaks, you're the one who has to come up with an excuse to the manager," I warned.

"Yeah, yeah. Try it. You need to be able to do this on your own more than once."

I wanted to argue, but she was right. I didn't trust Gramps, and I didn't want to be at the mercy of anyone else. I also wasn't thrilled about having to get naked.

"Turn around for a minute," I said.

Margrite rolled her eyes, but obligingly turned.

I shucked my clothes fast. I didn't care for this part of the operation at all.

Closing my eyes, I pictured myself as the dragon. Nothing happened at first. Then, I could feel the tingling, the awareness, that I'd felt before.

When I opened my eyes, I was the dragon.

Margrite was in the corner of the room.

"It's all right," I said in dragon-voice.

"Wow. It's hard to believe it's you," she said.

"You can come closer," I was annoyed. "I'm not going to eat you."

Her eyebrow went up, but the scared look left her face, which is what I wanted to see. "You sure? You look like you could."

"I'm still stuffed from breakfast."

I took a breath and tried not to gag. Everything smelled so

much stronger. I could smell the food on my clothes from the diner.

"You okay?" Margrite peered at me.

"The sense of smell is so much stronger that it takes some getting used to."

She didn't respond and then understanding flooded her face. "Oh, shit. Does everything smell? Do I smell?"

"Everything smells. You don't stand out," I said.

Her face relaxed. She did stand out for me, but it wasn't a bad thing. So I wasn't going to tell her that. But I could pick out her scent. It was one of shampoo and soap and right now, maple syrup.

She smelled like my friend. Since I wasn't being completely honest, I guessed I couldn't get on her anymore for the "I don't tell you everything" comment.

"How are you feeling?"

"It takes a minute to get used to this," I said.

"Yeah, and that voice."

"I know. It's weird to hear it."

"Can you change back?"

"This second? I don't know."

"You need to try. What if you need to be Aodan—human," she corrected herself, "Quickly?"

"One step at a time, for Pete's sake," I said.

"Try," she insisted.

I closed my eyes, and focused on becoming me, the me I was used to, again. It felt weird, like a coat that doesn't fit right.

The change wasn't finished when I opened my eyes. Like magic—I guess it was magic?—my hands were forming from the large claws. It was like watching a movie. It didn't feel like this was happening to me.

Margrite crossed her arms. "You did it."

"Let me put my clothes on," I said.

She turned away, and I hurriedly got into pants. "Okay, I'm halfway decent," I said.

Margrite laughed and said, "Only halfway. How do you feel?"

"Completely off balance. I don't like changing like that."

A smile remained on her face. "It's hard to believe we're having this conversation, but we are. You'll get used to it."

"That's easy for you to sit there and spout." I pulled on a tee shirt. "You know, since you're not the one who is dealing with it."

"No, I just get to haul your dead weight around when you fall over."

"Not the same thing."

"Thank god you haven't been a dragon when that happened. I would have had to leave you."

"Well thank god for small favors," I snapped.

"Simmer down. It's going to be fine. You know it. I know it. Whatever is going to happen will happen. You're just stressing over the loss of control. No Aodan boss in this."

I glared. "Whatever."

"Go take a nap, grumpy. I'll get you up in time for us to get there and scope shit out."

How did my good mood just disappear like that? I curled up in bed, my good mood gone like a penny in my 'hood. Maybe this was my bitching about my loss of control. Of all the things that could very wrong.

There didn't seem to be much that I had control over lately. Which sucked.

I knew that Margrite would crawl all over the warehouse. It was part of why she was the planner. I closed my eyes and tried to allow myself to relax.

---

*W*hen I woke, my eyes flew open, and I could feel my heart beat in my chest. What had I missed? Something was going on.

The room was darker. I sat up carefully, listening.

"You're finally awake."

Margrite was sitting in the ratty chair by the window.

"What time is it?"

"We're not late. It's after four."

I'd slept for nearly six hours.

"What did you find?" I asked, trying to reorient myself. But reorient to what? The feeling that I'd woken and missed something wouldn't leave.

"Although I don't have your sense of smell, it stinks in that place. You must hate it. But it's a good spot. There's no one around, no neighbors. So if something goes to hell, or your weirdo family gets feisty, puts on a magic show, I think we're fine."

"I don't think there's going to be a magic show," I said, swinging my legs out of bed.

I could hear her shrug, the rasp of material loud in my ears. "No one would have expected you to have a tail either, so let's try to keep an open mind, okay?"

"What are you going to do? And do you have a bag I can use?"

"I found a place that I can hide out and still see everything. If something goes wrong, I'm going to run to you and try to drag you out of there. It may not be a pretty sight if you're in dragon form, but," she shrugged again. "We'll do what we need to. What do you need the bag for?"

"Not very inspiring. I need the bag to store my clothes."

"When is it ever? It's a stacked deck most of the time, A. You know that. A tail doesn't change things."

"Why are you obsessed with the tail?" I asked, my temper close to spilling over.

She made a sound that almost sounded like a giggle. "I don't know. I'm not trying to mess with you, just the thought of a tail is funny."

"Says the person who doesn't have to deal with it."

"It could turn out to be a good thing. You just don't have your dragon-fu in order," she said.

"Whatever. I'll be ready in a bit." I went to the bathroom and closed the door firmly.

Why did being a dragon have to be so lacking in dignity? I remembered the fall on my face when I was trying to walk on all fours. And now my friend was laughing over my tail. Weren't dragons supposed to be fierce, and dignified and shit?

I didn't see any of that happening here.

As I stared at myself in the mirror, a thought occurred to me. Maybe it was up to me to change my dragon narrative, find my dragon-fu, as Margrite said.

Okay. This I could handle. When shit was my responsibility, I found a way to get it done. I couldn't control the fact that I was a dragon, or the dual personalities of my grandfather, but I could control how I put myself out there.

Just like I'd always done. Only now, as Margrite said, it would involve a tail.

So be it. I'd be the same badass with skills that I always was.

With a tail.

I grinned at myself in the mirror. I was Aodan, and that meant something, no matter what form I was in.

Too bad I couldn't wear my kick-ass coat as a dragon. But I didn't need it. I had amazing scales.

Happier, I got ready, splashing water on my face, and brushing my teeth. The years of nagging from Tina weren't forgotten even though I'd lived without her for the past five years.

Thanks, Mom, I thought.

When I took a last look at myself, inspecting myself for any visible cracks, any signs of weakness, I didn't see any. And while I was confident in who I was, and what I could do—I was also honest when I was weak.

I didn't see it. In fact, when I winked at me in the mirror, I saw a flash of bright green.

The dragon was with me.

It felt good.

"Let's go own this shit," I said, and I walked out of the bathroom.

Time to get serious.

Margrite didn't say anything. She could sense the change in me. It's one of the many things I loved about her. We'd been friends for so long there wasn't always a need for words.

Didn't stop her, or me, I thought. But we didn't need to. We were friends, and family.

The only one I had.

I pulled on my red coat, ready to go meet my only other known family.

Hopefully, he wasn't the jerk he'd been lately.

13

We took our time heading into the warehouse. Margrite made a circuit around the building. She reminded me of a wary alley cat, prowling cautiously, ready to take a bite out of anyone who got in her way.

When she got back to me, she nodded.

"Didn't see anything. There have been cars here recently. I saw tire tracks on the other side of the building."

"How can you tell?"

"It rained two days ago. These are in the dirt, dry."

I wondered where she picked up this information. It wasn't like we lived in the woods.

Then I decided it didn't matter at the moment.

"Okay, let's go in, and get set up where you want it. Then I'll call him."

She nodded again and led the way. We stepped quietly, like we were breaking in.

Margrite moved purposefully, stopping at a place a distance from where I'd done my practicing the day before.

"You go out there. It's not far for me if I have to get to you," she pointed. "Here's the bag." She handed over one of her messenger bags.

"Thanks."

"I didn't pack any clothes. You didn't mention that."

"That's fine. I don't need you to. I put my clothes in it," I grabbed the collar of my coat, shaking at her. "I'm not ruining this for a dragon, even one as handsome as me."

Her mouth dropped open. "You need to get naked?"

"How did you think I shifted?"

"I don't know. I didn't think about it. You made me turn around, remember?" She clamped her mouth shut and looked away.

"Well, I did. I don't care about my clothes other than the coat, but it's a pain to have to keep packing new stuff. Better to plan to get naked if I know I'm going to shift."

"Makes sense," she said, still not looking at me.

I took the bag and moved out to the open warehouse floor. "No pictures," I called out.

I heard her make a noise that sounded a lot like a snort, but she didn't speak.

Taking my time, I carefully removed my clothes, and put them in the bag. It felt... I don't know. Vulnerable? Knowing that someone was watching?

I'd need to get used to it. Like I told Margrite, the dragon wasn't going anywhere. She was my best friend. If we were going to stick together, she'd have to get used to seeing me naked. Just like I'd have to get used to taking off my clothes. I wasn't sure that I was ever going to feel casual about that.

Neither one of us was there yet.

The drill I'd used several times seemed the best bet. I closed my eyes and imagined myself as the dragon. I could feel the tingle before it happened—it was like my body was waiting for it.

Like the dragon wanted to come out.

It made sense. I'd felt like I was ready to go since I'd seen the flash of green in the mirror back at the motel. This shit was going to stop. I'd find out what I needed to, and then I'd be able to decide if my grandfather was worth the effort. He'd been a hinting pain in my butt up till this point.

"I'm going to call him," I said to Margrite. My dragon voice rumbled through the empty space.

She didn't respond, but that was all right. I knew she heard me.

I think the entire block heard me, I thought with a grin.

Good. Hear me and be concerned. Is it an earthquake? Is the building falling down? No, it's just Aodan the dragon.

I had to make this a skill like my other skills.

I'm here, I thought. I sent my thought out to the edges of my mind.

There was silence.

Then, *Good. I am coming to you.*

I felt my heart speed up, and the adrenaline began to surge through me. It was more intense as a dragon. This was like what it felt to complete a job, that point where you have the thing, whatever the thing is, and you now have to get out of the place without getting caught.

I was concerned for what might come next, but it was a rush all the same.

Would he come in dragon form?

A light burst in front of me—it was like the light in the warehouse when I stole the box—and it got bigger and bigger.

I just knew a guy would step out. Would he kick a woman again? Was this the same guy I'd seen?

Oh shit. That guy seemed mad and nasty. Was he connected to me—to all this—in some way?

As the light got bigger, I saw the form of a man, and then as expected, a man stepped out and the light winked out.

I let out a breath, and a puff of flame shot out about two feet in front of me. The fact that the things I'd seen in the warehouse were probably really connected to me scared the living daylights out of me.

The man was tall, and very dignified. If I saw him on the street, I'd want to steal from him for his attitude alone. It was dismissive and condescending. I could feel it, without him saying a word.

It was in the fall of his clothes—like some kind of renaissance faire look, with a robe, and then another robe over top of it. Lots of gold thread. The robes were various shades of red, and he had a large gold chain with a pendant that hit about middle of his chest.

The pendant was interesting. It looked alive, like there was smoke and something living moving around in it. Like his robes, the pendant was reddish, but the shade kept shifting.

It was mesmerizing.

"Aodan," he said, holding out his hands and coming toward me.

He didn't seem bothered at all that I was in dragon form.

"You are magnificent," he added, stopping right in front of me, hands still out.

I looked down at his outstretched hands and didn't move. I wasn't taking his hands.

"You do not greet me as a friend?" He asked. His tone didn't change, but I felt the shift in him. He wasn't pleased.

Having him in my head for a while made it easier to feel what was going on with him. I wondered if he could sense the same thing in me, and I steeled myself to show nothing.

"I'm not sure," I rumbled.

"It's good to hear you," he smiled, his irritation apparently vanishing.

I didn't trust it.

"I wondered what you would sound like."

"What did you expect?"

"You sound like your father," he smiled.

I was reminded of a crocodile. I was the dragon here, at the moment anyway, and everything about this guy told me to be careful, to be on my watch.

He was dangerous.

"I wouldn't know," I said.

"I realize that. He died shortly after you were born."

Aodan! The shout in my head made me blink.

You don't want talk with words? I asked.

What do you mean? How can we speak with words? We are not together.

Oh, for god's sake, I thought. *Enough with the games and bullshit. You're right here in front of me.*

What? I am not with you, Aodan! Who is with you?

I wasn't imagining the anger, and the fear, in the voice in my head.

Shit.

A dark-haired guy dressed in red robes, with this necklace and this crazy, moving pendant—

Get out of there.

His voice was deeper, more dangerous.

Why? What the hell is going on? Who are you? Who is with me?

I am your grandfather, Fangorn—

Did he just say Fangorn?

Yes, I did. The man with you is—well, I don't want to speak his name, I don't want to alert him—but he is not your friend, and he will not do anything to help you.

Who is he?

"Aodan?"

Shit. I'd forgotten necklace guy.

"I'm sorry. I'm—I'm thinking about my father. Tell me about him," I said.

Was I imagining the look of irritation that crossed his face? It was gone so fast I couldn't be sure.

"He was strong, and very brave. He lived in the human world for hundreds of years before he met your mother."

"What was she like? Was she a dragon too?"

He frowned. "No. She was a mere human. But somehow, she and your father fell in love."

"Isn't that a good thing?"

"Humans are weak, not set for the rigors of the Fae Realm. Lionel, that's your father, he knew that. But he brought her back, anyway."

"What happened?" I asked, wanting to stall him. I couldn't hear the man in my head. I knew it. I knew something wasn't right with this guy, from the moment he'd walked out of the light thing.

I wasn't sure that he was the guy I'd seen in Caleb's warehouse, but that wasn't a good thing, and if this guy was connected to that at all, it was something I needed to get the hell away from.

But there was no way to signal to Margrite right now. Not with this guy practically in my lap. He was eying me with great enthusiasm. Not in any kind of pervy way, but in a way that reminded me of a collector.

He wanted me, but he wanted the dragon me. I don't know how I knew, but I did.

Shit.

You there? I asked.

I am. I am coming to you.

No! Not with this guy here!

I will not let him have you, he said.

What does he want?

Everything, he answered.

I could hear the depth of anger and sorrow in that one word.

Not yet, I said.

No, Aodan. I will not lose you. Not just as I have found you.

I couldn't hear anything else for a minute because Necklace was talking. Now I understood why there was a sense of Jekyll and Hyde. Because it wasn't my grandfather switching personalities. It was two people. This guy was one. He was Hyde.

"Your father and mother came back to the Fae Realm, to my—my former Realm, the Dragon Realm. Yes, there is a Realm that is just for the dragons," he said with a smile.

"Who are you?" I burst out. I hated that no one used names. And that I hadn't asked before now.

"I am the… King of the Dragon Realm. I am Eilor," he said. He smiled, and I understood why Fangorn had warned me. All the danger that he'd tried to convey came through in that one smile from Eilor.

Not to mention, Eilor had the strong smell of crazy. It oozed from him. He hid it well, but I'd seen his type. And how was he the king of a realm he called his former realm? Something wasn't adding up. Well, that's not true. It added up to something crazy.

"What happened after that?"

"Your mother was close to birth. She was ill, because humans are not always healthy in the Realms of the fae, and then she gave birth to you both."

To us… both? What?

"What do you mean?"

"Are you unfamiliar with the idea of birth? It's not a difficult concept," he snapped. "Once you were born, your father tried to take you away. I believe he meant to kill you," he added. "Dragons are fiercely protective of their territory."

This didn't make any sense. He wanted to kill me? I knew that all my foster parents had thought my dad was a deadbeat wastrel, but this was taking it a bit far.

My head spun.

Aodan, do not listen to him. We're coming to you.

Who is we? I thought.

"Your mother tried to protect you, but in the process, she was killed. By your father," Eilor added with relish. "Had it not been for me, you and your sister would have died at the hands of that monster."

Sister? My father was a monster?

I had a sister?

I shook my head. "This doesn't make sense," I said slowly.

"I know that it may not at the moment, but it will. You have been fed the lies of the Human Realm, and whatever your mother might have told you. Where is she?"

He didn't know what happened to her.

"You didn't keep track of her? Or me?" I asked.

"No. I have been searching for you. Only when you activated one of the portals was I able to locate you."

"What do you mean, one of the portals? I don't know what you're talking about."

"Yes, please, Eilor, share with the class. Let us all know what you're talking about. I'd very much like to know where the portal is," another voice said.

I whipped my head around at the same time Eilor did. He had his hands up, and I could feel the energy gathering in him.

Maybe it was a reaction to the danger, but I could feel a similar energy in me as well.

That and relief that the man walking toward us came from the other side of the warehouse, the side that Margrite was not hidden on.

I wondered what she was thinking of this, and I hoped like hell she had the sense to stay put.

This man was tall, and dark-haired as well. He had the same sense of danger that I felt from Eilor, but his was harder. With a sharper edge. He was dressed all in black, dark jeans and a leather jacket.

And behind him was Caleb, the amazing shit-bag weasel.

"What are you doing here?" Eilor asked the guy.

He had stones, I'd give him that. He wasn't afraid of this guy even though the guy made everything in me scream *Kill him and get out!*

"Is that any way to greet your brother, the one you have not seen for many years?" The man held out both hands in an opening, welcoming gesture.

Eilor was a cool customer, and I got the impression from the way he carried himself that he wasn't surprised or caught off guard very often. But he sure was now.

"What are you doing here?"

"Where else would I be, brother? I couldn't stay in my Realm, now could I? I'd been banished, and you didn't lift a finger to help me. Why would you when you had the Dragon Realm at your disposal? And what do we have here?" The man's sharp gaze slid over to me.

I felt like someone was leaning over me, that sensation you get when someone's breathing down your neck, trying to intimidate you.

It was working. This guy was scary as hell. I watched him watching me, and I felt a shiver of fear ripple through me.

Then I remembered—I'm a dragon. One wrong move, and I can breathe the breath of death all over their asses.

"How did you get one here?" The man asked Eilor.

"Stefan, go away. Or at least, leave this building. I will oblige you and your questions once I have concluded my business here, but you are in the way!" Eilor apparently wasn't afraid of his brother.

The intense gaze of Stefan transferred from me back to his brother. Caleb was still staring at me like he'd seen a ghost.

"He's not going to eat us, is he?" Caleb asked softly.

"Shut up," Stefan said. "You aren't here to talk."

Caleb closed his mouth. I found a grin creeping across my face.

"Holy shit, he's baring his fangs!" Caleb pointed.

"Stop! Stefan, leave! Take your humans with you!" Eilor shouted. "I will not allow you to interfere!"

"You won't allow me? You've already interfered with my plans, Eilor! You think I don't know that it was you who stole the portal?"

"What are you talking about?"

I could tell that Eilor was surprised again.

"The portal. The casket that opens the portal. I had my man steal it. You had it stolen from me. Return it at once. My man had already secured it," Stefan gestured at Caleb.

It was all I could do to hold my laugh in. I didn't think a dragon laughing would be discreet.

The box that I stole for Luke—that must be what they're talking about. What had Stefan called it? A casket? A portal? Weird, but it fit the box thing. Sort of.

But Caleb hadn't secured shit. You didn't lock your girlfriend up in the same place you kept your stash. He was as stupid as the day was long.

"I do not know what you're talking about. Why should I need a portal? I am capable of traveling on my own with portals that I open." Eilor shrugged. "It is of no concern to me whether you have one of the caskets."

"Then where is it?" Stefan was getting angry.

"Why are you wishing to return now?"

"That is not your concern," Stefan said.

It was so clear that he and Eilor were from the same stuck-up family.

"Oh, I think it is. There is the small manner of your banishment. Why are you here? How did you happen to be here right as I came to—" Eilor glanced at me and stopped.

"Yes, what are you doing here, in the Human Realm, with a dragon? Are they not all supposed to be locked away somewhere? Why do you have one out? Does the Fae King know what you are about?" Stefan smiled, and it was a sly, knowing grin. "You are not as hidden as you think, brother."

"The Fae King does not tend to my affairs," Eilor retorted.

I could tell that Eilor did not like the fact that Stefan knew anything about it. I was glad to see that Eilor was rattled.

"Give me the casket, and I'll forget that I saw you."

"I don't have a casket. Use your magic, or a stone," Eilor shrugged.

He really wasn't concerned with anyone's problems but his

own. What a jerk. I'd bet these guys weren't close even before Stefan got booted from wherever.

What I also noticed was that Eilor didn't seem to be aware or wary of the danger of his brother. It oozed from Stefan. Eilor was either unaware, or stupid.

Aodan! Stay where you are!

The voice rang out through my head.

What? I thought.

I had no time for anything else. A small light, like the one that Eilor had come through, blinked into existence to the right of me. It got larger a lot faster than the one I'd seen with Eilor. It kept getting bigger, but before anyone could do anything about it, a dragon came through. There was a person behind the dragon.

But I only got a glimpse of whoever it was because the dragon—blue like me, but larger—planted himself between me and Eilor, and opened his mouth and spewed fire.

Holy.

Hell.

Eilor and Stefan jumped with what looked like more than normal reflexes. Stefan disappeared. Caleb caught on fire, and he ran in the other direction screaming.

"Eilor! You dare!" The dragon roared.

Eilor might be snide, and snobby, and act like a bratty kid around his brother, but he wasn't completely foolish. He threw out his arm. A large light circle burst open, and he stepped through it. The look he gave the dragon was pure hate.

"Aodan! Go! We will find you!" The dragon roared again.

I didn't need to be told more than once. I looked to where Margrite and my clothes were hidden, and I ran away.

With my dragon hearing, I could tell that she was moving with me, trying to keep up.

Ineedtobehumanagain Ineedtobehumanagain Ineedtobehumanagain.

No time for closed eyes, relaxing breathing or any of that

woo woo stuff. I thought about being human, and I fell on my face.

My human face.

"Clothes!" I yelled, holding out a hand.

Pants sailed over a rusted piece of machinery. I stepped into them as quickly as possible, and once I had both legs in, I started to run. Ducking over toward where I knew Margrite was —she was sweating, and it was nervous sweat—I held out a hand.

"Shirt, please!"

She handed it to me as we ran and I shrugged into it. Then came a shoe, and another, with me stopping for a heartbeat to step into them.

"Motel," I hissed.

We ran.

I kept hearing all the noises of the night, and footsteps of people I was sure were following us. But we made it to the motel, and when Margrite opened the door, I pushed her in and slammed it behind me, leaning against it and bending down, trying to catch my breath.

"What the hell was all that?" She asked.

"I don't have the faintest clue. But I think we need to leave."

She nodded, and silently, we both set to packing our things.

When we were done, I went around the room to make sure there was nothing left that would indicate it had been us staying in the room.

My head was whirling with all that I'd seen and heard tonight—and the dragon! And the person with him!—but we had to get out of here.

"You check out," I said.

I pushed the motorcycle away from the room and stood at the corner of the motel in a shadow while Margrite handled getting us out of there. I didn't want anyone to see me, or to see me with her.

We were well known as a pair, but tonight, it would be better if she weren't seen with me.

I was getting fidgety when she finally came and joined me.

"That jerk. He charged me for another night," she fumed.

"It doesn't matter. Not right now," I said. "Where should we go?"

Margrite sighed. "There are plenty of roach coach places in this neighborhood. Take your pick. Can we please try to skip bedbugs?"

"How will we know?" I frowned at her.

"Can't you tell if there's creepy crawlies?" She snapped.

I was about to ask her why she was mad at me and stopped. She'd been supportive of this whole weird freak show from the get-go. Tonight was stressful. Margrite had earned the right to be a little snarky and snap at me.

"Come on. Let's see what we can find. I'll see if I can spot the creepy crawlies," I added. I had no idea if I could, but I didn't want to needle her.

I pushed the bike around the corner, and only when we were out of sight of the motel office did I start it. Margrite got on behind me and arranged all our bags so that she could hang onto my waist.

I pulled out into the road, hoping like hell that we'd be able to find somewhere safe.

At least for the night.

After that, I knew, without being told, that being safe was going to be something hard to find.

But I could take being safe for tonight and be grateful.

14

We rode in the darkness, neither of us speaking. Not that you could talk much on a motorcycle, but tonight, I could feel that she was as lost in her thoughts as I was.

About two miles from the first motel, I spotted one that was small, and set back off the road. We were moving into a nicer area of town, and I could tell that this motel might be better. Less chance of bugs, or any of the things that Margrite was worried about.

"Will you check us in?" I asked. I didn't want to be seen. "I'll go stand by a room and see what I can find out."

She nodded and slid off the bike.

Margrite wasn't usually so quiet for an extended amount of time. I wondered if dealing with all my shit was finally getting to her.

Selfishly, I hoped it wasn't. Trying to navigate this without her made my heart sink into my shoes. I couldn't do this on my own.

But if it was too much, I wouldn't blame her. I don't know that I could have handled all this whatever it was as well as she did.

Pushing aside my own whining, I stood outside a door and listened.

Which was a mistake. I did not need to hear how Jay and his hot sexy mamacita Leeanne felt about each other. All spoken in broken gasps, of course.

And I decided right then and there I'd have to do something about my sense of—no. I wasn't going to think about it.

Thankfully, Margrite came toward me, and rescued me from myself.

"Anything?"

"There are creepy crawlies, but they're all human and they are presently occupied," I said, taking her arm. "Where's our room?"

Margrite stared at me, not understanding at first. Then, "Ew," she said.

"Yes. Very ew. Where are we?"

Hopefully on the other end away from Jay and Leeanne.

Please, if there is any sort of God. Please.

She walked in the opposite direction, and then up a flight of stairs.

"The penthouse, then?" I asked.

She didn't reply. Only walked to the door and opened it. I followed her in. She tossed her bag onto the bed and sat down with her head in her hands.

"Hey, what's going on?" I asked.

"I thought you were going to die," she said. "Those two—Stefan and what was the other guy's name?"

"Eilor," I said.

"Yeah, him I thought they were going to kill you. Was that your grandfather?" She looked up then.

"No. It wasn't. I don't know who it was. The dragon who came through after?"

She nodded.

"That was my grandfather. He told me to run, and that he'd be in touch later."

"So which one have you been talking to?"

I shrugged. "I'm going to take a guess and say both of them. I'd bet the asshat was Eilor. I can't tell, and he didn't say, though, whether he's a dragon. Why didn't he shift?"

"The dragon was bigger than you are."

I nodded. "I thought he was. Was I seeing things, or was there someone with him?"

Margrite didn't answer right away. She stared at the window next to the door. I sat down next to her.

"There was," she said slowly. "I had to think about it, because I was focused on getting us out of there in one piece, I couldn't remember. It looked like a woman."

"I couldn't tell," I said.

"She was sort of hidden, almost sheltered by him."

When she said that, I thought back to the moment when Fangorn came through. A zing of awareness went through me. Like there was something I knew, and forgot, or was supposed to know.

"He told me he'd get in touch later."

"That was some crazy shit," Margrite turned to me. "There's a lot more going on than just you being a dragon."

"Like that's not enough?"

"It is, and it's more than enough for us, but that whole showdown says you're part of something bigger." She sighed. "It's what Nala told you in your reading. There's more at stake here, and you have some decisions to make." She took my arm. "I know you don't want to admit it, but it's right here in front of you."

"No, I don't, but not for the reasons you think," I said.

"Then why?"

"I don't want to be involved in someone else's drama," I said. "Our whole lives have been one time after another of avoiding drama, and dancing around the drama of others, and trying to keep the mess from landing on us. This looks like more drama, and I just want to follow our plan and get the hell out of here."

Margrite regarded me, and then said, "I don't think that's an option anymore, Aodan. I want the same thing, but I don't think you can do that anymore."

"You don't have to," I said, thinking back to my earlier thoughts on what she might be feeling.

"Don't say that to me. I have no choice. You're my best friend. If you think I'm going to leave you—would you leave me?"

"No."

"Then don't be stupid and insulting and suggest I might leave you. It's not on the table."

"All right." I felt relieved although I had to admit I was worried.

Which was stupid. We'd been stealing together for the past five years. There was always danger present.

I couldn't put into words why this felt different. Worse.

But it did.

"So what now?" Margrite scooted back onto the bed, leaning against the shabby headboard. It creaked as she made herself comfortable.

"I guess we wait. Did you see what happened to Caleb?" I asked. "I was trying to watch the little weasel, but I was concerned about shifting, and lost track of him."

"He ran screaming off like the baby ass that he is. First sign of trouble, or problems—he's out of there," Margrite said.

"Well, he was on fire," I said. "That might be an acceptable reason to run off screaming. But I didn't see the thug patrol," I said referring to the huge guys Caleb usually surrounded himself with.

"Me either," she said, "I think that was his boss, the one that everyone's so afraid of."

"And he wanted the box I stole. Did you hear what he called it? A casket?"

"He also called it a portal. A portal to where?"

"To the other place, the realm they keep mentioning."

"They?" She looked at me suspiciously.

"Well, I thought I was only talking to one person, but I think I was talking to Fangorn and Eilor, and I just couldn't tell the difference."

"Don't they sound different?"

"Not in my head," I scoffed.

"You really couldn't tell?"

"No. I wish I could because who knows how much I shared with Eilor. That dude is scary."

She nodded. "He and Stefan both were. I can see why he makes Caleb pee his pants."

I laughed. It was mean as hell, but it was also accurate.

"So what exactly was it you stole?"

"I don't know," I let myself fall back on to the bed. "But look how much that couple paid for it. And this guy Stefan— he's pretty pissed that Caleb lost it. Guess he didn't notice the missing diamonds," I grinned.

"What?" Margrite sat up. "You have diamonds? Where? Why haven't you told me?"

"I forgot about them, dumb as that sounds."

"Only you, Aodan."

"I know, I know." I thought about where I'd put them. I had to go back to the night I'd stolen the box—was it really less than a week ago?

In a pocket. I remembered pouring them out of a pouch into my hand. Then I put them where?

I put them in a plastic bag, the kind used for lunches. And I put the bag in my jeans.

My bag was in one corner. "They should be in the pocket of my jeans," I said.

"Good thing we haven't done laundry recently," Margrite said. "Speaking of which, we need to."

"Kind of low on the priority list," I said, digging through my clothes. I only had four pairs of jeans, so it wasn't like disman-tling a closet or anything. Thankfully, this was not the pair I'd been wearing the first time we tried to leave. I found the pair I had been wearing the night of the heist and felt in the pocket.

"They're here," I said, pulling the small bag out.

"Let me see," Margrite got up and came over to me.

I handed her the bag, and she opened it and inspected them.

"He's going to miss these," she said.

"I don't think so. I think he's got a little stash going. It was in a pouch in a box of jewelry. There was lots of good stuff in there. The pouch is still there, and probably half of the stones."

"This is only half?" She gaped at me.

"I know, right? With our payment from Luke, and this, we're going to be fine."

Margrite glared. "That's if we can get out of here. We haven't been able to do that yet, and all your relations are trou-blesome and not helping."

"For the record, I don't think Eilor is a relation."

She waved a hand. "He's troublesome just like everyone else in this mess. Even you. Who forgets diamonds?" She gave me a cuff on the shoulder.

I smiled. "Why don't you keep those then? That way, my dumb ass can't lose them?"

Margrite inhaled deeply, a sign of being greatly put upon. But she took the baggie and put it into one of her bags inside her big bag..

We both knew that I wouldn't lose them. But if it made her feel better, I wasn't going to worry about it.

I went into the bathroom, and splashed water on my face, and into my hair. Where was Fangorn? He needed to get in touch with me. This limbo thing was making me a little stir-crazy.

Once I'd cleaned up a little, I went and lay down. Margrite was doing something with the bags, and I closed my eyes and let my mind go back over the scene.

Fangorn was huge. I wasn't small, at least, I didn't feel like I was. But next to him, I looked like the little kid dragon.

Which was fine—as long as he and I didn't have to fight? I didn't know who to trust anymore, but I didn't think we'd be fighting. At least, I hoped not.

There had been someone with him. I'd have to take Margrite's word that it was a woman.

Aodan.

I swear to hell there was no peace.

Who is this?

It's Fangorn.

How do I know this?

What do you mean?

Because I've obviously been talking to two of you—

I am sorry. Eilor—

There was a tone in his words that came through even in this manner of communication. He hated Eilor. Like, serious, let-me-kill-you kind of hate. I could hear it.

Eilor has a pendant that allows him access to us.

That red one?

Yes.

What does that mean? Access to us?

I am not comfortable speaking like this knowing he still has it. May I come to you?

Sure it will be just you?

This time, yes, Aodan, it will be only me.

I considered.

"M?"

"What?"

"You up for a visit?"

"Who?"

"Fangorn."

"Who?"

"The dragon."

"You really think he's going to fit in here?"

I didn't have to open my eyes to see the expression on her face.

You're not going to fit in our motel room.

Don't worry about that.

It's me that has to pay for things you break.

I'll fit, Aodan.

I hesitated. Did I want him to come? There was no turning back. Up till this point, I kept the illusion that there was choice that I didn't have to do anything. But if I let this guy in, it would be a lot harder to shut the door on him if this didn't turn out in a way I liked.

Sighing, I decided that I had to take the chance. I wanted to find out about this whole dragon thing, and I really wanted to find out about my family. He knew.

If I needed to cut him off, then I'd deal with it. Just like I'd dealt with everything that came my way.

"I'm going to let him come here," I said, sitting up.

"You sure that's a good idea?"

"No," I admitted. "But he has things I want. There's no way to get them without this. If we need to, we'll deal with that."

"There's no way around this?"

"I don't think so."

"I don't trust it, or him, or… or anything," she finished.

"I know. I don't either." I didn't like the options. I didn't like the people in my head. I didn't like that I sounded completely crazy when I even thought things like that.

But there was no way around it.

Margrite sighed. "All right. Call your madman. We'll see who shows up."

I nodded. *I'm ready,* I thought.

Very well. His reply was instant, as though he'd been waiting.

How will you get here?

In the same manner I did earlier. Via a portal.

The light thing?

Yes.

Okay. What now?

Nothing. Let me focus on you.

I saw Margrite watching me. "He says he's coming. The light."

"That big light ball thing? Great. That is totally inconspicuous," she rolled her eyes.

"I'm not the one driving the bus," I said.

To my surprise, she grinned. I didn't see that from her often.

"It's driving you crazy, isn't it?"

"Yes."

Margrite laughed. After a moment, I laughed with her. Every time we met one another's eyes, we laughed harder.

Which was totally inappropriate for the situation, but seriously, what else could I do? If things went to shit, I'd go dragon, and get Margrite out of here.

A knock on the door made us both stop immediately.

"What the hell?" Margrite whispered.

"You think it's him?"

"Who else?"

"This is one of those times I wish we had a gun," I said.

Margrite rolled her eyes. It was one of our few arguments. She hated guns. I was ambivalent. They served a purpose. But she was right in they did complicate things, so we'd never kept one around. Not that I couldn't get one. It just wasn't worth the hassle. Not from Margrite, or anyone else.

"Can you look out the window?" I whispered.

She walked carefully over toward the window as the person outside knocked again.

"Aodan," a man's voice said. "It's me. We spoke very recently. Please open the door."

"Does that sound like the warehouse guy?" Margrite hissed.

"No, but…" I shook my head.

"Open the door."

15

I carefully turned the handle, ready to slam it into the face of Eilor if it was him. Whatever he was, I was done with him.

A man stood on the doorstep. He was tall, and had dark hair, and the greenest eyes I'd ever seen.

Margrite stood up from where she'd been crouched next to the window.

"Oh, my god," she said.

"No. I am not any sort of god," the man said. "May I come in?"

I opened the door wider. "Yes. Who are you?"

He stepped in and closed the door behind him. "I am Fangorn, and you are Aodan." He looked me up and down.

His eyes glittered.

"You look like your father," he said quietly.

No one spoke. I could almost hear the walls breathing, the silence was so heavy.

Then Fangorn shook his head slightly. "I am sorry. I hadn't thought that seeing you would remind me so strongly of Lionel."

"That was his name? Lionel?"

He nodded. "Yes."

"What happened to him?"

"Is that really what you want to know?" His green eyes pierced me.

"Yes, it is," I said. I meant it. "Did he try to kill me?" That rang in my head, and I couldn't shake the words. I needed to know if Eilor had been telling me the truth in any way.

"May I sit down?"

"Please," Margrite said, moving around next to me and away from the small table and chair that sat under the window.

Fangorn looked at us both, and then carefully lowered himself into a chair. It was interesting to watch him. He didn't move like other people.

I took a few steps and sat on the bed across from him.

"Tell me everything. About my parents why I'm a dragon. This is your chance."

"Don't lie," Margrite said. She'd moved over between the two beds and stood glaring with her arms crossed.

Fangorn gazed at her. "I do not lie. I may not tell everything, although I will certainly try this evening, but I do not lie, young lady. Who are you?"

"I am Margrite."

"Is she your mate?" Fangorn asked me, turning the eyes onto me again.

It was disconcerting.

"No. She's my best friend. Anything you can say to me, you can say to her," I said.

"Best friend?" Fangorn's one eyebrow raised the tiniest bit. "That is a good thing, Aodan. Friends are hard to come by. Best friends even more so. Where would you like me to start?"

"Who's the other guy? Why has he been talking to Aodan?" Margrite asked.

"Eilor has been talking with you?"

I nodded. "You both sound the same in my head."

Fangorn looked down, saying something in a language I didn't understand. He was pissed. That much I could tell.

When he looked up, he'd gotten past the anger, although I could see a spark in his green eyes. "I am sorry. I did not know that he still had the pendant. Honestly..." he looked away and then back at me. "I was under the assumption he was dead. I am not surprised he's alive, although I am extraordinarily disappointed."

"What, is he a bad guy?" Margrite asked.

Fangorn smiled, but there was no humor in it. "Yes, very much so."

"My parents," I said.

He gazed at me. "You do not trust me."

"I've had voices in my head for the past week. Now I find out they were from different people. I'm weighing my options," I said, trying to keep my tone neutral.

"That is honest. I appreciate it. Your parents," he sat back, sighing. "Lionel was my son. His mother was one of many women—"

"You played the field," I said.

"No," he said forcefully. "No," more gently this time. "To answer your question, no, your father did not try to kill you. I should be surprised that Eilor would lie so blatantly, but I am not. He is without morals or convictions outside of his own. Lionel loved you. He and your mother were very happy that they were expecting children even though there was a risk."

Fangorn stopped, and looked at me. "It's important that you know that. You were wanted, and loved. But your parents were fighting against something that began long before they met."

"To explain, I need to go further back. I am a dragon, and I am also a shifter. I can shift to fae form. I am from the Dragon Realm within the Fae Realm. This, where you live, is the Human Realm. Long ago, the dragons ruled our Realm. But we were greedy, and careless. We started a war with the other Realms, and the Fae King, who also rules over all the Realms, banded together with the other Realms and fought us." He looked down again.

I could see that he was talking, but he wasn't seeing us. He was seeing whatever memories his words stirred.

He sighed. "We were not the victors in the war we began. Most of us were destroyed. I was left alive, as were ten of my brethren."

"Why?" I asked.

"As you have experienced, dragons can communicate without words, over distance. We share our consciousness with one another."

"That's what I've been seeing? Your life?"

He nodded. "Mine, and the others. For hundreds of years, the others slept. I was woken because I was a shifter. And Eilor, who took the Dragon Throne after we were defeated, wanted my—our power."

He looked down again. Now I felt a mixture of anger and sadness from him.

"What power?" This from Margrite.

"The fae, and the other inhabitants of the Fae Realm—the trolls, the goblins, the dwarves and the dragons—all have power. Magic. It's different for all the races. We all have our own form of magic. The dragons have always had strong magic, and we'd always kept it hidden. To hide and to hoard is the way of a dragon. That all disappeared when we lost the war."

To hide and to hoard. I'd been doing that for a large part of my life.

Fangorn sighed. "When one is defeated, there is nothing but the mercy of the victor. Eilor was not merciful. He wanted to harness the power of the dragons. He wanted our magic. It did no good to tell him that since he was not a dragon, it would not work. He is many things and determined is one of them."

"Asshat," I said.

"I do not understand," he said.

"Bad and nasty," Margrite said helpfully.

Fangorn smiled again. "That is apt. When I wouldn't give him what he wanted, he determined that he would take it. That pendant he wears? It has my blood in it. He is able to speak with you because you are of my blood. He used it to monitor me, to keep me from even the barest amount of privacy."

"That is horrifying," Margrite said.

I could tell that she was getting interested in spite of herself. And she didn't hate him, which I think would have surprised her if she'd been thinking about it. Fangorn's story was compelling. I wasn't getting a sense of dishonesty from him.

I wondered if it was possible for dragons to lie to one another.

No, his voice said in my head.

Get out of my head, I thought.

I cannot help it when we are this close.

Okay. Don't comment then.

Fangorn smiled at me. He didn't comment further on our side conversation, but continued his story. "The manner in which he determined he could take the dragons' power was through a child. So he began to bring fae women to me and force me to mate with them."

"That's disgusting," Margrite said. "Why did you go through with it?"

"Because he killed the first one in front of me." Fangorn's words were flat.

"What?" She whispered.

"When I refused to touch the woman—the girl, really, he cast a spell and killed her. At that point, I realized I had no choice. I told him that I would relent, but that it was to be on my terms. He was to bring the woman to me, and I would take the time to become known to her, and allow her to feel more comfortable with me."

He looked down. "There were many women. And some became pregnant. None of them lived. None of the children lived. I watched the women, the little ones—" he stopped, and rubbed his hands over his face. Then he looked back up at both of us. "They all died. Until Lionel. He lived. His mother did not, and I was sorry. I cared for her. Once Lionel was born, and he survived, and kept surviving, Eilor took him from Leona——"

"That was my grandmother's name?"

Fangorn nodded. "She was a servant in the castle. An orphan. Eilor only chose the orphans. Because they wouldn't be missed. Carrying my child was difficult for the fae women. While I can shift into a fae man, I am a dragon. We are not the same."

"What do you mean, fae?" I asked.

"Fae. I'm told by——well, by a woman raised here in the Human Realm that you see fae as fairies."

"Where are your wings?" Margrite had moved to sit next to me. She had a look on her face I didn't see often.

I probably had the same look. I couldn't look away from Fangorn. What he was saying was enthralling——the idea of another world. It was horrifying as well. I could see the hurt on him. It was a part of him, all these women and children that hadn't made it.

"Fae do not have wings. Dragons do. Fae do not. And the two are not meant to mix. But Eilor was determined. He allowed Lionel to be with me as he grew, but not much, and rarely unsupervised. Lionel learned, as you did," Fangorn smiled suddenly, "That dragons can communicate without words. So even when we were apart, we were able to speak. Eilor knew that——all the fae who fought us in the war did——but he didn't realize that Lionel could as well. Then he caught Lionel trying to shift. That was the beginning of the end," Fangorn said.

"What do you mean?" I asked.

"I told you Eilor wanted the magic of the dragons? We are stronger than the fae. Our magic is wilder, more primal and fierce. Used with fae spells, it enhances and strengthens magic that fae do. He wanted that, because he wanted to conquer the other Realms, and rule them alone."

"Do they all have kings?" I asked.

Fangorn nodded. "The Fae King rules them all. While he was part of our defeat, I have come to see that the Fae King is a man of honor. We have settled our differences. Eilor hated him and plotted his downfall. He didn't succeed," he added, the grin returning.

"What happened?" Margrite asked.

"That is far too long to share in one sitting. I will be happy to do so at a later date when we are not pressed for time. Suffice to say, we all believed Eilor dead. I didn't worry about the pendant, because if he died, the pendant would be lost. But as he lives, and is still able to use the pendant, we must help you to shut him from your consciousness."

"That would be nice. First finish telling me about my father. And my mother."

Fangorn sighed. "Your father, once he reached the age of adulthood, and he could shift, and fly, and make fire, realized what Eilor sought. Eilor wanted to bind him with magic and make him a vessel for Eilor's own magic. So when he could, he ran. He discovered how to make a portal—that's how we travel—"

"The big ball of light?" Margrite interrupted.

He nodded. "Yes. And Lionel came here. I was sad to lose my son. I lost all my family in the dragon wars. None of them wanted peace. My former mates, my children—they all wished to overthrow the fae. So they perished. I loved Lionel. I understood why he left. He was safe, here in the Human Realm, for several hundred years. Then he met your mother, Maria. He loved her dearly. He was so delighted when she became pregnant. But worried, as well. He knew my history, knew what carrying my children had done to the women Eilor forced to mate with me."

Fangorn ran his hand through his hair. "Well, Eilor had not

forgotten Lionel. He kept watch for him. How he found him here, I do not know. But he did. And somehow, he managed to find Maria as well, and bring both of them back to the Dragon Realm. When he did, he was delighted to find that Maria was pregnant, close to the time of birth. I thought," he said, rubbing his chin, "That she would be one of the humans who would survive."

"What does that mean?" I asked.

"There is something about the Realms of the Fae Realm that is deadly to humans. Most humans do not survive. There are children—not so many anymore—who are wished away to the Goblin King; and most of them do not live. Those that do become fae. But their numbers are small. I thought Maria might be one of the humans who would survive but once she had you both—"

"What do you mean, both? And why are kids wished away to a goblin?" I'd forgotten that he'd mentioned that before.

"You have not felt her? You have a sister. The Goblin King is also for another time," he added.

"What?" I whispered. "Was she with you tonight?"

"Yes," Fangorn said, and I could see his pride. "Aine was with me. She is a strong woman, and she is also the Dragon Queen. She's recently married the new Dragon King."

"Aren't you the Dragon King?"

"Didn't Eilor say he was the Dragon King?" Margrite asked at the same time.

Fangorn shook his head. "Eilor was once the king. He was removed when his treachery was discovered. I was never the king when the dragons ruled our Realm. Only one of us advisors. After our uprising, we were banned from the throne. The former king—my friend," Sadness flashed in his eyes, "Was executed. Now, there are only eleven of us, thirteen if I count you and Aine. I no longer wish for a throne, or a kingdom. Now that the other ten dragons are awake, we are happy in the far mountains of the Dragon Realm. I see Aine, and am with my brethren, and I am content." He smiled.

His words rang true.

I have a sister.

There was so much to take in, I didn't know where to go first.

"What happened to Aodan's parents?" Margrite said.

The smile faded. "Once you and Aine were born, Maria began to fade. She kept you with her, and she gave you your names. Eilor made sure that Lionel was unable to be with her, but he knew she'd given birth, and he broke free of the prison Eilor had him in, and found Maria and the two of you."

Pain crossed his face sharp as a knife. I could feel his pain as though it were my own. I winced at the strength of it.

"I do not know everything that happened. All I know is that Lionel went to see you and your mother. He was sharing with me. I saw him lean down to both of you, touch you with his snout. And then Eilor's men burst in, and took him away. I was never able to communicate with him after that."

"Why didn't you help him?" My voice came out cold. "Where were you in all this?"

"In a cage under the Dragon Castle. A cage I could not break free of. With the last of the dragons, who slept. Do you think I would not have helped my son if I could have? That I wanted to see all that happened, and know that I was losing yet another child, another member of my family, and know that I was powerless?" His voice rose.

The dragon was speaking within him. I could hear it, feel it in my bones. I looked over and I could tell that Margrite could feel it too.

"Then what?"

Fangorn recovered his composure somewhat. "I think because you and Aine have dragon blood, and you shared that with your mother, I was somewhat able to see through her. It was not clear, not like you and I, or your father, but Eilor came to her. He took Aine, telling her that he wanted Aine for something special."

Fangorn spoke in the other language again. A puff of smoke escaped from his mouth.

"That is so freaky," Margrite breathed.

"I am sorry. I am ashamed to share this with you even though I am not the creator of this. Eilor took Aine and raised her with his child. She was intended for me. Eilor felt if he crossed the dragon and fae blood once more that he would gain the child he needed."

"Ew! He wanted you to hook up with your granddaughter?" Margrite asked.

"Yes. That was his plan. Thankfully, other things he had in motion set his plans awry. He lost the throne and disappeared. Most thought him dead. Aine was able to free me, and the other dragons. The new Dragon King and I made a pact, and for the first time in years, we were free. I did not think to search for you, because when Eilor took Aine, your mother escaped with you. I assumed she returned here, but I had no way to seek for her. Eilor didn't focus on you as far as I know because he had Aine, and a viable female was his goal."

"Disgusting," I said.

"Very much so. What happened with your mother?"

"My mom? She died when I was two. I was put into foster care until Margrite and I were old enough to get the hell out of the system. I don't remember my mom much. She left my dad's coat for me."

"A coat of red leather?" Fangorn's eyes brightened.

I nodded.

"Do you have it still?"

I got up and went over to where I'd tossed the bag I'd carried this evening. The coat was underneath it and I pulled it up, giving it a little shake. The red of the coat was so satisfying to me every time I saw it.

"May I?" Fangorn stood, holding out a hand.

I walked to him and passed it over. He ran a hand over it, smiling. "Lionel crafted this. It is made from dragon hide. Eilor had some in one of his workrooms, probably left over from the wars, and Lionel stole it when he left. He didn't want Eilor to have any of us." Fangorn frowned.

"This was someone you knew? He thought it was best to make a coat from it?" Great. Now my coat was going to be all creepy.

"Perhaps. I no longer know. But when you wear this, it is as though you have the hide of a dragon. It protects you. Or anyone who wears it," he flashed a brief smile at Margrite. "Wear this with pride. If the dragon who gave it had to die, they would be pleased it was another dragon who wore it. Even more pleased that Lionel stole it from Eilor, who has only ever defiled us. We always protect our own," he added. I am glad your mother took it that she was able to give it to you." He ran his hand over the back of the coat once more, and his eyes glittered.

Then he looked at me. "I miss him. My son. He was a good man, and a smart man. He would have been good for us now."

"So you really didn't know about me?"

"I could not feel you. I only sensed that you had shifted. How did it happen?"

"We tried to leave," I said. "We were on our way out of here, out of the hell we've lived in, and I couldn't leave. Why can't I leave this city, Fangorn?"

"This is where your parents met and married. This was their home. Lionel cast a spell that wouldn't allow you to leave, not Maria, and not you or Aine, unless you were with family. He knew what Eilor wanted, and he and your mother did what they could to protect you. When you were taken to the Dragon Realm, you'd not yet been born, so you could leave. Your mother brought you back. But since then, you've had no family."

"What, what? He can't leave?" Margrite was on her feet, and right in front of Fangorn.

16

"Not without family. Only family can break the spell."

"Then break it," I said immediately.

"It's not that simple. I am not the architect of the spell. I would need time to study it, to see how to break it. It's easier if you just let me take you from the city itself."

"That's easy enough. You can walk me over the line, and then we can be on our way."

"On your way? To where?"

"To where we planned to go," I said, not wanting to give that information. "But first, you need to tell me how to manage this dragon."

"It's not that simple, Aodan."

I held up a hand. "Yes, it is. I didn't ask for this. Your world is not mine. My world is mine. I don't want to be involved in all your history, and your wars, and all the shit you just told me. My family is Margrite. I'm glad to have met you, but I'm not happy that I'm a dragon. I need to know how to deal with it so I can live a normal life."

Fangorn didn't speak immediately. He studied me, and walked back to the chair, taking a seat. "I am not sure if there is such a thing for you. Oh, I will gladly escort you from this city. I understand your desire to leave. It doesn't sound as though you have the happy memories that your parents did. But I do not think you can run from who you are, what you are," he added.

"That's not your call to make." I crossed my arms. I wasn't ready to sit down again. Standing allowed some of the anger to bleed off.

"You are correct. That doesn't make me wrong," he said. "You are what you are. You are a dragon. You are a shifter. It's not something that happens often. None of my children with dragons were able to shift. Only my child with a fae. If I did not despise him, I would understand why Eilor seeks my children. They are unique. You and your sister both."

My sister. I'd forgotten her. And I needed to consider that, but it was too much right now. I didn't even know where to start with all the family history. Better to put it aside and deal with practical matters.

"How do I control the shifting?"

"How have you been controlling it so far?" He leaned back in the chair, arms crossed.

"I close my eyes and concentrate."

Fangorn's eyebrows went up. "That's very good, Aodan. Aine has not yet shifted, although," he stopped, waving a hand. "It is not important."

"No, it is. Why hasn't she shifted? Is it because this isn't a good thing? Everything shitty that's happened in my life has been because of this. My parents were hunted down, my father was killed, my mother nearly died, my sister was taken from her, and my mother and I had to run here and she didn't live long." I could feel the anger rising.

"I am sorry. I did not know Maria well, but Lionel told me much of her, and when she was still carrying you, she could participate in our communication."

"Why?" The thought distracted me.

Fangorn shrugged. "I'm not sure. I think it was because her

blood was shared with you and Aine. That's my best guess. I was not able to be in her presence, and Eilor distorted everything that he could for his own gain."

His green eyes darkened, and I could literally see the dragon snarl inside of him. It was the strangest thing, and at the same time, it make complete sense.

I didn't know if Margrite could see it, but she could sense the change. It was like a cloud had blocked out the sun on a summer day. She edged a little close to me.

"He sounds horrible," she said quietly.

Fangorn brought those eyes onto her. "He is. He spent hundreds of years killing women and children to further his own gains. He made sure that I could not look back on my life and have any peace. I see them, still, when I sleep—" he closed his eyes. Then they shot open. "I will kill him for that. Sadly, I thought he was dead. The Fae King—well, it doesn't matter. I was right. I suggested that perhaps it was all a ruse, and it seems it was." He sighed. "Aine was going with Drake to share the news." Fangorn laughed suddenly. "I wager the Fae King will be rather put upon this evening." He laughed harder.

"I'm missing the joke," I said.

He didn't answer as he was still chuckling to himself. When he calmed, he said, "You cannot understand. I am, as are you, tied to the Fae King, and the Goblin King, and the Dragon King. Not alliances I would have sought. But as Aine has wed the Dragon King, and he and the Goblin King are the sons of the Fae King, we are reluctant in-laws." He smiled again. The smile reached his eyes.

It was disconcerting to see the range of emotion that he showed. His emotion was so strong, and so… committed. Like he threw his all into everything he said, or did, or felt.

"I have learned that time is not what you think, Aodan. It passes, and it drags. Those we love are often not here for as long as we'd like. You learn that you must enjoy life as it comes, waiting for no one."

Stop it, I said in my head.

He smiled again, wider this time. "I told you, with us this close, there is no way to shield our thoughts from each other."

"I can't read yours."

"Of course you can. You don't realize it. Your awareness of how deeply I feel—that is based on the fact that we share a consciousness."

Fangorn looked at Margrite. "What am I thinking?"

She started. I don't think she was expecting him to turn his attention to her.

"How would I know?"

He looked at me. "What am I thinking?"

"You hate Eilor, you love Aine, and you like all these kings more than you expected," I said without hesitation.

"You are correct. I do. As I fought the Fae King, intending to kill him, it is a rather unexpected outcome. I will say that perhaps the siring of children changes one. When he and I fought, he did not have his sons. And like me, Jharak has known tragedy."

"Such as?"

"Again, that is more than is needed. Let us focus on your request. I will help you work on your shifting. Then I will walk you past the boundaries of the city if you wish to leave."

"I do. We are done here."

"We need to leave," Margrite said. "That other pair of guys? They're after Aodan. For something he stole."

"I was not focused on them. Only Eilor."

"Well, you should be," I said. "The one guy, the one who wasn't pissing himself in fear? That was Stefan, who is apparently—"

"Eilor's brother lives? He was banished."

"Yeah, and he's not real thrilled about it. He wanted the box that I stole. Said it was his way out—"

"What sort of box?" Fangorn sat up. "What did he call it?"

"A portal," Margrite said.

"You stole a portal casket?" His eyebrows went up to his hairline.

I shrugged. "I guess so. I have no idea what I stole. All I know is that's when things went sideways... wait."

"What?" Margrite asked.

I sat down as I thought about it. So much had happened since I'd stolen the box. "I think I saw Eilor that night."

Margrite quietly sat next to me. She was on the other side of me, away from Fangorn, and she gave my hand a squeeze. We'd get through this. Like we got through everything.

"What do you mean?" Fangorn leaned forward.

"I haven't had any problems like I'm having now until I stole that box. I had to go to Caleb's warehouse, and when I was in there, a guy tried to come out of one of the light circles—"

"Portals," Fangorn said.

"Okay, portals. Anyway, I'm in the rafters, and a portal shows up, and he kicks a woman and tries to step out, but then the light disappears. That's when I noticed the smoke coming out of my nose, and my throat was on fire."

"When did you shift?"

"After I got home."

"Did you handle the casket? The box?" He added when I didn't answer right away.

"Of course. It was in a backpack, and I had to make sure it was there. I left the backpack and took the box."

"You had not experienced anything surrounding your dragon up until that point?"

"No. Never."

"The portal, the closeness of something from the Fae Realm, someone attempts to portal near you—it allowed your fae and dragon side to waken," Fangorn said, talking more to himself to than to me.

"So if I'd never taken the job, none of this would have happened?" I couldn't keep the bitterness from my voice. "We could be gone by now."

Fangorn shook his head. "No. The spell put on you by your parents would still be in effect. That might have triggered it also —did you attempt to leave before or after you shifted?"

"Before," Margrite said. "We went past the sign for the city limits, and he fell off the bike, passed out. I got him home, and when he woke up, he was a dragon."

Fangorn looked at us both and then burst out laughing. I could hear the man laughing, and behind it, the dragon was laughing too. It was a deeper awareness. He had a bone-deep rumble to his voice.

He leaned forward, laughing still. When he sat up, he had calmed down. "I do not mean to make light of your predicament, Aodan. However, you have the worst luck I've heard of in some time. You shift at the most inopportune moments. Are you always so unlucky?"

"No. I'm good at what I do. Luck has nothing to do with it. It's skill."

"What do you do?"

"I'm a thief."

He smiled, but at least he didn't burst into laughter again. "That makes sense. Dragons are good at acquiring what we want. No one gets in our way."

"No one ever has. Back to the dragon thing. What do I do with my clothes?"

"What?" He was surprised.

"My clothes. I can't get naked every time I want to shift. It's not done here, running around naked."

"It's not done in the Fae Realm, either," Fangorn said dryly.

"So, wise one, what the hell do I do?" My frustration welled up. I couldn't tell why I was getting all shitty, but I couldn't stop it.

"See yourself as putting the dragon on over your clothes."

"What?" I said.

"That sounds like a drug-induced suggestion," Margrite said at the same time.

Fangorn didn't reply right away. When we both stopped talking, he said, "The dragon is part of you, Aodan. So imagine that you're just adding another layer. That's all it is."

"I don't want to end up busting out of my clothes, and I really don't want to lose my coat," I looked over where I'd put the red coat on the other bed.

"No, I cannot blame you. The coat is a wonderful piece. Lionel was so smart," a look of wistfulness crossed his face. "It would seem you have inherited his ability to thrive no matter what the conditions."

"Oh, the skills conversation," Margrite rolled her eyes, and got up. "I'll be right back. Don't OD on ego."

She walked out of the room.

Fangorn watched her. "She is very loyal to you," he said.

"It's mutual. We're loyal to each other."

"You have been friends for some time?"

"Almost ten years," I said.

"Friendship like that is priceless," he said.

"Yep."

"You need to try shifting now that we've discussed the clothing concerns."

"Um…" I wasn't feeling confident.

"What did Margrite mean by skills conversation?"

"I'm good at what I do. I always have been."

"Isn't it less than honorable to be a thief?"

I shrugged. "Yeah, sometimes. I steal for all kinds of reasons, not just my own gain," I said, thinking about the shop owner's daughter.

He laughed. "You have a conscience?"

"Doesn't everybody?"

"No, and if you operate in a world where thieving is accepted, you know this. Stop stalling, Aodan. Try to shift."

I glared. He sounded like a parent there, and I was way beyond needing or wanting a parent. I stood and pushed the beds apart to give myself some space. I closed my eyes and envisioned putting on the dragon like a coat. I could feel the response that I normally felt, and then I felt a zing.

"That will be because I am here. We are more powerful together."

"Oh yeah?" I got out.

"Yes. Had Eilor come upon us together like this, he would have been lucky to get away with his life."

Why was he still talking? Couldn't he see the things going on with me over here?

And then the tingling stopped. I opened my eyes, and I was my dragon.

There wasn't a pile of shredded clothing next to me.

"Where are my clothes?" I asked in my deep voice.

Fangorn didn't answer. He'd stood and come over closer to me.

"You look so like him," he said in a broken voice. "Aine looks like him, but it's different seeing my son in another male. And your dragon is like his. Like mine."

He bowed his head slightly. Shit. Was he crying? I didn't know what the accepted protocol was here. Fangorn was more formal than anyone I'd ever met in my life. He had an air of something special around him. Like royalty, or something. I found that I wasn't as flip with him—and I hadn't even realized I was doing it.

To think he might be crying was… weird.

Like every other damn thing since I'd taken the job for that damn box.

I am glad that you did, I heard him say. *I would not have found you had you not shifted. There are too many barriers between our Realms without a point to focus on. I thought you and your mother dead.*

Half right, I thought.

I am sorry. I liked her, and your father loved her very much. She loved him as well. I was growing to care for her a great deal, and then she disappeared with you. I was still caged, and I chose to put my efforts into trying to help my granddaughter. Your life has been hard, and I am sorry.

Her life has been difficult as well. Eilor was not a good person to raise children.

He has kids?

He did. A daughter. His insanity contributed to her death. No, do not be sorry. She was evil and cruel, like he is. There is only one end for people such as that.

"So why is Eilor still alive?"

He sighed. "I wish I knew. I wish that I'd been free when he was still in the Realms—but that could not be helped."

"How did you get free?"

"Turn around. Let me see you."

"What?"

"Turn. You're smaller than I, but you are similar in size to Lionel. It's interesting that we are all shades of blue."

"Um… genetics?"

"Not necessarily. There is something within us that shifts colors for each dragon. Their colors match their personality. Blue is usually associated with a calm, but fierce being. We are not hotheaded like the scarlets, and the greens are the more caring of our kind. We have a golden left—she is like a mother to all. You will see that when you meet the others."

"What do you mean?"

He looked surprised. "You don't want to come back to the Dragon Realm? To meet your kind? Your sister? Your family?"

"I told you, your drama is your drama. I want no part of it."

"I think you should at least meet others like you. Then you can decide."

"Then what?" I took a step toward him. Even though I was taller as a dragon, having to bend down from the ceiling, he didn't flinch. I guessed he wouldn't.

"What am I supposed to do about my life here? Leave my best friend? The one person who's been my family? I don't think so."

"There might be a way for her to—"

"No. You said most humans die in your world. I'm not

risking my friend who has been my only family for a family I don't know that showed up like five minutes ago. Sorry. Meet and greets are not worth the risk."

"You don't have to bring her," he said.

"Not an option either. So far, you're failing all the family tests," I said.

"That is a shame, Aodan. I think it would be good for you and help you and Margrite in your plans. But you must do what is best for you."

"I plan to."

"Then shift back. I do not expect to see your clothing torn."

What?

He was an ass.

I can be. Do it. He crossed his arms.

Shit. I couldn't even think in private. Another reason not to—

Stop stalling.

Get out of my head!

I glared at him, and then took a breath, closing my eyes.

"No. Open your eyes. You need to be able to shift effortlessly. If you are under attack, you must not close your eyes. It allows your enemies too many advantages."

"What, you think I'm going to be in a war?"

"Aren't you?" His response was swift. "Eilor is not going to want you competent. And if Stefan is involved, your situation is much worse."

Oh, for Pete's sake. I glared and imagined taking off the dragon suit. The tingling hit me, but this time it was fast, like a lightning strike. Then I was me again, and all my clothing was still intact.

"That's amazing," I said, looking at myself.

"It is easy once you realize it's natural for you. A skill," he added.

"Why can't Stefan go back there?"

"You really need to know this right now?"

"Yes," I crossed my arms and gave him my best stink eye.

He threw it right back at me.

If he wasn't such a pain in my ass with regard to my plans, I would like him.

I like you, too.

"Out of my head!" I yelled. "Don't you listen?"

"I am the head of our clan," he said.

"I am not in your clan," I shot back.

"You are, no matter how you wish to fight or deny. You're a dragon. That's not going away. It's not something you can decide to leave off." He had the nerve to grin.

"Then I don't want to be with your clan, or whatever, right now. I want to manage my life."

"As I told you, I don't think that's possible."

I turned away. "Don't start twisting shit to make your wish list look better."

I heard him walk back and sit down. I didn't turn.

"Why do you think Eilor is here? Why do you think he allowed you to think he and I were one?"

"I don't know that he knew of you—"

"He knew. The pendant allows for that. He wants you for some scheme, Aodan."

"And you don't?"

"I am not Eilor. I want nothing for you but your safety and freedom. Do not equate me with that monster." His voice deepened to a growl.

When I looked at him, I could see that he was pissed. His dragon was looming over him, behind his words and his anger.

It was weird that I could see it.

"You're not him, okay? But you both want something of me that doesn't take into account what I want, and I won't be controlled by anyone. I had enough of that growing up."

His dragon relaxed immediately. "I am sorry. That is not what I'm trying to do. But I know about being a dragon. I know what you will need. You will have a better chance of getting it in our world."

"This is my world, this one, right here! I've built something for myself, and—"

"Do you think that Stefan and Eilor will allow you to keep it? Stop, please, before you shout again." He held up a hand. "Use your skills. You need to approach this logically."

I raised an eyebrow. Here we go. Cue the bullshit.

"Eilor is presumed dead—or was, until today—in the Realms. Now that we know he is back, his plans must become more active. He cannot hide anymore. We will be seeking him out. Somehow, you are vital to his plans. I would guess he felt your dragon also since he showed up at the place you were attempting to steal from."

"Don't judge. And it wasn't an attempt. I succeeded."

"My apologies. Then there is Stefan. He was banished here many hundreds of years ago. Eilor is the kinder of the two. And Stefan is seeking a way back to the Realms. He believes you have that portal. It sounds as though he believes you are Eilor's creature. Do you feel safe from that?"

I didn't answer. Fangorn didn't seem to care because he continued.

"Between the pair of them, you will be lucky if you make it away from them alive."

"I'm doing fine so far."

AODAN! The shout was so loud in my head I put my hands over my ears.

"What?" I glared at him.

He stood and immediately went into a protective crouch. He put a finger to his lips and moved closer to me.

"Respond," he whispered "That was not me."

What the hell? Why was this douche still in my head?

What do you want?

I want to talk a trade with you.

You have nothing I want.

Oh, but I think I do. Say hello, my dear.

Aodan!

I heard her scream, and I roared as I came off the bed, knocking Fangorn away from me.

He had Margrite.

17

"*L*et her go!" I roared. I could feel the walls shake as I shifted, my dragon on alert. "Let her go now!"

I will let her go when you come to me.

Where are you? I thought.

"Can you hear this?" I whispered to Fangorn.

He nodded, but didn't speak.

Thanks to Fangorn, I am back where I belong, safe in the Realms. I didn't even need to open a portal. Much better for escaping detection.

His gloating made me want to strangle him.

But we know where you are.

Do you? The Realms are vast, and there are many Realms. No one has found me yet. No, Aodan, you shall not find me, not until I am ready for you to do so.

What do you want, asshole?

You. Come to me, and I will release the human.

I remembered how he'd spoken of humans. I couldn't be one-hundred percent sure, but I was pretty sure the shade had come from Eilor.

If she is harmed, I will kill you.

He laughed. He actually laughed.

That is why I want you. You are going to help me get what I want.
What's that, asshole?
Everything.

Did he really just say that? What. An. Asshole. He was that entitled rich guy who you wanted to steal from on principle only. Because he was rude just standing there.

So come to the Dragon Realm. Talk to your grandsire. He will help you get here. And meet me when I call you. Or she will die.

The door in my head slammed shut. It slammed so hard it made my head hurt.

"Holy shit," I breathed, sitting down and having trouble because my tail was in the way. I stood back up, and keeping my eyes open, took off the dragon. The inevitable zing, and I was me again.

"What the hell?" I asked. Sorry, Tina, I thought. I'd been cussing a lot lately. She'd smack my head if she could hear me.

I thought, though, that she might give me a pass on this one. At least this week. It had been a week that cussing was literally designed for.

"He has made his move based on his assessment of your weakness."

"How did he know? She went out to get a soda, or something. I doubt she left the motel."

Fangorn shrugged. "I gave up attempting to understand how Eilor would know so much. He has the pendant, and I am uncertain as to the extent of power and understanding it allows him. But it allows him a great deal. If he was in your head, he has seen how you feel for Margrite."

"I'm going to kill him."

Fangorn gave a hard chuckle. "As my in-law Iris says, you will need to get in line. There are a number of people in front of you waiting for that chance."

"He's pissed off everyone, hasn't he?"

"He is a creature of no morals, no conscience, and no feeling for the cares and concerns of others. To say that he has angered everyone around him is a statement of fact, but does not do the facts justice."

Yeah. He was a rich guy who deserved to be stolen from. I didn't know what I was going to steal from him, but I would take something and make sure it was something that would hurt to lose.

"What do we do?"

"We are a we now?" Fangorn looked smug.

"You know we are. Besides, if it gets you what you want," I said.

"What do I want?"

"For me to go to… wherever it is with you."

"To the Dragon Realm. That is where we will find him. It's where he's hiding. He was the king for over a thousand years. He knows the hiding places."

"Better than you?" I asked.

"No. But he's good. Our goal is to find him before your friend comes to serious harm."

That was one thing I didn't want to face, but I didn't have a choice. "You think she's going to…" I trailed off. I couldn't say the words.

"Not if we move swiftly." Fangorn looked at me expectantly.

I turned away, picking up my coat, and adding a few things to the pockets. Damn it. Damn it to hell. This was not what I wanted.

"All right. All *right*," I said. "We do this so that Margrite and I can come back. I don't want to just take off and then we don't have anything to come back to."

"Very well. What can I do to help in this?" Fangorn's expression was neutral.

"I'm going to pack up our things. Then we're going to the bus station. They have lockers there. We're going to stow our stuff so it's not lying around waiting for someone to steal." After my last shift, I was surprised someone hadn't called the cops. No sense in staying here.

"I didn't think you had an issue with theft."

"Not when I'm doing the theft. I prefer not to be the person stolen from," I rolled my eyes and then went back to packing up the few things we'd pulled out.

We hadn't even been here that long. But better that anyone watching thought we were holed up here. It gave us time to get away.

"We're going to need to sneak out," I said. "Can you manage to sneak anywhere?"

Fangorn made a noise that sounded like a snort, but it had dragon undertones. I could feel the rumble in my feet. He held out a hand for one of the bags. I handed over the large one of Margrite's and then turned off all the lights but the bathroom light. It needed to look like someone was here. I also turned on the TV, setting the volume on low. I messed up the beds, bunching the pillows around so it might look like someone was in them, if anyone happened to peek in the window.

But I made sure the dusty curtains were tightly closed. No one could see in, but it would look like we were here.

When I came back to my bag on the bed, Fangorn was watching me carefully. His scrutiny made me uncomfortable.

"What?" I asked.

"What are you doing?"

"Making it look like we're still here."

"This will fool someone?" He looked around, scorn on his face.

"We're not dealing with rocket scientists, here. Eilor, and his creepy brother might be smart, but the rest of them? Thinking is not high on the list of skills."

"I hope you are correct." The doubt was apparent in his expression.

"We don't have to put on a show. Just a distraction."

"Where are we going?" Fangorn whispered as we walked out the door, and I closed it softly behind us.

"The bus station. Follow me. And tell me if you notice anyone hanging around."

"There are many people hanging around."

I glared over my shoulder. "Don't you have some kind of spidey sense, or something like that?"

"I could answer that if I knew what it was."

"Never mind. Stay quiet, and we'll be out of here soon."

I scanned the parking lot as we moved down the stairs. I couldn't see anything, but there were a lot of bad smells. My sense of smell was maddening now. Everything was so much stinkier. This was not one for the plus side of being a dragon.

Maybe this other place—the Realm—smelled better. Or at least not as dirty.

There is dirt no matter where you are.

This bad?

I felt his shrug next to me.

Once we'd left the motel lot, I moved faster, less concerned about making noise. Now we were just two more people on the street.

"Keep your head down and stay with me," I said.

He moved closer, his pace matching mine.

Within ten minutes, we were at the station. I went to one of the corners of the locker stands and opened up two lockers. "In here," I gestured at one. The bag he carried would fit perfectly.

My bag fit in the other locker. After getting the keys, and tucking them carefully into one of my coat's inner pockets, I turned to see Fangorn watching people moving in the station.

It was a typical downtown station. A couple of homeless men and one woman who looked like she was homeless as well. She had a small shopping cart piled high with plastic bags. They were full of something, but I couldn't tell what.

A few more people were sleeping on benches. I didn't think they were homeless, and I hoped that they weren't anyone I needed to worry about. Most were curled up as though they wanted to disappear, so I didn't have any way to get a look at them.

"What now?" I asked.

"Are we done here?"

"Yes. I'm ready to go when you are."

"This is a bit too out in the open. I prefer to use a portal in a more secluded area."

"Um," I said, thinking. "I think I know a place. Come on." I walked through the back doors of the station to the field beyond. There were a few abandoned buildings back here, and we might get privacy. At least for enough time to summon the light ball thing and get the hell to wherever we needed to go.

I hoped so. I hoped that Margrite was all right. I hoped I wasn't making a mistake in trusting Fangorn. He didn't seem shady, but he had his own fight, his own agenda. People with their own stuff often didn't put as much importance on the things of others.

And that worried me.

What choice did I have? I couldn't abandon Margrite. I was all she had.

So off to woo-woo land it was.

I kept walking, hands in my pockets, thinking about Margrite and hoping like hell that she'd be okay. The whole 'humans don't survive in the Realm' thing was on auto-play and repeat in my head.

"Will I be able to function?" I whipped around to face Fangorn, who was behind me.

He pulled himself up, so he didn't run into me. "I am sorry?"

"You said that humans don't usually live over there. Will I be all right? I can't help Margrite if I'm laid out."

Fangorn chuckled.

"This is not the time for laughing." I turned and jammed my hands back into my pockets again, walking faster.

"I am laughing because you are part of over there, as you

call it." He caught up with me easily. "You are part fae and part dragon, in addition to being human. You were born there. Your sister, who shares your origins, thrives there. You will be fine, Aodan."

"I hope so. No screwing around. We go and arrange to get Margrite."

"We will need to have a plan, Aodan. If you think that Eilor is just going to give her up and let you go on your way, you haven't grasped the danger he embodies yet."

"We can plan. How to kill him, for starters."

"We will."

I spread my arms. "This is it. No one will see us here." I'd led us to an open space between two buildings. There could be people roaming around, but it wouldn't be anyone to worry about.

"Very well." He held out his hand, and I could hear him whisper something. A small flash of light, and then a small, glowing circle appeared. It great larger and larger. When it was as tall as Fangorn, he looked at me. "We are ready. Follow me."

Then he walked into the ball of light.

Feeling like I'd landed in the worst sci-fi film ever, I took a step into the circle. It didn't feel hot, or burn me. Not that I'd admit it, but I was kind of worried about it.

"Do not tarry, Aodan. This will not remain open forever."

Fangorn sounded annoyed.

I moved forward and where it had been dark, we were now in a room lit with late afternoon sun and candles.

Did time move differently here too? I shook my head. Part of me kept waiting for me to wake up, to see that it was all a bad dream.

It's not, Fangorn said in my head.

Stop it.

He gave me a brief smile and said something in the language I didn't understand. The light behind us was gone as though it had never been there.

Without speaking, he walked further into the room. He looked like he was waiting for something.

Times like this made me wish I had a gun, or some kind of weapon. I felt danger all around. More so than usual.

"What are you doing here? What happened?" A woman's voice came from off to the right, and after, the woman herself.

She was my height, with dark hair, and dark eyes. She wore a dress that came down to the ground, and it was some shade of purple. She was gorgeous. Her arms open, she went to Fangorn.

"Grandfather, I've been worried. You were gone too long. What happened?"

He turned and held a hand toward me. "I have brought your brother with me."

The woman dropped her arms and faced me. Her mouth fell open. "Aodan?" She breathed.

"Yeah. You are?"

"I am Aine." She held her arms up again, and came at me, wrapping them around me before I could say anything or get away. "I never thought I'd see you."

Her voice broke, like she might be crying. I patted her back, not sure how I felt. Part of me felt right, felt as though I belonged here.

The other part of me had never felt more out of place.

Aine stepped back. "It's like looking in a mirror. Except the eyes. And you need to shave," she brushed at my face. "I'm so glad that you're here," she whispered.

There were tears in her eyes.

"I didn't want to be."

That stopped whatever emotional thing that was going on. "Then why are you?"

She could shift to all business just like I could. It was a quality I appreciated, and I felt my mouth turn up in recognition.

But Aine didn't notice. She was glaring.

"My best friend has been kidnapped."

"By Eilor," Fangorn added.

Aine's mouth twisted, and she turned from me, striding away. Not walking. Striding. Angry walking. She made it as far as a small table and kicked it.

"Will he never go away? Haven't we all suffered enough?"

"As soon as I get Margrite back, I'm going to kill him."

Aine whipped around. "He's powerful. More than you know. We thought he was dead."

"I know——" I started.

"He fooled us. All of us. Well," she glanced at Fangorn. "Almost all of us. Grandfather didn't believe it, not even after the body was found. He's outsmarted and escaped the Fae King, the Goblin King, and the Dragon King. Yet somehow you will succeed where they have failed? Don't be arrogant, brother!"

"Don't make assumptions about someone you don't know, *sister*," I shot back.

*a*ine's brows came down as she frowned at me. "Oh, you're one of those. Isn't that perfect?" She rolled her eyes. Then she turned to Fangorn. "I'll get Drake." And she whirled away, skirts flaring out.

A moment later, I heard the door slam.

"That was well done," Fangorn said, walking over to look out a window, his hands clasped behind his back.

"I'm not going to pretend this is some kind of happy family reunion. I don't know any of you. My goal is to get my friend back. You said you'd help me. That's it. That's all there is."

I ignored the warm flare I'd had in my chest since I'd stepped into this room. The one that felt at ease immediately. It was like something inside of me knew this was somewhere I belonged.

That I'd once belonged. My mother had been so frightened, she'd taken me and run. Run back to her world where she never got better. I didn't have many memories of her—most of the ones in my head were good, and of a woman signing to me in a soft voice—but I knew she was tired. She didn't run, or play, or do a lot with me.

She sat in a window. That memory flashed in front of me like it was on a TV. She was sitting on a couch, looking out a window. I'd come in the room, and she didn't move. It was like I wasn't there.

She must have heard me because she turned quickly. When she saw me, her face broke into a smile. Even though she smiled, from this distance, I could tell that she was sad. She opened her arms to me, and I crawled up on the couch next to her. Cradling me to her, she began to hum into my hair, her sadness enveloping us both.

What the hell? I hadn't thought about my mom in years. Was it this place? I didn't have the time to go through ancient history. I had a job to do. And then Margrite and I had a plane to catch.

Well, a plane to reschedule, and then catch. I could almost hear Margrite correcting me.

The door opened again, and a man strode in with Aine behind him.

"Fangorn! I'm glad you're back." The man clapped Fangorn on the shoulder. "How did everything go?"

Fangorn nodded his head at me.

The man openly appraised me, taking my measure. I met his eyes, not moving, not flinching. He was measuring me.

As I was him. He wore leather... armor, it looked like. A sword hung at his side. He was as tall as Aine, and he had an air of command. Like if he told you to hop it, you'd better do so.

I wasn't hopping it for anyone.

He gave a short nod as though he'd come to a decision, and took the steps toward me, holding out his hand. "I am Drake. I'm married to your sister. That makes you family. I am grateful you are here although sorry that bastard Eilor is the reason."

I studied him and then reached out my hand. I was expecting him to shake, but he reached past my hand and clasped my forearm. I did the same.

"Aodan."

His face changed as he smiled. "I would have known even if you'd only passed me in the market. You and Aine look like mirror images—although you're much more attractive," he tossed that last bit over his shoulder.

I heard rather than saw Aine make a noise of impatience. "Be quiet. There's more."

Drake dropped my arm and immediately looked to Fangorn.

"Aine told you of when she and I went through?"

Drake nodded.

"Not only did we see Eilor, very much alive, but his brother Stefan was there."

"That doesn't mean anything to me," Drake said.

"It wouldn't. He was banished before your time. We will need to notify Jharak."

"Because I haven't sent him enough bad news today," Drake said, with a twist of his mouth. "I love adding onto that."

"Stefan is worse than Eilor—"

"How can anyone be worse?" Aine interrupted.

"He is. That is why he was banished."

"And sent to… to the human world?" I asked. "That was really good of you guys. Thanks."

Aine glared at me, but Drake smiled briefly.

Apparently my sister didn't share my sense of humor.

Fangorn shrugged. "Fae are less powerful in the Human Realm. They are not as capable, and magic doesn't work as well. It was the safest place for him."

"I'm not so sure about that. He's a serious crime boss, and he scares the shit out of anyone who has to work around him. That doesn't sound safe for any of us."

None of them responded.

Then Aine said, "Your point is fair, and probably accurate. The fae don't always," she looked at Fangorn, "Make the best decisions. But when they find they have made a mistake, they fix it."

Fangorn didn't say anything but the look he gave Aine made my heart twist.

He loved her. He loved her very much. It was the look of a grandfather to a beloved grandchild. It was a look of shared history, of a past, of pain and suffering and triumph.

I looked away.

You are my grandchild as well.

Go away.

No. This will need to be addressed. Your feelings, the past, all of it. Ignoring it or attempting to negate it via bluster and rude behavior will not change a thing.

It might get you slapped, another voice chimed in.

My head shot up.

Aine had her hands on her hips, glaring.

"No."

The sound of Drake's voice made all three of us look at him.

"I hate it when it's the two of you and you do that head talk business," Drake said. "Now I have to put up with three of you? No. I'm drawing a line, right here." He made a motion like he was drawing a line in front of him. Then he continued, "I'm going to have to tell Brennan. Which means I'll also be telling Iris. Which means," he looked at me and grinned. "Whatever else is going on, you're going to have to spare some time to meet the family. There's probably going to be a baby, as well. She doesn't let it out of her sight. I don't need the three of you chattering behind my back." He rolled his eyes.

Aine laughed. "You love that child, so stop pretending otherwise."

"This doesn't help Margrite. My friend. The one that Eilor kidnapped. Fangorn told me that humans don't do well here. She doesn't have a lot of time."

"She has more than you think. If Eilor took her to use as leverage against you, he will make sure she stays alive and well. She's of no use to him dead," Drake said.

"That was helpful," Aine said.

"What?" Drake looked at her. "I don't mean to be insensitive, but he's horrific in his practicality. You both know that," he looked at Aine and Fangorn. "If Aodan has something he wants, he'll keep dangling the friend over Aodan. No sense pretending otherwise. Let's use that to our advantage."

Everyone looked at me. I didn't like to hear Margrite dismissed to leverage, but what Drake said made sense. He was being practical, and I appreciated that, even as my worry for Margrite rose.

"All right. What do you suggest?" I asked.

Fangorn smiled.

Aine crossed her arms.

Drake said, "I'm going to, as I said, contact my brother. We take the fact that Eilor is alive rather personally since we thought we'd found his dead body. I hate being wrong," he grinned at me. "So I'm offended on that count, too. You're not alone in this, Aodan. We're going to get your friend back. Eilor won't let her die. Trust me on this."

I looked at him. "All right."

Drake pulled a small silver mirror from a pouch on his belt. "Brennan," he said to it.

"What?" The mirror barked back.

"I need you."

Silence, and then the mirror began to wail. Like an angry baby.

"I have my hands full at the moment," the mirror said. The voice sounded kind of snotty. But that could be due to the screaming kid.

I covered my mouth so no one would see me laugh. These people were a lot more formal than I was. I didn't want to offend them—all right, I didn't want to offend them more than I already had.

Well, maybe it was just Aine. Fangorn and Drake seemed okay with me.

Here I thought I'd be delighted at meeting my brother. But you're kind of ruining that, her voice said.

Well, you're not the best chips and guac, either. Sorry that my agenda doesn't match yours. But I'd like to keep my friend alive.

I think you insulted me, but I can't be sure. She sounded frustrated. *What are chips and guac?*

Not you, I thought.

I grinned when she glared.

Stop, the voice of Fangorn said.

How come I can tell the difference now? I asked.

What do you mean? He thought.

Before... I couldn't tell the difference between the two of you. But now, you and Aine sound completely different.

What are you talking about? Aine interjected.

"You're all doing it again!" Drake threw up his hands. Then he spoke to the mirror. "Now there's three of them that head talk," he sounded really put upon.

"I'm on my way. Have you let Father know?"

Drake nodded. "Aine did when she returned. You coming alone?" He laughed as he asked.

"Must you?" The mirror asked.

"Yes," Drake said. "Bring your entourage, brother. We can handle the invasion."

The mirror said something I didn't understand, but the other three laughed as Drake put the mirror back into his pouch.

"I'm guessing he told you to piss off," I said. It was amazing how you could tell what people said just by tone.

"Something along the lines of he hoped my progeny never allowed me to sleep again," Drake said.

The laughter that came after his statement—laughter that included me—reminded me of Tina. A pang hit me. She'd always told me that I was so much more than what I let others see. I'd gotten into a fight at school, and she had to go to see the principal. The other kid's mom was all offended and told Tina that she ought to do better to keep those foster children in line. Tina had told her she hoped she stepped on a Lego. I could still see the woman's outraged expression. I'd stepped on Legos. It hurt. The other mom must have stepped on them too because she was more pissed about that comment than the fact I kicked her kid's ass.

Tina told me then that I was not just a foster kid, but Aodan, who was amazing and smart and worthwhile. That while family seemed hard right now, it would change.

Looking around at these three people, I had a glimpse of what she'd meant.

I had to turn away. I could feel a lump in my throat.

"Are you all right?" Drake asked.

"He's fine," Aine said. Unlike before, her voice wasn't annoyed. It was softer, and I knew she'd heard some of my thoughts.

For the first time since I'd learned this kind of thing happened with dragons, I didn't mind.

"Let us alert the staff that we will need some things for Iris and the baby," Fangorn said.

I could hear footsteps as he and Drake left.

Aine came up to me and put her hand on my shoulder.

"Your life has not been easy, either, has it?" She asked quietly.

"You can't read my mind and tell?" I wasn't ready to get all touchy feely.

"No. I felt your emotion then. It was strong. When we're close like this, physically close, it's hard to keep emotion to yourself. Fangorn's better at it than I am. But he's starting to let me in more. He was in a cage for over one thousand years. He had to shield himself. So did I. And so did you. Habits die hard." Her hand squeezed my shoulder. "But you are safe with us. When we find Eilor that will be different. Here, however, you can let down the shields."

I felt the lump in my throat increase to painful proportions.

It was stronger than the feeling of smoke that was always with me. I reached up and put my hand on hers.

When she wasn't annoyed, Aine spoke with a quiet confidence. I found it comforting.

A lot better than the snarly side, I thought.

She made a noise.

Shut up.

I held her hand tighter.

19

We stood together until the door opened. I could hear a buzz of conversation. Drake, Fangorn, and someone I didn't know.

Aine let go of my hand and went to greet the new arrivals.

I watched.

A woman entered who was small, blond and attractive. She held a baby. A dark man was right on her heels and talking to Drake even as his hand guided the woman.

Then two more people who fanned out around the couple. They were women carrying trays—one with a pitcher and cups, and another with food. It looked like bread, at least. They headed for a table against the wall that I hadn't noticed before.

"Anything else, m'lord?" One of the women asked.

"That's all," Drake said.

The women hesitated.

"Oh, all right. Go on," he added. "It's like a sickness," he said to the dark haired man with him.

Both women went to the woman with the baby. "Y'majesty," they curtsied as one spoke. "How is the little one?"

The blond woman smiled. "See for yourself," she held out

the baby, and the older of the two women, who must be servants, took the baby.

Both the women bent over the baby. Thankfully, it wasn't crying. As I watched, a small, pale arm reached out and grabbed at the scarf around one woman's head.

I could feel the pleasure from these two women. They were obviously servants, and the man and woman were royalty, if that's what being called 'majesty' meant. Yet none of these people acted like royalty.

They were just... people.

Your family, Aine said.

I didn't respond. My family was Margrite. She'd been my only family since Tina was killed. I wasn't ready to—

Stop it, Aine spoke again. *Just let the shields down. That's all you have to do. Don't be such a man.*

I am a man, I thought.

This is the Goblin King and Queen, and the baby is their son. There hasn't been a baby born to one of the ruling couples since Brennan, over seven hundred years ago. People are thrilled to see a baby.

I could hear the tone. I could actually hear it even though she wasn't speaking. Aine was as fond of this couple and the baby as everyone else seemed to be.

"Thank you," one of the women said as she handed the baby back to the blonde woman. The Goblin Queen, Aine had called her.

She didn't look like what I thought a goblin looked like.

She's fae, and human. Brennan is fae. He rules the Goblin Realm. But he's not a goblin.

Are you trying to give me a history lesson?

I'm trying to make sure you don't make a fool of yourself in front of people. We're related, after all.

Point taken, I smiled in Aine's direction.

Good. Don't embarrass me or Fangorn.

I will be fine regardless, Fangorn chimed in.

See? I thought smugly. *He's fine.*

"They're doing it again," Drake said, gesturing around at me, Aine, and Fangorn. "It's like they can't help it."

"We can't," Fangorn said.

"You're Aodan? Aine's brother?" The blonde woman came toward me, the baby cradled on her shoulder. "I'm Iris. You're part human, aren't you? Is this the first time you've been in the Realms?"

"I didn't even know what the Realms were until a couple of hours ago," I answered her.

"Then don't let all the weird stuff get to you. It takes some getting used to," she said with a smile. When she smiled, she went from attractive to beautiful. She turned, the smile still on her face. "This is Brennan." She pointed at the man. "And this," she patted the baby, "Is Kenric."

The baby didn't stir.

"I am glad you're here," Brennan said, offering his hand.

Thanks to Drake, I knew what to do now.

I clasped his forearm. He gave mine a squeeze.

You need to let me know what's expected, you know, with manners, I thought.

Oh, we care about that now?

Figures it was Aine. Sarcasm must be a family trait as well.

Aine will need to be your guide. Dragons have their own rituals.

That's a lot of help. I shot a glare at Fangorn.

"I'm not sure," I said to Brennan. "I'm only here because I have to be."

"What's happened?" He looked from Drake to Fangorn.

Quickly, Fangorn filled everyone in on what had happened from the point that he came to see me. Thankfully, he didn't include all the details of our conversation. That was a good thing. I didn't want everyone to know everything about me.

No one here is your enemy, Fangorn said.

Well, that's on me to decide for me.

Very well. Try to start from a place where trust is possible.

For Pete's sake. I rolled my eyes.

Aine met mine, and she smiled in understanding.

I looked away. All the family things, all the comfort—it was coming too fast.

"See? They're doing it!" Drake pointed at the three of us.

"You're really bothered by this," Iris said, patting Kenric and rocking back and forth slightly. "It might lead one to believe it's due to something personal."

"Be quiet, ladyship," Drake said.

Iris only smiled into the baby's hair.

"It's natural for us to engage in this form of communication," Fangorn said. "It's not meant as discourtesy in any way."

"He knows that," Aine said. "He likes to complain."

"Yes," Iris and Brennan said together.

There was a moment of silence, and then everyone but Fangorn and I started to laugh.

Drake must make this kind of complaint regularly.

Fangorn smiled. *He does. But do not be fooled. He is a fierce warrior, and intensely loyal. He was Brennan's second for years, before he was given the Dragon Throne. He and Iris are both fierce. They rescued Brennan when—well, that doesn't matter at the moment.*

He is a good man. And he hates Eilor, Aine added.

You're not biased or anything, I thought.

I'm very much biased. But that does not change the truth.

"Did you converse with Eilor?" Brennan asked me.

It pulled me from the head talk.

"I did. I thought it was Fangorn. They sound similar. I mean, he's definitely got a douchebag edge to him—"

Iris laughed. Everyone looked at her.

"I don't get to hear human slang much anymore. It's a funny word to describe what a hateful and arrogant man Eilor is," she added. "It's pretty accurate," she said to me. "I'm sorry. Go on."

"Now I can tell the difference between Fangorn and Aine. When Eilor told me that he had Margrite, he sounded different from Fangorn. I could tell the difference between them now."

"I envy this form of communication," Brennan said. "We

have the mirrors but if we could talk between minds, it would be faster and private."

That was something I hadn't thought about. I'd been stuck on the fact I had voices in my head like a crazy person.

Maybe a change in perspective is something to consider. Aine wasn't looking at me.

You going to drop in all the time like this?

Fangorn gave me what Margrite called the side-eye. And he wanted to laugh, but he didn't.

Perhaps your elders are worth listening to.

"What did Eilor tell you, Aodan?" Drake said.

"He said... uh..." I had to stop thinking about a comeback to Fangorn. "He said when I came here, to the... uh..." I waved my hand around.

"The Realms?" Iris asked.

"Yes. The Realms. He said he would contact me." I frowned. "How much time does she have?"

"Your friend?" Brennan asked.

He reminded me most of Aine. They were both quieter than everyone else in this room. Watchful, careful, deliberate. Those were qualities I appreciated. All the noise was getting to me. Margrite and I knew how to be quiet with one another.

I nodded. "She's human. Fangorn said she couldn't make it here."

"No, she may not," Fangorn corrected.

"That is not what you said," I frowned at him.

"She has a chance," Brennan said. "Most of the people here are more human than anything else."

"What? Aren't you all magical woo woo and shit?" I was so surprised I spoke without thinking.

Iris started to laugh. Everyone else smiled.

She handed Kenric to Brennan, and leaned over, laughing. "You guys are missing out on the way humans talk. It's been so long, Aodan! I miss it!"

"What is wrong with the way we speak?" Brennan went all frosty on his wife.

"Whatever, Bren. Save your indignation. No, I just miss listening to people who talk like I did. It's not personal."

He didn't look convinced, but he cradled the baby, doing the same rocking back-and-forth thing Iris was doing earlier.

"Brennan is right. She does have a chance. The Realms are not good for humans. There's something in the air, basically." She shook her head. "Don't ask. I got a lecture that lasted all day when I asked for specifics. But she can live. And Eilor is a practitioner of magic. He'll keep her alive. He needs her."

That was the second time someone had said she'd stay alive as long as she was useful. Another thought struck me. "Who else is human?"

"I am," Drake said immediately. "I was wished here seven hundred years ago. I didn't die, and my parents adopted me."

"Me, too," said Iris. "I'm a quarter fae, thanks to my grandmother."

"I'm half human," Aine said. "So are you. Our mother was human, and our father half fae, half dragon."

"So she could live?"

Everyone nodded. "There's no telling why some people live and others don't."

"I think you should alert Eilor that you are here. But before you do, may I ask you a few questions?" Brennan asked.

"I guess?"

"Tell me about the box you stole. Fangorn tells me that Stefan wanted it. Called it a casket. I haven't heard that in a long time."

I shrugged. "I got word of a really good paying job. It was halfway easy, with the complication that I had to steal it from another guy who'd already stolen it. When I went to find it, I saw Eilor—at least I think it was him. He was in a portal, and he kicked a woman in the face."

Brennan and Iris looked at one another. "Eleanor," she said

softly. Then she looked at me. "That's another story. It's not important now. Please go on. I'm sorry for interrupting."

The thief in me wanted to dig, to find out the details, the information. One thing I'd learned was that information was a valuable as any physical thing. There were so many stories within stories here.

"I stole the box. I got to my fence, and he called the client."

"Who was it?" Brennan asked.

"A woman and man. Young. She was one of those good-looking snotty women. He was good looking, and," I thought about them. "She was in charge but he calmed her down when she started getting angry."

Brennan nodded. "I think I know who that might be. They are of no danger. I'd be surprised if they had any clue what was going on," he added to Drake.

Now Drake nodded. Then he looked at me. "Where does Stefan come in?"

"When I arranged to meet Eilor, thinking he was you," I said to Fangorn, "This Stefan guy shows up, and starts yelling that Eilor's this and that, and he set him up and stole the casket for himself and lots of drama stuff." I rolled my eyes. "I think Stefan is the boss that the guy I stole from works for. He's supposed to be dangerous, and he puts off that vibe for sure. But when he started ranting at Eilor, it was kind of pathetic."

"He is dangerous," Drake said flatly. "Very much so. But like Eilor, he gets mad, and he acts when he's mad. So he wants to come home," he looked at Brennan and then Fangorn. "That would be very bad."

"There are now two fronts. The mysteriously back from the dead Eilor, and his equally mad brother," Aine said.

"Oh, come on. You were getting bored," Iris teased her.

Aine crossed her arms. She didn't answer.

I glanced at her, brows raised in a question.

Maybe.

It nearly killed me, but I didn't smile.

"Well, we must first concentrate on the safe return of Aodan's friend Margrite. Then we can focus on Stefan." Fangorn didn't seem ruffled. "Do we have a plan? It would not be wise to let Eilor have the upper hand."

"As a matter of fact, we do," Drake said. "But everything is easier over food. Let's eat, and we'll talk it out.

This further delay was going to make me crazy. At the same time, it made me think of Margrite. I hated delay, and she made me plan with her, account for all possibilities before I did a job.

She would appreciate this.

I'd have to tell her, when we got her back.

If we did.

20

*W*hen these people ate, they did it right. As the tray of bread, and cheeses, and fruits that I didn't recognize, along with cuts of meat got low, one of the serving women came in and refilled it.

Not that I wanted to say it but it was like magic.

I listened. That's how I planned best—to hear the plan and make it work for me.

"You don't think he'll be suspicious that I'm yelling for him?" I asked, tearing my millionth piece of bread. It was so good.

Aine was the one who answered. "No. He's very, very clever, and has an amazing sense of preservation, but he's not good at assuming others will be smarter, or even as smart as he is. He'll assume you're just a human, and you are panicking and not thinking rationally."

"He knows I'm with you, though. He told me to ask you to get me here. He knew that I'd have to. There was no other way to get me here," I turned to Fangorn.

He nodded. "He will expect me to be with you. No doubt he

has a scheme that involves both of us. All three of us," he looked at Aine, "If he can manage it."

"She's not going with you," Drake said.

"She is," Aine said.

"He'll know you are close. He has the pendant still," Fangorn said.

"You have mentioned that but I am unfamiliar with the pendant. Why does that matter?" Brennan asked.

"If you recall, one of the things Eilor always wore was the ring of the Dragon King, which he thankfully no longer has, and a large pendant with a red stone. That stone has my blood in it. It allows him, when he wears it, to hear the thoughts and collective awareness of the dragons. It allows him to participate like a dragon. He used it to insure I had no privacy after Lionel escaped and he realized that Lionel and I were speaking over distances." He looked down at his plate, which only had fruit on it.

Aine put her hand over his. Neither spoke. Then Fangorn looked up. "We must get that pendant from him. And I insist—" he stressed the word, looking between Drake and Brennan, "That it be returned to me. It will not go to either of you, or your father. It is my blood. I will not have the last of us used in any way by another."

The dragon rumbled in his words. He was deadly serious. I could tell that something bad had happened with him, with other people using him. I knew about Eilor, but I wondered what he had against Brennan, or Drake, or their father.

Jharak, their father, is also the Fae King. He is one of those who put me and the rest of us into the care of Eilor. And never bothered to check on us again, Fangorn's words rumbled through my head. *Brennan already covets our communication.*

He thinks it would be useful. He doesn't covet it, Aine objected.

Useful leads to reasons why someone should have something, regardless of whether it is right. Fangorn wasn't budging. *Do not go against me on this. I will not allow it.*

"Are you dictating terms?" Brennan didn't look bothered, but something in him shifted as well. He was also deadly serious.

"I am. If you will not agree, I will help Aodan with no assistance from any of the leaders of the Fae Realm. Given all that my kind have suffered at the hands of yours, there is no reason to deny my demand."

Brennan took another bite of cheese. "You're right. Jharak might have something to say about it, but we were not good stewards to the dragons. It is reasonable."

I felt Fangorn relax next to me. "Then the pendant is mine."

Brennan nodded. "It is. Although I would ask if you would work with me on something when this is over?"

"What is that?"

"Some way to improve on communication. The mirrors work, but they are not easily concealed, and they can be lost or stolen.

"Or given away like they were some sort of treat," Drake said, glaring at Iris.

She ignored him.

Brennan ignored them both, talking to Fangorn. "We need a better way. Since the dragons have been using a different form of communication, I would welcome your help in this."

Fangorn stared at the other man. I was glad I wasn't on the other end of those green eyes. He was intensity with a capital 'I'.

"I will."

I felt the entire table relax.

"That doesn't explain why I can't be with you," Aine said.

"Because he will know. And it's better that he believe Aodan and I are alone."

"Can't he hear us now?"

"How have you kept him out?" Fangorn asked.

"I imagine shutting a door and putting him on the other side of it."

Fangorn nodded. "I've felt you do that. It's crude, but effective."

"You know a better way?"

"Of course. I'll teach you. I've taught Aine, so that we are safe from him."

"Then bring it," I said. "I don't want him in my head."

"We do not have the time now. Keep your door closed. Although you will need to let him know you are here. We should not be here, in the Dragon Castle," he added, looking around the table.

"You think he can tell?" Iris asked.

"I think it unwise to assume he will act carelessly. He has managed to escape all of us and avoid death. He ought to be dead several times over, and he is still alive." Fangorn sighed.

"Yeah, he's annoying and a menace," Iris said. "Will you go back to your home?"

Fangorn nodded. "I am sure Eilor has an idea of where we are. The caverns are well guarded against him. The others would tear him apart should he come near," he added.

He sounded like he relished some tearing apart himself.

I could understand that.

"So we call him tonight?" I asked.

"Yes. And that is another reason you must stay here, child," he said to Aine. "We need you to relay what is happening to Drake and Brennan."

She nodded, although she didn't look happy.

"We'll have portals ready. We'll get her out of there," Iris said to me.

I believed her. While I wasn't ready to throw in with these people, I didn't think they were lying to me. They were too pleased to have me here. It wasn't gushing, or over the top. I could tell they were happy—not just for themselves, but Aine and Fangorn.

Aine was right. This was a family.

Of course I'm right.

Go away.

Across from me, she smiled.

*A*fter the meal, Fangorn and I used a portal to go to the caverns where the dragons lived.

"Will the rest be there?" I asked. "Are they shifters, too?"

"No. I am the only shifter. A few will be there. All of them know of you. All of them are very happy that you are here, that you have come back to us, for however long. There are so few of us left, all of us matter even more than we did before."

I looked at the opening. It didn't look big enough for dragons to go in and out freely.

Come, Fangorn thought.

I followed him, and there was some sort of barrier, but it wasn't solid.

Only dragons can pass, he added.

Ah. This was magic and woo woo.

Thinking about that made me think about Nala. I'd pulled the Dragon deck. The memory of all the dragons flashed through my mind. They'd been beautiful. I hoped the dragons I was about to see were too.

We walked down a long hallway, or corridor. It was dark, but my eyes didn't seem to be affected. When Fangorn glanced over his shoulder, I could see the green glint of his eyes.

Ready?

"As I'll ever be." I squared my shoulders and tried not to be too nervous. Something told me they would know.

I could see a doorway up ahead. There was a light on the other side of it. Fangorn walked steadily on, and before I knew it, we were walking through it into a large cavern.

When I moved through the door, I could feel them.

They were huge. I knew that before I saw anyone.

You're here.

Welcome, child.

You have returned to us.

Step into the light and let us see you.

The voices came fast, each distinct. Everyone was excited, though, and I couldn't feel any negative energy. Joy, happiness, relief.

Fangorn held out his arms and shifted.

It was seamless. One moment he was a man, and then he was a dragon.

We have found our lost one. He has come back to us.

He turned and looked at me, his green eyes even more brilliant as a dragon.

Join us, my child, I felt from him. *Let us see you.*

Keeping my eyes opened, I imagined the dragon moving over me, the dragon suit closing around me. When I looked down, I was my dragon.

Ah. The sigh was collective.

You are small, but you are strong, said a voice that sounded like it belonged to an older female.

I thought you might be smaller with so much human in you, but you are not.

Welcome, Aodan. Welcome home.

Fangorn faced me. *We welcome you to the Cavern of the Ancestors,* he said. *This is your home for as long or as little as you choose to make it so. But now that you are with us, will you share?*

What do you mean? I shook my head a little. There were so many voices even though I knew there were only eleven. Everything about them was huge.

You have felt how we share and communicate with each other. Share your life with us. Let us see.

I—it's not great, I thought bleakly.

It is yours. That is what matters. There was no hesitation in Fangorn's response.

How?

Open your mind. Let us in. It will not hurt, but it will feel... overwhelming at first. Then it will not. Let us see you, Aodan.

I could feel the forces warring in me. Part of me wanted to be part of this—a family, a part of something bigger. The other side of me was scared to let this many people—beings—see all of me. I knew there would be no hiding.

This was the Devil that Nala had seen. And the Hanged Man. I had to change, and if I didn't change, it was because I couldn't get out of my own way.

How I remembered that, I couldn't even take a guess. But I did. If—when—I got home, I would need to see her. Take Margrite's notebook and find the ways that her reading had been correct.

I thought that I should have listened better. The whole damn thing was turning into a see-the-future kind of thing for me.

Fangorn's thoughts brought me back to the present.

Aodan, no matter what happens, we will always be here. You are always a member of our clan. We are always with you. Fangorn sounded gentle.

Has Aine been here?

Yes. She has not yet shifted, but she has shared with us. It is why we know we must end Eilor. It does not matter if the Fae King decides other-wise. We know. We know what he is and what he can do. He dies.

That decided me. We were on the same side. *All right. What do I need to do?*

This time, close your eyes. Picture yourself opening a door—

What if Eilor comes in? I didn't want him to see any of this.

He will not, another voice said. *We will protect you.*

I felt the hum of agreement at those words, and the deep thread of anger that his name stirred. I had a vision of things he'd done, pictures that flashed through my brain like the old flip cards we used in school. In all of them, he was hurting a dragon. Some were blue. Some green, A large red one who looked like he or she had tears falling from its golden eyes. Dark blood glistened at the side of the dragon.

He will not come to you here, a third voice said.

I didn't know why but I thought that might be the red dragon.

Why?

He knows we would kill him, the same voice said. *He very much wants to live. In all the time we were held by him, and he knew of this place, he never ventured here. It's not just our home, it's the place our ancestors came to die. When we lost the war, we were allowed to bring our fallen here. They are all here. This is a dangerous place unless you are a dragon.*

They're all here? Like ghosts?

Spirits. Power. Protection. That was Fangorn. *Are you ready, Aodan?*

Yes. I closed my eyes and let the doors open.

I could feel them. They were on the edges of my consciousness. Not doing anything other than looking. Seeing. Pieces of my life moved through my memory.

My mother, sitting in the window and crying. Holding me, and speaking to me in a language I didn't understand.

She knew the stories, a voice whispered.

What stories? I asked.

The stories of us.

Lionel must have told her. I shared many with him, Fangorn said.

Then my first foster home, and the first time anyone ever hit me in anger. Then another foster home. And another. And another, until I came to Tina.

The first time I stole, and how I defeated Brandon, the other boy who was in Tina's home with me. The one who hurt the girls. Sara and Tara. That had been their names. Sara and Tara. He'd hurt them, and I'd stopped it.

My life with Tina, and then with Margrite. We both laughed then, when Tina was alive, and Margrite spent all her time with me.

The cops who came and told me that Tina had died.

Margrite and I when we left her foster parents' house.

Our apartment in our old, rickety building.

Burning with anger when Caleb humiliated me in the local bar. Wanting to kill him. Margrite holding me back.

Me hiding my stashes all over the building.

Finally, they saw me stealing the box.

A portal?

Was that when you first shifted? Fangorn asked.

Right after that. That's when I saw Eilor for the first time, I added. *I didn't know it was him then.*

Show us.

21

*T*his didn't feel entirely natural, but I could see why Brennan envied this form of communication. It was fast, and by being in a collective, shared quickly with many. I couldn't have talked as quickly as I'd let them see all my memories.

Aodan?

Oh, shit. I was supposed to be sharing something specific.

I went back to when I was hanging off the beam, trying not to sneeze my head off. The smoke in the back of my throat, like someone was blowing the smoke from a fire into my face. Seeing Eilor in the portal light and then handing the box over to Luke. His snotty clients.

There was some discussion when they all saw the man and woman who paid for the box. I didn't pay attention to it. I wanted to watch what happened next.

I went to bed, and woke up on the floor with a broken bed underneath me, and I was a dragon.

Margrite screaming when she came in.

Practicing shifting in the warehouse.

I stopped focusing on what was happening. I let them see

without letting myself watch. Worry for Margrite washed over me as did shame. I'd spent the entire evening getting to know all my new family, and the family who'd stood by me since the day we'd met was somewhere in danger.

We will find her. This was a new voice, a male.

We have to. I can't let her down, I thought. Even I could hear the panic in my thoughts.

We will not. We will get her back.

Before she gets sick or... I couldn't finish the thought.

Yes. Before.

It was hard to tell who was talking. It didn't matter. This was why Fangorn had pressured me. This was a part of me, and something that was supposed to be in my life. I knew it.

I didn't know how this would work with the life I'd planned. Maybe that didn't matter right now. We'd get Margrite back and go from there.

Thank you, Aodan, the older female who I'd picked out earlier said.

You're welcome. Thank you, I added. I meant it.

You were right, Fangorn, the stern male said. *Our lost ones have returned.*

We made the right choice, Fangorn thought. *We all did.*

Now let us find Eilor. We must get Margrite back, the male said.

Can she come here? Even though she's not a dragon? I wanted her safe. *Just until we can get back?*

I think we can manage it. While you are fetching her, we will make a place for her.

What if she's ill? Not doing well?

We have our ways of healing. They are not the ways of the fae or any other creature of the Fae Realm. We will be able to help her, Aodan. This was the female again.

Thank you, I thought. I sent out all the gratitude I was feeling. I wanted them to know that I was appreciative, and not an ass or an ingrate.

"Let's do this," I said. "Help me find that asshole."

"We need to leave this cavern," Fangorn said. "I don't want him to have any sense of what is here."

"All right. Back out the way we came?"

"No. Follow me."

I was doing a lot of that. Normally I led. The control thing, again. When Margrite was back, she needed to look up that reading from Nala. I felt like there was a lot going on that would end up falling into some of the things she'd seen in the reading.

Holy shit. Had I just thought that? Thank hell I hadn't said it. But I tucked it away for when I saw Margrite again. She'd appreciate it.

We came a stairway and Fangorn leapt up and flew.

"Um," I said. "I don't know how to do that."

"You do. Spread your wings."

I'd forgotten that I was in dragon form. I'd been so caught up in all that was going on around me that I'd completely forgotten I was a dragon.

That's because you're as you're meant to be, Fangorn thought down at me.

"I can't—"

"No. Fly, Aodan. Don't think, just do it."

This had the makings of me walking on all fours all over again. Except I was pretty sure I was going to end up on my ass *and* my face.

I hadn't done anything with the wings that were tucked next to me. I hadn't even thought about it. Four legs was intimidating enough.

"Why are there stairs here—?"

"Do not tarry, Aodan."

I opened my wings. At least, I thought I did. When I looked over my shoulder, they were open. Okay. First step down. This was good. I could do this.

Flap them. Make them move.

I thought about them moving, and I could feel the rush of air from them moving. Okay. I had some control over them.

Wasn't there some skill involved in flying?

You will never learn it if you stay on the ground, Fangorn said.

"Damn it! Ease up!" I shouted.

The entire cavern went quiet. Great. Now I had an attentive audience.

One. Flap. Two. Flap. Three. Flap. I kept counting, speeding up my wing movement. I was so busy counting that I didn't notice I'd risen off the ground.

The surprise made me lose count, and I sank down.

No, no, no! Count! I ignored everything else, and forced myself to count, and to keep speeding up the count.

Slowly, I rose up again, and kept going.

Holy hell. I was flying. Thirty-seven. Flap. Thirty-eight. Flap, flap. Thirty-nine. Flap.

When I reached sixty-two, I saw that the wall of narrow stairs ended and there was a ledge, or something, above. I gave a final flap and landed on the ledge, nearly losing my balance in the process.

Looking around, I could see that it was night, and we were at the top of the Caverns.

This is the easiest way for us to come and go, Fangorn said. *You did well.*

"I'm dying," I rumbled. "I need to lose weight, or something."

"No. You need to practice flying. Your wings are not used to moving you through the air. With practice, flying will become as normal as walking."

"You know I fell on my face when I tried to walk with all the legs?" I was pretty sure they'd all seen that down there when I was sharing things with them.

He shrugged. "It is always so when one is learning to use new things. You are a dragon, and these are instinct for you. You will need to practice. However, your time of feeling awkward will be short." Fangorn nodded off in the distance to the front of us. "This is the edge of the Dragon Realm. There," he pointed left, "Is the Goblin Realm. And there," he pointed directly before us, "Is the Fae Realm. The Fae Realm sits at the center of all the Realms. It's why they are all part of the Fae Realm. The Fae King rules not only his Realm, but over all."

"What's he like?"

Fangorn was quiet. I could feel him considering his words. "He is a good man. He was harsher, more strident when I last knew him. Time and circumstances have allowed him to be less so."

"That's a good thing, right?"

"Yes. Enough of him. Let us summon Eilor."

I sighed.

I didn't want to. He was creeptastic before I knew all the shit he'd done. Now he'd stolen my best friend, and I knew what a terrible person he was. I wanted to just kill him and then take Margrite home.

It will be all right, Fangorn thought.

Hey! Eilor! I'm here. I'm in… I'm in the Dragon Realm.

I needed to sound scared. I wanted him to think that I was afraid, and unsure of myself.

Eilor! I'm here!

I sounded angry and worried. Good. I could feel the other dragons around me, almost like a protective ring.

"He won't know you guys are here?" I whispered. I didn't want to head talk with Fangorn until I was done with Eilor.

Fangorn shook his head. "No. He knows a great deal about us, but he does not know everything. We did not write our lore down. It's passed from one to the next. So he does not know all our capabilities." He grinned.

If you've never seen a dragon grin, it's a little unnerving. Especially when the grin is full of teeth, and you know that the dragon grinning wants very badly to rip something—or in this case, someone—to bits.

I am glad to see you've made it, Aodan. I was beginning to wonder if you would.

I felt guilt wash over me. I wouldn't—I stopped myself.

The human is still alive although she doesn't seem to be at her best. That shouldn't create too many problems since you're here now. Where are you?

Fangorn brought me like you said he would.

Scared scared scared scared.

I want to get Margrite home. What do I need to do?

"He is going to trap you," Fangorn said next to me.

I will open a portal. You will come to me alone. Once you do, I will open a portal to your world, and send her home.

How can I trust you?

How can you not? You don't really have a choice.

He was enjoying this, the smarmy bastard.

I need to see where the portal light thing goes. When you send her home.

Done.

What now? I let myself sound plaintive.

I will open a portal for you.

"Hide," I said to Fangorn. "He's opening a portal."

"You cannot go." He put his larger, clawed arm on mine.

"I have to." I shook him off. "Can't you track me or something?"

Fangorn huffed and stalked away from me. Something was going on in his head talk, but his door was shut to me.

I shifted. He didn't need to know that I was more comfortable in my dragon. I needed to look as weak and as small as I could.

He was not much different from the assholes I'd been fighting all my life.

"What are you doing?" Fangorn hissed, feeling my shift.

"Looking weak."

He nodded. But he wasn't happy about it.

I waited to see the light, and finally, it appeared. As it got larger, I could see the shadow of a man within it.

"This is it," I said. "Back away, so he doesn't see you right away."

"I won't leave you there," he promised.

"I know," I said. "That's why I agreed to this."

He put his claw on my head. "Be careful, grandson."

I felt it for the benediction it was.

Then I walked forward and into the portal.

The room was brightly lit with candles. It had been dark when I stood on top of the Caverns. Now it seemed like day.

That was a lot of candles. Where did he get the support for this? Living on the edge made me keenly aware of what it cost in money and supplies to keep yourself going.

I searched the room, looking for Margrite.

"Where is she?" I said.

Eilor came forward from my right. "She is safe."

"We take her back now."

"Or what?" He clasped his hands behind his back. "You have put yourself into my hands. You have no control here."

He was one of those kinds of guys too—the ones that got off on having more power than everyone else. It was like he was a complete stereotype.

"Wouldn't your plans go better if I was willing?"

Eilor raised an eyebrow.

I shrugged. "I can be willing, or I can fight. It doesn't matter to me. But you honor our agreement, or I will be as difficult as possible."

"You don't need to be alive."

I made sure to shrug more noticeably this time. "Then I'll be dead."

"You value your life so little?"

"What I value is none of your damn business. I deal in facts. You made an agreement. We send Margrite home now." I'd wanted her to be here, with me. The dragons would make somewhere safe for her to hide. I was changing the plans. But they needed to change.

He didn't speak, only gazed at me.

Dude. A staring contest? How in the hell had he lasted this

long? He was like a petty villain. Although according to Aine, he was lucky and sneaky, which aided greatly in his survival. I couldn't forget that.

"Very well." He turned, heading for a door off to the side of the room.

I didn't move. With him focused elsewhere, I took the time to look around. I could shift in here if I needed to. But getting Margrite out of here was the most important thing.

This looked like a dining room. There was a table against the wall, and another closer to the center of the room. Books and paper were scattered across the center table. Off to the left, a curtain surrounded a bed.

Then there was the room Eilor had just gone into. I leaned forward, trying to see. All the walls were stone, which made me think we were in a castle or something like it. Something really well built.

Eilor came out of the room carrying Margrite. Her head lolled against him. I hated that he was touching her. I just knew he had some kind of shitty bad guy funk. Aura. That's what Margrite called it. You just know, sometimes. And I knew his aura was bad.

"Is she alive?" I kept my voice steady.

"She is. But the Realm is not good for her. We should get her back," he put on false concern.

I had to focus to keep my breathing steady. "Give her to me. You open the portal."

"No, that's not how this will work, boy."

It's already started. I'm not Aodan anymore. Just 'boy'.

"Then how will it work? Because I sure as hell don't trust you."

"I will open the portal. Then I will step through and put her back. I will then close the portal. During that, you will not harm me, or attempt to change things in any way. Should you do so, she will die."

I let my mouth fall open. I'd been talking too much like me. "That's not fair."

Eilor laughed, a mean, hateful sound.

"It's entirely fair, for me. As the victor in this situation, I get to decide what is fair. I am allowing this because it suits me to have you willing and unwilling all at the same time. Makes it sweeter somehow." He smiled. That was hateful, too.

This guy had no redeeming qualities.

He waved a hand from under Margrite, and a portal began to open. Once it was larger, he held her closer to him and looked at me. "No tricks. No attempts of anything. Or she dies. I hope that we understand one another."

"We do," I said, clenching my jaw. I made sure to clench my hands, too.

Margrite stirred, mumbling something. Then she slid down from him.

"Stupid girl," he said. "Put your arm around me."

She mumbled again. Then lifted her head, and said, "Pancakes."

"Now girl, or I'll kill you and be done with this."

Slowly, her arm reached up around his neck, then the other one joined it. I saw her fingers weakly trying to link together. One of her hands fell from his shoulders.

"Never mind, girl. Hold still."

"Can I say goodbye?" I asked.

"No." He stepped into the portal, and I could see him bend down and kind of toss her on the ground.

At least he didn't kick her, like he had when I'd seen him before.

He stepped right back into the room, faster than I thought he could move. I saw Margrite sit up, a glint of gold in her hands as she held them to her chest. She looked at me, and then the portal closed.

She'd said what I thought she'd said. Now the question was, what did she have in her hand?

I looked at Eilor.
Then again.
Holy shit.

*E*ilor! I yelled as loud as I could in head talk.
Nothing.

Eilor! Is she alive? If she's dead, we do not have a deal!
Nothing.

EILOR!

I looked at him. He was gathering something together off of the center table. Without looking up, he started to speak. "I will be moving forward with my plans, Aodan. You figure into those, and since you're here, no sense in waiting. I want the dragons. I will have your magic." He pulled a single sheet from the mess and holding it up. "This should do nicely."

He stepped away from the table.

EILOR! I thought again, trying to shout.

He didn't even flinch as he came toward me.

Can you hear me, Eilor! Fuck you!
Nothing.

She'd done it. She'd taken it. When—I realized when. And I had to stop myself from laughing.

I tried again because I couldn't believe it.

Eilor!

He came to me and waved a hand in front of me. I felt all my muscles freeze. I could still breathe, but I couldn't do anything else. Okay—I could sort of still breathe, if I took shallow breaths.

"That's better," he said. "First, I will need your blood."

I tried to ask why, but since my lips wouldn't move, it came out as an unintelligible sound.

"There's no need for talking," he said. "That's why you're immobilized. I neither want nor need to hear from you."

Fangorn!

Yes? His reply was instant.

No time to explain, but he can't hear us. Change of plans. Open a portal. Come and get me.

You're sure?

Yes. But I don't have much time. I can't move. You need to hurry.

"Once I have the blood I need, then you and I are taking a little trip. Where are we going? Why, you're going to take me to the Cavern of the Ancestors. I know you've been there. It's the only place Fangorn could hide you from me. But no more. With you and your blood, they will let me in."

He wants the Caverns, I thought. *Hurry!*

They all heard me. I could feel it, feel the anger.

We're coming.

I forced myself to slow my breathing. *Oh, shit. You'll have to move me. I can't move. I don't know what kind of magic he used. There's no time to look. Just so you know. I won't be any help.*

We will be fine. That was the male I'd heard in the Caverns.

Eilor was back at the table, checking a small bottle with a cork, or something like it, in the top.

"This should be enough. Then you will be mine forever." He looked up and smiled at me.

I tried to shout "No!" but like before, it was garbled.

Widening my eyes, I did my best to look scared shitless. He liked that, and it made him careless.

Don't mess with the people who have skills, I thought. We

will kick your ass every time and be gone before you even realize it.

It was good that I couldn't move. I wanted to laugh, which would blow the whole thing.

"Are you ready? You're only here because of me, boy. If it weren't for me, your father would not have been born. Nor would you. You're mine, and you will never forget it again."

Okay, crazy.

As he walked close to me I noticed he didn't have anything that resembled a needle. I wondered how he planned to get blood.

The possibilities weren't pleasant.

When he was about five feet away from me, the ceiling burst into flames.

He looked up, his hands flying over his head and blue flame shooting out from them.

That was a pretty impressive defensive response. He'd been hunted for some time. That and he knew he was up to shit. Made a person a little jumpy.

A bunch of dragons fell through the flames, mouths open and roaring, spraying fire.

Shit! Don't burn me! I head yelled.

Be still Aodan. You will not burn. That was Fangorn.

Oh. That's right. I wouldn't. I'd already tried to burn myself and nothing happened. I was just panicked.

Eilor was shouting something. A large green dragon came through the flames and knocked the shit out of him with one claw. I would have laughed if I could.

Then it looked at me and winked.

That felt good.

I bet. Get me out of here!

The girl is safe?

Yes!

I felt claws grip my shoulders.

Relax, Aodan. I will not cut you.

That sounded more female.

As she rose, lifting me up to the hole in the roof, I tried to look down. The whole room was in flames. The dragon carried me out of the house, and I could see that it wasn't a castle, but it was an impressive looking stone house, nonetheless.

It was also well hidden in the side of a cliff.

Yeah, this shitbag was good.

I felt the dragon increase speed, legs moving as her wings moved faster.

We will be there shortly, she thought to me.

Good. Is there someone who can unfreeze me?

Do what to you?

Allow me to move again.

Oh. I'm sure there is.

That lack of completely surety could be problematic.

I have him, she thought. *Do not tarry.*

We're coming. That was Aine.

No! I thought. *Aine! Don't!*

I worried about her getting caught by Eilor. He obviously had more of his weird experimenting in mind.

We need to finish this.

I think the dragons are doing that, I thought, remembering how much of the place was on fire when I was pulled out of the roof.

We need to be sure.

I didn't answer. This was the plan. The fae would come in after the dragons. The only thing that had changed was how they got me out of there. And thanks to Margrite it was a lot easier than what we'd planned.

With Eilor freezing me, I'm not sure our plan would have worked, much as I hate to admit it. Part of what we'd planned needed me to move freely. So this was good even though I generally didn't like changing things mid-stream.

The dragon carrying me slowed, swooping toward the ground. I could see that we were approaching a cliff, and I hoped like hell it was the one Fangorn and I had been standing on a little while ago.

When she dove, I felt my stomach venture up to my throat. Gross. I couldn't even close my eyes.

Thankfully, she flew fast enough that there wasn't time for my stomach to decide that it was time to puke. She put me on the ground lying on my back.

Dear sweet hell, thank you. Thank you for letting me not puke in my mouth.

Okay. Medic! I thought.

What is a medic?

Someone who can take care of medical—health issues, I amended my thoughts. They might not know the terms. The dragons spoke more formally, like people from one hundred years ago. I found myself falling into it at times.

I lay in silence. There was nothing to do but wait.

Are the others back? I sent the question out to whoever might be here.

They are on their way. That was the female who had carried me out.

What is your name? I asked.

I am Imi. It means Tender One.

If you're tender, what is fierce?

She put off a sense of power and strength.

Imi laughed. *It's not my only quality, Aodan.*

I could hear her laughter in my head.

I am fierce, another—male—voice joined in. *I am Kyldret. I am the Life Giver. And the Life Taker.*

He sounded fierce. He was the one who'd sounded ready to drop Eilor when we were talking before I portaled to him.

As am I, a female voice I hadn't heard before said. *I am Ymri, the Taker of Life. I give nothing.* She sounded proud of that.

Except death, Kyldret added.

They all sounded amused.

This was a better ending than I'd expected.

Fangorn?

I am nearly there.

Is everyone else all right?

They have checked the dwelling, and it is now burning.

Is Eilor dead?

Silence, and then, *No.*

What do you mean?

He was not in the dwelling when the fae searched it. Aine went over the dwelling carefully. He was not there.

Jeesh. He's like a cockroach. And you blew the place up?

We set it alight.

Same thing. Where could he go?

I wish that I knew, Aodan. We are still not safe with him here.

Damn it. None of us were safe. Margrite and I weren't safe. Why couldn't he just die like anyone else in the same situation would?

I could hear a flurry of wings, and then Fangorn landed near me. There were other dragons, but they retreated quickly.

Voko? Fangorn was looking around the main cavern.

I am here.

That was the older female I'd heard before.

More shuffling, and then I could see a pale, golden-colored dragon leaning over me.

I remembered that Fangorn had mentioned her. The mother of all was how he described her. And the closest thing to a dragon doc, apparently.

What did he use? Fangorn asked.

She got closer.

This is an old spell. She looked up at him. *It's a variation on one of ours.*

Doesn't he make the connection that you're dragons? I asked.

Voko shrugged.

I would never get tired of a dragon saying 'whatevs.' Not ever. They didn't need to speak. Their body language did it so well. I'd have to practice that move. Because it was so very cool.

We are merely a tool and because he held us captive for so long, I don't believe he sees us as capable beings. That doesn't matter. Can you break it, Voko? Fangorn sounded irritated.

I got it. I couldn't believe the cockroach was still alive.

Voko inhaled, and then leaned down to me, touching my forehead with her snout. A golden light blinked in front of me, momentarily blinding me.

Try moving, she said.

I tried to blink, and my eyes hurt. My eyelids wouldn't close all the way.

Then I tried to lift my arm.

It came up and patted Voko on the side of her face.

Thank you, I said. *I wasn't trying to be rude.* I dropped my hand immediately.

Her mouth curved upwards. *I know that, youngling. Take your time, but get up.* She turned and moved away.

Fangorn huffed and a small flame shot out of his mouth. Then he shifted.

"You are all right?"

"Stiff but yes. I'm fine. How the hell did he get away?"

Fangorn shook his head. "I don't know."

Aine! He called out to her.

I am here.

Any sign of Eilor?

No. The fire burned all the books and paper he had, so that's potentially good.

Why potentially? I asked.

We may have need of the information that was in the books. He has stolen much from the Realms.

She was pissed, too.

I hadn't thought of that. I could see where that would be a negative thing.

"Aodan, why did you tell me that the plans had changed? I trust you, and it was wise to do so, but I would like to know why?"

I could tell that all the dragons were listening. I could feel the weight of their listening.

"Because I remembered what you said about the pendant—the one where Eilor added your blood?"

He nodded. His movements were short, a sure sign of his anger.

"He wasn't wearing it. I don't know where it was. But I took a chance."

"How could you know?"

"I yelled at him, cursed at him."

"I heard that."

"He didn't answer, he didn't even flinch. If someone head yelled at me like that," I said, using Drake's words to describe what we did, "I would at the very least flinch. It's like yelling in someone's ear. It made *my* ears hurt. He didn't even show a sign that he heard me."

"That was what made you change plans?"

"Yes. It's a good thing I did, too."

"Why?"

"Because had we stuck to our plan, I'd still be there. He immobilized me. I wasn't able to move. Not to speak, nothing. I couldn't even blink!" I was starting to feel like this had moved to an interrogation, and a less than friendly one.

Our plan had called for me to shift and disable, or at least distract, Eilor. Once I was a dragon popsicle without all the ice that wasn't possible. I didn't want to have to explain all this. It's why, even with the best plans, you still had to be able to change, and adapt.

Nala's words came back to me.

"Part of Strength is being able to accept the new, or things that are outside our norms." Is this what she meant?

Fangorn studied me. "It was a risk, but it was a wise risk. He might yet still have the pendant. I will keep seeking it, and him."

I do not have any idea why I didn't tell them I thought I

might know where it was. I couldn't be sure. It was a calculated guess on my part. That was all.

"I think you should try calling him, baiting him."

"Why?"

"Because that guy is a total arrogant douchebag. He really likes the sound of his own voice. I kept waiting for him to head talk with me, but he wanted to talk about how he beat me and what he was going to do with talking. He was gloating, the smug bastard."

"That's like him. What are your plans now, Aodan?"

I hesitated before I answered. "I'm going back to my world."

There was a moment before many voices burst forth in my head.

Why? Fangorn silenced them all.

"Because that is my world. My friend is there. She and I have an agreed-upon meeting place whenever we are separated. I need to see that she's okay."

"You belong here."

I shook my head. "No. I'm part of another world. There is part of me that is here. I can't deny that." I thought about Aine, and Fangorn, and all the dragons here. Of Drake, and Iris and Brennan. They were family as well.

"Before you go, you must meet with the fae. They are part of you as we are." He was firm.

Damn it.

I only had a limited amount of time here.

Margrite had said "Pancakes."

That meant she'd meet me at the shed at the back of the lot of one of the diners at the edge of the city. They had the best pancakes ever, and they made banana pancakes for Margrite. It was one of our code words. If we got separated, we'd do what we could to share the code word. The shed had a cellar. I thought it might have been an old root cellar or something like that.

We had a couple of hiding places to meet. I wasn't trusting.

It wasn't our property, though, and it wasn't abandoned. So she would have a day, two at the most, before she'd have to leave.

I also wanted to know if she had the pendant. I could call out to her, but she wouldn't be expecting it, and I didn't want to expose that she might have stolen it.

There was no telling what my dragon family might do.

I didn't want her to get backlash from it if she did in fact take it. Better that Margrite have it rather than the cockroach. But I couldn't forget how Fangorn had faced down Brennan and made it clear that no one would ever be able to use the pendant again.

Then I thought about what else Fangorn had said. That people in need would find ways to justify the things they did. Wasn't that what I was doing right now? I shelved these thoughts and concentrated on the discussion in front of me.

"Okay. That's fair. Can we go now?"

We'd hoped you would stay with us for a time, Voko said.

I want to, but I have things I need to take care of in my world, I said. *I can't just leave them. It's not just Margrite, but there are other things— things that I need to address.*

Like what Margrite and I would do now. She'd said she wouldn't split, but everything had changed. I had a place that she couldn't go.

Fangorn sighed noisily. "We do understand obligations. But you are a dragon, and this is where you belong. We are here always, Aodan."

I looked around. I couldn't see any of the dragons. The main room of the cavern went up—as best I could guess was that we were in a mountain—and there were openings along the wall as the wall went up.

Thank you, I thought. *This has meant more to me than I ever thought it would. I am a dragon but I am also human. Can I stay connected when I am in the other Realm?*

Didn't we speak while you were there? Fangorn was irritated again.

Yes, but I'm checking. That's what I do. Check to make sure things are the way they need to.

He huffed. I guess that was a kind of response.

Then let us say goodbye for a time, Imi said.

A song, just a single voice, sang a few notes. Then another joined in until the Cavern echoed with song.

It was not the song of birds, or anything sweet. This was the song of dragons, and it filled me with... strength, and fire, and how great it was to be a dragon.

As quickly as it had begun, the song was over.

Goodbye, Aodan George, a voice whispered.

I thought it was Voko.

Then everything was silent.

"Wow," I said.

"Let us go now," Fangorn said. He turned and led the way out of the main cavern toward the stone corridor we'd come in initially.

I knew he wasn't happy with me.

That couldn't be helped. I had to get Margrite and see what could be salvaged from our life.

"Are we flying or using a portal?"

"Portal. It will be faster."

Well, okay.

Once we were outside the Cavern, Fangorn opened a portal, and stalked in.

Yeah, he was mad.

It had been a long time since I worried about disappointing any sort of parental type. It still felt as crappy as it had before.

I followed him, and we were back in the room where I'd first come with him.

Aine was there talking with Drake.

"You're here? What happened?" She asked.

"Did you find him?" Fangorn was blunt.

"No. Nor did we find a body."

"I don't know how he escaped," Drake said.

"I think he plans for plans within plans," I said.

"What?" Drake looked at me.

"I kept hearing that he's so smart and whatever, but I didn't get that impression. I think he's hard and ruthless, and has no regard for anyone not working for him, but I don't think he's a genius or anything."

Aine crossed her arms. "Why?"

"Because he brags too much. He really does love the sound of his own voice. Like, way too much. People like that, they miss things when they're too busy talking."

Aine looked at me and nodded. "That makes sense. So how is he always one step ahead?"

"He plans like a guilty man. He knows everyone and their brother is after him. He knows all of you want to kill him. He plans for it."

This seemed simple to me.

"In what way?" Brennan came in.

"If it were me, I'd plan for every worst case scenario. I'd have an escape plan for each room, you know, so if I got caught somewhere, I could still get away."

I ran my hand through my hair. "That's how Margrite and I had our place set up. We had multiple exits, and hiding places, and escape routes."

"Has life been that dangerous?" Brennan asked.

"I lived in a building that wasn't mine. No one was supposed to be there. I steal for a living. That pisses people off. I'm in this predicament now because someone isn't happy with the last job I did. Anyway, that's what I'd do if I was Eilor. And I think that's what he's doing. It makes him seem smart, but really, he's more of a good planner."

No one spoke after I finished. Maybe my reasoning wasn't making sense to them.

"It would be smart to plan. We would all happily kill him." Aine tapped her lip. "I don't think we should ever underestimate him, but this makes his cunning a little less intimidating."

"It does. Anything to take that bastard down is good with me," Drake said.

"Where is the casket that you stole before this all began?" Brennan asked.

I shrugged. "I don't know. I was hired to do a job. I did it and delivered the item to the client. In the process, I had my own issues pop up, but those have been resolved as well. So I don't have an answer for you."

Brennan found. "I am not comfortable with a portal in hands I am unaware of. Those caskets are supposed to be well-guarded," he finished and glanced at Drake.

"Well, there was that problem with some of the Keepers," Drake said.

"Which won't go away. I need you to find the couple who purchased the casket," Brennan turned to me.

"Whoa, hold up," I held up my hands. "I wasn't kidding. I did the job I was hired to do. I don't know who my clients are, or what happens after I deliver. Besides, wouldn't they come here? I mean, isn't that what a portal does? Brings you here?"

"So you have no morals in what you steal?" Fangorn asked.

Playing dirty? I asked.

He didn't respond, only crossed his arms, waiting for my answer, I guess.

"I have quite a few. But this couple didn't do anything to me, or Margrite, or even the guy who set up the job. She was kind of stuck-up, but that's not a crime. They paid well for my trouble."

"Then I will hire you," Brennan said.

"I need to get back. Margrite was taken back, but she wasn't looking so good. I need to see if she made it to our spot and make sure she's okay."

"Your spot?" Aine asked.

"When we get separated, we have a predetermined meeting place."

Brennan smiled. I wasn't expecting it, and it transformed his whole face.

"You're a planner, too."

I nodded.

He continued, "I like that. I am also a planner although I suspect you may be far more detailed. I have a job for you, Aodan. Once you get home, please contact Aine, or Fangorn. Then we can talk specifics of what I need you to do."

"I'll do that," I said.

"I hope you find her and she's better," Aine said, coming to me and putting a hand on my arm.

"That makes two of us," I said. "Thank you." I looked at everyone. "Thank you for helping me. I'm not trying to be ungrateful, but I need to make sure the only family I've ever had is okay."

"You have nothing to explain," Drake said.

I turned to Fangorn. "You still mad at me?"

His arms were crossed, and he didn't move. Then he sighed. "I am. But I understand. I have gone to extraordinary lengths for the remaining dragons. They are my family, and I would fight to the death for them. But before the war, we were not related, nor were we in the same clans. Only those of us completely disconnected were left." He looked out the window, then back at me.

"Family is more than blood ties. I feel more strongly for you and Aine because you are my blood, and I have not had that pleasure for many years. I am not mad. Disappointed."

"Disgruntled," Aine said.

"Perhaps," Fangorn didn't look at her, but he wasn't mad at

her either. He smiled at me. "Go and find Margrite. I like her. I think she is a good friend to you."

I nodded. "Can I get some help? I don't know how to get back."

"When you've found her, and she has healed, you need to come back. You need to learn how to portal, among other things. No matter where you live," Fangorn finished.

"I'll do it," said Aine. She came next to me and took my hand. "Imagine where you want to go and let me see it."

"Oh, okay." I stared at the wall, seeing the block that the diner was on. I didn't want to show anyone the diner.

Not yet.

Aine held a stone out in front of her and said something. A light popped in front of us, and when it was large enough to fit me, she squeezed my hand and let go.

"I am glad to meet you, brother."

"You, too," I said.

I hugged her, surprising us both. Then I gave a wave to everyone else and stepped through the portal.

Once I was on a familiar street, the portal disappeared behind me.

I was home.

Now all I needed to do was find Margrite.

Turning, I headed for the alley that was behind the diner. That was the easiest way to get to the shed.

When I reached the back of the diner's property, the little shed sat right where it was supposed to be.

Looking around, I crept inside—it was never locked; they'd given up on that—and felt around for the small pull in the floor that would open the hatch.

"Ouch!" I sucked at my index finger. I'd found the hatch and hit my finger right on it.

Carefully this time, I felt for the hatch ring, and pulled it open. A sliver of light shone through. Good. She was already here.

I opened the hatch further and slid down into the space.

There was a small bed that barely fit in the room. I could stand up in here, but my head brushed the ceiling. A single light bulb was installed on the side of the wall, turned off and on by a chain hanging down. The chain hung motionless in the still air.

Margrite wasn't here.

I looked around. How could she not be here?

Then I looked at the bed.

There was a torn piece of paper, brown paper, like from a shopping bag. On it was one word.

'Peaches.'

Shit. This meant she was in trouble, and couldn't stay. I knew where she was headed, but this next stop wouldn't be easy.

What sent her from here? Even though bums liked to hide out in the shed, most of them didn't know about the door in the floor.

Something had happened.

Taking my time, I searched the rest of the room, hoping she'd left another clue.

She hadn't.

Peaches was enough.

I clicked off the light and left the small room.

Making sure to conceal the hatch, I took care not to make a lot of noise, or draw any notice to myself. I inspected the door, and then eased out of the shed, checking that no one was around.

I had to go.

Next stop: Margrite.

EPILOGUE

*N*ala sat in the back room of her store, idly shuffling cards. It soothed her to handle them, to feel the smooth surface and hear the snick of the cards as they brushed against one another.

While it didn't always happen, she often felt that in shuffling the cards, the outcomes and futures of many were in flux. Only when a client came in and held the cards themselves did their future take on a solid form with a confident outcome.

She sighed. It was a shame she had to lie to so many, but most people didn't want to hear the real truth. The real truth often hurt, and carried pain and struggle. People didn't come for a tarot card reading to discover pain or struggle.

Most knew more than enough about that.

When she first began reading the cards, it had broken her heart to be unable to help people. For most, it was that they made the same poor choices and decisions. Then they showed up on her doorstop, wanting change, but unwilling to do the things necessary to get what they wanted.

It was a vicious cycle.

But it was a cycle that paid the bills.

She looked down at the deck in her hands. It was the Dragon deck, the one she'd used for the reading for Margrite and her friend Aodan. It kept turning up in her hand, even though it wasn't her favorite deck, or one that she used much.

Nala had been reading the cards for too long to not recognize a sign when it was being paraded in front of her. There was a reason these cards wouldn't just sit in the box where she kept her decks. Why they kept moving to the top, so that they would be pulled out and used.

It was a gorgeous deck, both on the back of the card and the illustrations themselves. She'd bought it on a whim after seeing the artist's work at a show. But the cards were intimidating. She didn't talk about it much. Another reader would understand.

There was so much power, so much intensity in each of the cards. Those who were drawn to them were people with immense strength. She had not been surprised with the Strength card appearing in the spread.

That had been an intense reading, too. The hair on her arms stood up the entire time Margrite and Aodan had been in here. She hoped that she'd conveyed the importance of the spread to Margrite at least. Aodan didn't seem like he believed it although she would swear that he had been shaken by some of the cards.

"What do you want?" She asked the deck. "Why are you always on top? What do you need to tell me?"

The cards didn't answer. It would be so much easier if they did.

As she continued to shuffle, and glare at the non-cooperative cards, she realized she hadn't seen Margrite in some time. The girl came in at least twice a week. She would sometimes watch the register for the shop out front, and she and Nala would sit and talk.

Not about anything major. Margrite was the very definition

of a closed book. But she showed up regularly. And she hadn't been there in over a week.

The cards exploded out of her hand.

Something was very wrong.

ACKNOWLEDGMENTS

I say it every time, but no author is an island. This story has been percolating in the side of my brain for at least a year. I had other things that had to be written before Aodan could show his face to the world.

Thank you so much to my family. You all continue to support and cheer me on. And to my extended family - to my ladies - you know who you are! My writers group, RMFW. I have so many wonderful tribe members that I never would have found had I not joined RMFW.

To my cover designer, Steve Novak. The fact that he creates such beautiful covers and puts up with my plethora of emails is a testament to his professionalism.

To Dean Samed of Neo Stock Photography. When I saw this photo shoot, I knew this was Aodan and my Dragon Thief.

And to Daniel Gemsa. He's the amazing model, and I have had so much fun working with his Neo Stock portfolio.

Thank you thank you thank you to all my readers. I could not do this without all of you.

ABOUT THE AUTHOR

Lisa Manifold is a USA Today Bestselling Author of fantasy, paranormal, and romance stories. She moved to Colorado as an adult and has no plans of living anywhere else. She is a consummate reader, often running late because "Just one more page!" Lisa writes the things she does because she really, really wants to live in a world where these kinds of stories happen.

She is a fan of all things Con, and has an entire room devoted to the costumes created for Cons. She served on the board of Rocky Mountain Fiction Writers for four years, and in 2016, was named the 2016-2017 RMFW Independent Writer of the Year.

Lisa is the author of the fae paranormal romance series The Realm, the Grimm fairy tale retelling Sisters of the Curse series, the Djinn Everlasting series which follows a free-lance djinn, the

Aumahnee Prophecy urban fantasy series, and the urban fantasy series The Dragon Thief.

She lives as close to the mountains as possible with her husband, sons, and three attentive dogs.

Connect with Lisa online:
www.lisamanifold.com
Lisa@lisamanifold.com

Lisa Manifold
PARANORMAL | ROMANCE | FANTASY
Fiction With Flair

WRITTEN BY LISA MANIFOLD

Dragon Thief

Dragon Lost

The Realm Series

Heart of the Goblin King

To Wed the Goblin King

Realms of the Goblin King

Rise of the Dragon King

The Companion Tales, Volume I

The Companion Tales, Volume II (2018)

The Aumahnee Prophecy

with Corinne O'Flynn

Marigold's Tale (Prequel)

Eamonn's Tale (Prequel)

The Portal Keepers (Tales from the Veil 1)

The Gimcrackers (Tales from the Veil 2)

Watchers of the Veil

Djinn Everlasting

Three Wishes

Forgotten Wishes

Hidden Wishes

<u>Sisters of the Curse</u>

Thea's Tale

One Night at the Ball

Casimir's Journey

Do you like being in the loop? Sign up for Lisa's newsletter!
Shenanigans, book recs, and the latest news abound!